SIX

A Novel
by Calvin J. Brown

Copyright © 2012 by Calvin J. Brown
First Edition – November 2012

ISBN
978-1-4602-0175-6 (Hardcover)
978-1-4602-0174-9 (Paperback)
978-1-4602-0176-3 (eBook)

Published by:

FriesenPress

Suite 300 – 852 Fort Street
Victoria, BC, Canada V8W 1H8

www.friesenpress.com

Distributed to the trade by The Ingram Book Company

For Jane
With all my love

Acknowledgements

Although much of the writing process is extremely solitary, it nonetheless needs substantial support. I am very grateful to my daughters – Sarah, Laura, and Erin – for their unflagging patience in listening to years of my musing and muttering, and for their creative ideas for the book cover. I am additionally thankful to Laura for her effort and extraordinary technical skill in producing the cover design. I was very lucky to have my good friend, Craig Peterkin, provide his amazing talents in editing the book. For the time he spent meticulously combing the text and noting problems, and for the patient tutoring he provided in trying to improve my modest grammatical skills, I am extremely appreciative.

To my wife, Jane, it is hard to express my thanks sufficiently. She was extraordinarily diligent and insightful in providing feedback on the story throughout its development. She was the key to keeping our family running smoothly whenever I disappeared into a remote corner of our house to work on the book. Most of all, she was my own personal cheering section – her faith in my ability has probably never been justified, but her apparent confidence in me has always lifted me beyond what might have otherwise been possible.

And even with all of this support, I suspect that errors still lurk somewhere within. For those, I am clearly responsible. Perfection has probably remained unattained for a tad longer.

"In 1950, Alan Turing proposed the following method for determining whether a machine can think. His method has since become known as the *Turing test*. To conduct this test, we need two people and the machine to be evaluated. One person plays the role of the interrogator, who is in a separate room from the computer and the other person. The interrogator can ask questions of either the person or the computer by typing questions and receiving typed responses. However, the interrogator knows them only as A and B and aims to determine which is the person and which is the machine. The goal of the machine is to fool the interrogator into believing that it is the person. If the machine succeeds at this, then we will conclude that the machine can think."

– Elaine Rich & Kevin Knight. *Artificial Intelligence (Second Edition)*. New York: McGraw-Hill, 1991, pp. 24-25.

"...in the summer of 1956, a group of young scholars... gathered at Dartmouth College to discuss their mutual interests. Present... were most of the scholars working in what came to be termed 'artificial intelligence'.... During the summer institute, these scientists... reviewed ideas for programs that would solve problems, recognize patterns, play games, and reason logically..."

– Howard Gardner. *The Mind's New Science: A History of the Cognitive Revolution*. New York: Basic Books, 1985, pp. 30.

"The question of whether a mechanical device could ever be said to think – perhaps even to experience feelings, or to have a mind – ... has been given a new impetus, even an urgency, by the advent of modern computer technology.... What does it mean to think or to feel? What is a mind?"

– Roger Penrose. *The Emperor's New Mind: Concerning Computers, Minds, and the Laws of Physics*. New York: Oxford University Press, 1990, pp. 4.

In 1997, the IBM computer system "Deep Blue" won a six-game chess match against the reigning World Chess Champion.

In 2011, the IBM computer system "Watson" won a two-game, total-point match of the TV game-show "Jeopardy" against two of the game's best players.

Prologue

For most, the day would be like many others. But for two, the day would be transformational. Their lives – or more correctly their ideas – would be altered in subtle ways. And when small changes occur, who can predict the outcome? In a chaotic atmosphere of gases and energy, the proverbial fluttering of a butterfly's wings can cause a storm. What then are the possibilities for two small disturbances in an atmosphere of thoughts and ideas? And what could be the nature of the eventual storm?

"Hey, Les. Save a seat for me!"
"Helluva party last night. Did you see..."
"Stop pushing!"
"Look, there she is!"
"But his argument was flawed. Simple deduction would suggest..."
"Did you see them together?"
"He's my favourite. I like the way he..."
"How'd you do on the test?"
"Hope we get seats. There's some up there."

Bodies jostled through the entrances to the lecture theatre. The attraction was a public lecture at the university by Eric John Fillmore. Fillmore had a worldwide reputation as both a successful entrepreneur and highly respected motivational speaker. He had amassed a fortune through his formation, growth, and sale of several high-tech companies. Now, with his wealth secure, he spent most of his time lecturing audiences around the world on his techniques for success and his vision of the future. His speech on this day was to be in a four-hundred-seat theatre overflowing with interested students and faculty.

Ada Robinson settled into the seat beside her friend near the last row of the theatre. "I hope he keeps to his schedule," she commented. "I've got a ton of work to do."

Ada was twenty-four years old and working on a post-graduate degree in Computer Science. Although she had a heavy course load, was actively assisting with a research project, and had a part-time job, when she heard that Eric Fillmore was going to speak, she knew she should make time to hear him. She'd promised herself that she would partake of as many opportunities as she could while at the university. She found the entire educational experience exhilarating and wanted to get as much out of it as humanly possible.

A few minutes later, moments before the presentation was scheduled to begin, Jason Starr walked confidently into the room on the lower level. Even though the room was clearly crowded beyond its normal capacity, he calmly scanned the seats in the front row. Locating what he sought, he strode toward an empty one. "Good seats, Ken. Thanks for saving one. Looks like a standing-room-only crowd."

Jason was a business student. Any moments that were not filled with coursework were usually focused on his full-time position as editor of the campus newspaper. Nonetheless, when the announcement of Fillmore's talk had been submitted to the paper a few weeks earlier, he knew he had to attend. Fillmore's business achievements were a model for what Jason wanted to accomplish in his life. Even though Fillmore now seemed to have assumed a semi-retired lifestyle, Jason was still determined to find the time to hear what Fillmore had to say.

"Ladies and Gentlemen." A man was now in the middle of the stage facing the group. "If you could all please take your seats. Those of you in the aisles, please sit to the sides and leave a path." He paused while the crowd settled. "It's wonderful to see the turnout. But then we shouldn't be surprised given who we've got with us today. As you all know, our guest is in great demand around the world. We're very pleased that he could fit us into his schedule, and equally pleased that he isn't charging us his customary speaking fee, which is rather sizable." He paused again to wait for the few chuckles to subside. "He really needs no introduction and I'm sure you're anxious to hear from him. So, without further delay, I'd like to present – Eric John Fillmore!"

He gestured to his right as a tall, lean, and immaculately dressed man with well-groomed and slightly greying hair entered the room and mounted the steps to the stage. Fillmore held up his right hand momentarily to acknowledge the ovation. He assumed centre stage and surveyed the faces in the crowd. The noise soon subsided.

"Good afternoon. I'm very pleased to be given the opportunity to speak to you.

"I suspect many of you are here today to hear the answer to two particular questions: How did I acquire so much money, and how can you do the same thing? If that's true, I don't expect that you'll go away disappointed. However, before *I* start telling *you* things, I'd first like *you* to tell *yourself* something: Tell yourself what *you* want out of life. Tell yourself, and be truly honest, what it is that constitutes your fondest dream. Or set of dreams. Imagine yourself as eighty-five years old. What is it that would really make you pleased to look back on your life? So, it's only about a minute into my talk, and I'm already going to pause for a moment. I want you to ask yourself that question right now."

Fillmore clasped his hands in front of him and again carefully surveyed the crowd.

Like most of the audience, Ada was surprised to find that she was now expected to participate, albeit silently, in the presentation. She looked around her, only to find that many others were looking around. She turned her attention back to the stage. Fillmore clearly seemed to be waiting for them to decide. *"OK, what do I want?"* she thought to herself. *"To be happy, of course. But what would cause that? Lots of basic things: family, friends, health. What else? What motivates me? What do I really love to do?"* She again glanced at the mass of now-contemplative people around her. It occurred to her how much she enjoyed being in a place where so many people spent so much of their time learning. *"Given where I am and that I'm already enjoying myself, it seems pretty obvious. I love learning. Understanding how things work. Solving problems. Difficult problems."*

Jason was equally surprised to suddenly find that there were expectations of him in the presentation. He continued to watch the speaker for several moments after the question was posed to the audience. Fillmore was simply standing in the middle of a stage, in front of a few hundred people, calmly waiting. Jason turned in his seat to see the others in the theatre. Some were still looking at Fillmore. Some were looking down. Others were looking around the room. Everyone was quiet. Silence reigned in the room because of a simple request by a single man. Jason looked again at the speaker, still standing quietly on the stage. *"Simple,"* he thought. *"I want to be able to control people the way you do. I want the respect, and I want the power."*

After a minute of contemplation, the silence began to dissipate and Fillmore continued. He talked of the importance of having clear goals, of pursuing those goals relentlessly, and of making sacrifices to attain them. He spoke of his own personal goals, formulated early in an impoverished life, of gaining financial independence and complete control of his destiny, and of his single-minded pursuit of those goals for over forty years. He told personal stories of his minor failures, and more of his major successes.

"I've talked at length now about *my* pursuit of *my* goals. I'm going to change gears slightly for a bit and talk about the general process. How do you attain yours? What strategies should you employ? What principles should guide your choices? In talking about this I'm going to be a bit presumptuous. I'm going to presume that you've set yourself a least one tough goal. One that requires you to challenge yourself. One that isn't attainable simply by plodding along through life and simply *existing*. How do you actually get to where you want to go?

"You've heard the phrase 'Think out of the box'? Well, that's the key. But let's first realize what that phrase means. It means that you should think differently. Be creative. Don't follow the crowd. Be independent. Don't conform. Take a different fork in the road. Try a new approach. It means: Be original! None of the great people in history made their mark by being the same as anyone else. Einstein. Churchill. Confucius. Michelangelo. They all had goals, and they were all originals. They spent as little time 'in the box' as possible.

"Let's talk about this notion in slightly more specific terms. Let's suppose that your goals are in some way related to technology – to computers. Computers are everywhere. They're wrapped up in all aspects of our lives. They're at home, at school, at work, in the car, in your phone. And they do amazing things. They do our taxes. They make our plane reservations. They entertain us. Their capabilities have been developed and their use has been expanded at an unbelievable pace for decades. So if you expect to achieve something in the realm of computers, how can you possibly do it? What more could there possibly be to accomplish? If you're interested in making money, aren't all of the ideas already taken? Don't companies already exist to do everything? If you're interested in inventing new capabilities, what can possibly be left to invent? Don't computers do everything they possibly can already, and aren't labs around the world already filling in any gaps that might exist?

"If that's what you're thinking, then I have a suggestion for you – *Get out of the box!* You're stuck thinking like everyone else! Start exploring other possibilities. Look at the overall situation, and use it to your advantage. Find the gaping holes in today's approaches.

"If you're interested in the *business* of computers, try something like: OK, I accept that people and businesses are having many of their needs satisfied by computers. They're becoming *dependent* on computers. Everyone else is busy *making* them dependent. What can you do with the observation that they *are* dependent? Think wildly. Brainstorm. Do you do something to make them *less* dependent? Do you help them *cope* with their dependency?

Do you establish a chain of counselling services for computer addiction? Do you establish a remote resort, and feature it as a computer-free holiday heaven?

"If you're interested in the *science* of computers, consider how computer systems are built today. Look at what they do and how they do it. Amazing aren't they? They seem to do everything possible, and phenomenally fast. That's the result of the way everybody has been thinking up until now. *You* should think differently. Try this. I'd like you to think of characteristics not normally associated with today's computers. Here's an example. Do you ever consider a computer as creative? As inspirational? And then imagine what advances you can work toward that would foster those characteristics. OK, your turn. Think of some characteristics not normally associated with computer systems today."

He again folded his hands and began watching the audience.

Ada closed her eyes and mentally continued from the examples that Fillmore had given. "*Creative. Inspirational. Adaptive. Considerate. Thoughtful. Conscious.*" Her eyes opened. "Conscious," she said softly.

Before considering this particular question, Jason was processing the earlier comment. *"How do you profit from everyone's dependence on computers? Something worth giving some thought to later."* Jason refocused on Fillmore's question. In a moment, he chuckled at his idea. *"Destructive. Whoever thinks of computers as destructive?"*

After a few moments, Fillmore continued. He talked at length of how key people in history had made their mark by being different. He talked of their techniques, their perseverance, and their ultimate achievements.

Thirty minutes later, he was finishing up.

"And so now it's *your* turn again – your turn to go out and make your mark on the world, to pursue your dreams. I sometimes like to see myself as something of an enthusiastic gardener. I plant seeds in a wide variety of places and hope that some of them will germinate. It's one of my fondest dreams that some of you here today will take these ideas, approaches, and examples and make them work for you. I encourage you in the strongest terms to be creative, be ambitious, be passionate, and succeed in your own way and on your own terms."

As he bowed slightly, applause rose enthusiastically from the crowd.

Jason joined in momentarily and then stopped. Knowing there was nothing more to be gained by staying, he rose from his seat. The two notions of *profiting from their dependence* and *destructive computers* were lingering at the edge of his mind as he strode toward the nearby doorway. The applause was still in progress as he exited the room.

Ada joined in the applause for several seconds. As she clapped, her mind wandered back. Her hands came slowly to rest on her lap, and her gaze was blankly straight ahead as she became lost in the idea. After the applause had ceased and the crowd had wandered from the room, she was still in her seat, mentally exploring the possibilities for a *conscious computer*.

Chapter 1

Ten years later.

Ed Holland paused at the entrance to his corner office. Sipping his coffee, he admired the tenth-floor view of the city from the windows that ran along the length of the two outside walls. He had spent twenty years with the company attaining his current position and particularly enjoyed the office that came with the job. After the moment of reverie, his attention was drawn to the stacks of folders awaiting his attention at the side of his oversized desk. The job also had its drawbacks. It was clearly going to be a long day, but he felt good and ready to deal with anything it threw his way.

Holland was Vice-President of Information Technology for SimirageFX, Inc. In a movie industry that continued to rapidly embrace the benefits of generating sets, characters, and special effects via computer systems, SimirageFX was the undisputed leader. Its technical staff had developed highly sophisticated software that allowed imaginary worlds, characters, and actions to be simulated by computer systems. Additionally, the company's artistic design staff members were the creative experts at using the software. The software, the design staff, and the company's collection of high-powered computers they utilized had attracted numerous lucrative contracts from movie and advertising production companies. In addition, the company had recently released a more simplistic home version of its special effects software. It had caught the imagination of the computer-literate public and was selling at a furious pace. From almost any perspective, the future of SimirageFX looked bright, and Ed Holland was pleased to be a part of it.

He moved his bulky frame over to his chair, settled into it, and powered on his computer workstation. As soon as the system was initialized, it automatically displayed his daily calendar. As usual, most of the day had been planned for him by his Administrative Assistant and contained many hours of meetings. He noted approvingly that this included one with the Director of Product Development. Business trips, conferences, and vacations had prevented his talking with the Director at length for a few weeks, and he needed an update before his meeting with the executive management team the next day.

As Holland finished examining his schedule, he noted that the anti-virus software had automatically initiated its morning scan of his workstation. Running his hand absently over his short grey hair, he watched as it reported that no viruses had been found so far in the many files and hidden recesses of his system. He noted that this feature of their computer infrastructure was typical of most defensive systems: It was too easily taken for granted. Comfortable in the knowledge that theirs seemed to be working well, Holland directed his attention to the stack of folders to his immediate right. At the same time, he made a mental note to meet soon with the security chief to renew his understanding of the measures that were being taken to ensure the staff continued to work in a virus-free environment.

Later that morning, Theresa Chen, the Director of Product Development, arrived at Holland's open doorway for their meeting. She knocked politely on the door jamb to announce her arrival.

Holland looked up from the document he was reading. "Come in, Theresa," he said as he set the material down on his desk.

Chen sat in one of the chairs at the small conference table that was a few steps from Holland's desk. Holland rolled his desk chair over to the table. They exchanged pleasantries for a few minutes and then moved to the substance of the meeting.

"I thought the best way to bring you up to date on the latest would be to start with our division's support of the current projects," Chen began. "As you know, the Creative Division has three movies under development right now. They're all using Version 5.1 of the software on high-end platforms. Because these are the first projects to be based on the new release, we expected some bugs, but the results have actually been better than forecast. For example, our Everest project is the most technically challenging. In the last two months, it has generated no Severity-1 errors and only four Severity-2's. Each of the 2's was fixed within the standard 24-hour period, so the project barely even hiccupped."

"That's encouraging," said Holland. "Are there any significant technical problems outstanding with those three movies as of today?"

"Only the usual array of minor ones that arise out of these situations. And they're primarily to do with tweaking performance as opposed to fixing functionality, so the impact is minor."

"And the ad projects?"

"They all opted to stay with the previous version since there was nothing in their requirements that demanded the latest one. It reduced their risk by using the old one. They all seem to be moving along well and have reported no major problems at all."

"Good to hear. Any indication that our competition is catching up?"

"No. None. In fact, even better. It appears that our buddies in Denver have hit a speed bump."

"Explain," Holland interjected with interest.

"Reports as of a few days ago indicated that they were down for a while because of a nasty virus that had infected a number of their systems. Apparently they were able to disinfect their systems and were up and running by the next day, so the actual hit wasn't catastrophic. However, they had a major project in the works that was running into serious schedule difficulties, and the outage infuriated the production company. The company made a big fuss and seems to have generated concern with others that Denver may not be reliable. It has the potential to send some serious business our way."

"Interesting," Holland said thoughtfully, noting again how easy it was to take good security for granted. Having that talk with the security chief now seemed even more important. Getting back to the conversation at hand, he continued, "It's always refreshing to hear how well we're doing. It's a bit of a bonus to hear that the competition is having some unexpected difficulties. I'll get the latest schedule and budget on the Creative projects from Josie when I talk with her later. How are the latest stats on the home version?"

"I don't know the latest sales figures precisely. However, as of the end of last week, they were approaching the million-unit mark. The Help Desk is reporting that the call rate is only 50% of target so far, so that's a good sign. And only 2% of those have been requiring any assistance from the second-level support team. That's well within the expected norms."

"And is Version 2 on track?"

"We're about a week behind because of the late arrival of the hardware we needed for parts of our testing, but we should be able to make that up. I still expect to release it for beta testing in about six weeks, as planned."

"Any major problems I should know about?"

"None."

"It all seems too good to be true. Here's hoping the rest of the reports today are as positive as yours. Thanks, Theresa."

Holland returned to his desk as Chen left the office. "Cindy?" he called through the open door.

"Yes, Mr. Holland?" his Administrative Assistant asked as she arrived at his doorway.

"I need a fifteen-minute meeting with Frank Fontaine today," said Holland, thinking it would be good to be well-versed today about the Denver virus problem, just in case it came up at tomorrow's meeting.

"Yes, certainly," she responded pleasantly as she left.

Holland returned to his paperwork and awaited his next scheduled arrival.

"What's up, Ed?" Frank Fontaine asked as he settled into the chair in Holland's office.

"I wanted to meet for a couple of reasons, but we may only have time for one of them today," Holland began with his Chief of Security. "I've been wanting to talk in general about how things are going, just to ensure I'm up to speed on the latest. But my primary motivation today is to talk about the hit that our Denver competitors apparently experienced. Have you heard about it?"

"I have. I heard the rumour a few days ago so I thought I'd look into it a bit. I know someone who works there and who usually isn't too reluctant to talk to me. He didn't fail me this time, either."

"And..."

"Apparently, they were hit by what's become labelled as the 'Zinger' virus. It was a brand new one that's suspected to have come out of eastern Europe. It appears they were a bit lax in keeping their shielding systems up to date, and this one got through in a big way. It spread through a good percentage of their systems and triggered last Tuesday. Before they were able to get it under control, it had crippled a number of their systems."

"Why do you say it *appears* they were lax?"

"A good indication is that the anti-virus companies had already encountered the Zinger. Most of them had made the code available a few days earlier, and all that was necessary was for a company to download it and apply it to their systems. It looks as if Denver's systems were using virus descriptions that were at least a few days old. In today's environment, that's dangerous. The reason they were able to eradicate the virus so quickly – it took about a day – was that all they essentially had to do was get the code from the anti-virus companies, update their own software, and sweep their systems clean. That and a fair bit of reconstruction of what Zinger had zapped."

"How vulnerable are we? Could we have been hit by it?" Holland asked the real question that was on his mind.

"No. We were immune from this one. We keep our virus and other security systems as up to date as we can. Our virus patterns are updated daily – more frequently if a special alert is issued. If this virus tried to work its way into our systems, it would have been caught because ours knew what it looked like and were actively scanning for it – along with thousands of others. Of course, no security system is perfect. We're simply as good as we can be."

"And it's possible that we could be caught by one at some point."

"Absolutely. But let's keep it in perspective. The odds of a company with our level of protection running into anything other than purely superficial problems are very small. And I intend to keep it that way."

"That's good to hear, Frank. I'm afraid that's all I've got time for today, but I'll have Josie set up another meeting for us in a few days. I'd like to talk more. Thanks for freeing up some time on such short notice."

"No problem," Fontaine said as he rose and walked from the room.

Holland remained motionless and thoughtful for a few moments. He knew he should feel reassured, but even the tiny possibility of some young hacker on the other side of the planet screwing up his well run world left him feeling uncomfortable.

"C'mon, Ed," he chastised himself. "You've been at this too long to let a problem this small worry you. Get past it." He took a deep breath and resumed his reading.

Chapter 2

"How much longer?" asked Blaise, sipping his coffee.

"Only a couple more minutes," replied Ada as she continued typing at the workstation. "There's just one last parameter to adjust."

"I'm ready anytime," announced Rhonda.

A short while later, Ada was almost ready. While she reset the experimental system to its initial "ready" state, Blaise set up the first test.

"I'm all set," Ada pronounced.

"And… so am I," Blaise responded moments later. "Rhonda, do you remember what you're supposed to do?"

"I think so," she replied, trying to sound confident.

"OK, away we go. C'mon Six!"

"Six" was the name that had been given to the current version of the computer system they were testing. It was actually Version 6 of the software, and the version in which Ada and Blaise had added some significant new features – features that they thought held great promise for making a leap forward. Actually, they were now at Version 6.9 since they had been tinkering with it for several months, but it was still "Six" at heart.

Blaise held the first photograph up to the digital camera.

"Ford Model T," came the pronouncement from the system's speaker.

As Rhonda recorded the score for "Correct" in the evaluation spreadsheet, Blaise held up the next picture.

"A Great Blue Heron."

"Correct" was again recorded, and the process continued.

"A table with a book on it entitled The Geology of Mars. Behind the table is a shelf containing 20 other books," was the response to a more complex photo. Identifying this one had required more than just the simple ability to recognize a single object. This time, the system had to analyze the scene and break it down into its components. It was programmed to describe orally, using relatively simple terms, what it saw.

This test case was followed by numerous others. The process that they were executing was a test of the visual ability of their computer system. Among its many exceptional abilities was the capacity to identify static images of objects by collecting what it "saw" with one of its digital video cameras and relating this picture to a database it possessed containing images of hundreds of thousands of objects. Upon determining what the object appeared to be, it would "say" the name of the object via the speaker attached to it. By recording how well it identified objects, the team could give the system a rating of its ability for "visual object" recognition.

In this particular test, which took about fifteen minutes, the only objects the computer system failed to identify accurately were a Beluga whale, which it decided was a dolphin, and a scene from a ranch containing a bi-level house and some Arabian horses, which it mistook for a bungalow and some Clydesdales.

"And that's the last one. What's the score?" Blaise looked at Rhonda.

"98%." Rhonda read the result from the spreadsheet. "That was very cool! Don't you think so?"

"It's about what we've come to expect," observed Ada. "But I don't think we'll suggest using Six for any horse-judging contests in the near future. On to the next one."

"But how does it do so well?" Rhonda looked bewildered. "Sorry," she said, realizing her error. "I guess I shouldn't slow things down. I've been trying to hold myself back, but I'm blown away by what the system can recognize!"

"I suppose we do tend to forget how impressive even the basic aspects of the system can be when we work with it so often," offered Ada. "What you've seen so far is Six's capacity for recognizing static visual images. Behind that ability there's some very sophisticated AI programming, but it's one of the more rudimentary capabilities that the system possesses. We'll explain more as time permits. For now, we should press on to get this work done."

"OK, thanks," Rhonda conceded, barely managing to suppress dozens more questions.

The trio proceeded to set up the next test. This one was to test the system's ability to recognize *sequences* of visual images. To do this they played short video clips that were again viewed by the system's camera, analyzed by comparing their entire contents and components against a database of static and moving images, and finally categorized and described according to their most probable interpretation.

"Neil Armstrong taking the first steps on the Moon."

"A group of people of varied ages, possibly a family, eating in a park."

"Ada arriving at the lab with wet hair, wet clothes, and smeared eye makeup."

"Hey! How'd that get in there?" Ada gasped as the other two laughed.

"Oops, sorry. A small mix-up," Blaise tried to remark professionally. "I believe this was found by some entrepreneurial soul from the security video after that thunderstorm we had a while ago. I thought it important that Six be given a broad test. And please note that it gets full marks."

Ada crumpled a piece of paper and threw it at Blaise. "You're twisted! Delete that video clip now!"

"Consider it gone. But I must say I'm certainly interested to see what else shows up in the remainder of the sequences. Did you change your clothes in the lab?" He grinned.

And again the process continued. As with recognizing static images, the system behaved nearly perfectly.

Ada Robinson, Blaise Sanchez, and Rhonda Jenkins worked for IntellEdifice Tech, a company dedicated to devising and marketing "intelligent" systems for use in office buildings and homes. From its base in central Canada, the Winnipeg-based company had been very successful in the past several years selling products with individual capabilities. These included systems for voice-activated lighting, face-recognition security, and automated mail sorting. In providing these capabilities and numerous others, their building systems employed a great deal of leading-edge technology, including many parts that were constructed using so-called "artificial intelligence" or "AI" techniques. Voice-activated systems used voice-recognition and natural-language software; face-recognition systems employed approaches developed through the efforts of image-recognition researchers around the world; the sorting of company mail had been largely automated through the combined use of image-recognition software to examine the mail, and robotic arms to physically handle and sort it. The company had taken the approach that many of the advances achieved by the AI research community had reached a sufficient level of sophistication that they could be successfully commercialized. It had focused on automating and enhancing the functioning of buildings as its foundation for this business venture.

Ada and Blaise were employed by the company as senior researchers to develop ways to enhance the intelligent capabilities of the systems. Rhonda was a college student, newly assigned to a work-term at the company after having completed her first two years of study.

As head of the Research Department, Blaise had a staff of ten people, including Ada and Rhonda. The mandate of the department was to investigate ways of enhancing the product line marketed by the company, with most of his staff working on different projects in two other labs. Blaise delegated as much of the administrative work as possible to others in the department, in order to keep a large percentage of his time free for direct involvement in the details of the research. When he had joined the company earlier to form the department, he knew that he could tolerate being its manager only if it consumed a minority of his time. Six years later, he still managed to keep it that way, but often only by working extra hours to juggle the dual roles. Two years earlier, he had persuaded Ada to join the department. She, like Blaise, had a deep interest in AI research. Blaise had lured her from another company with the promise of spending more time on leading-edge research projects. They had found that their research interests and abilities were well matched and had worked as a team for most of the time since.

The lab in which the trio worked was a large and rectangular. Spread around it were desks, chairs, tables with stacks of papers, shelves filled with books, whiteboards, and a collection of computer workstations and other equipment. There was a row of equipment racks, each containing numerous vertically stacked, computer components. Some of these components were very powerful servers, some provided extensive disk storage, several were for communication, and a few were specialized electronic devices needed for their research. All were interconnected by high-speed cables that were largely hidden behind the racks.

When Rhonda had first arrived at the lab a few days earlier to assist them, Ada had tried to introduce her to their overall research approach. "Put very simply," she had begun, "we try to make systems smart, or we try to make already smart systems even smarter."

"Computers already seem pretty smart," Rhonda had immediately replied.

"Yes, I suppose they can seem to be," Ada had conceded. "There are some things that most computers have been made to do very well. They're certainly very adept at gathering raw data, storing it, moving it around, performing calculations, and displaying results. Because this is all done so quickly and, for most people, so mysteriously, computers certainly can seem to be *smart*. However, then there's the AI view. From that point of view, *smart* tends to mean the ability to excel at what are really more-basic human capabilities, but ones that are actually extremely complex. You see, for all of the wonderful technology that has been developed for computers, they're still not very adept at performing basic human activities. For example, they have trouble *seeing* and understanding what they're looking at, and they have difficulty *hearing* and comprehending what's being said. Some of the work that we do here is directed at building commercially viable systems that are able to use these sorts of individual AI skills. We do that primarily by tinkering with individual techniques developed and generally understood in the worldwide research community."

"What kinds of systems has the company built?" Rhonda had asked.

Ada had paused to sip her coffee before continuing. "Well, we've recently enhanced the abilities of some image-recognition software to be able to better recognize objects – including people – when only a portion of the entire object is visible to the computer system's video cameras. An example is the ability to identify an object as being a chair when only its legs are visible. This same capability is useful in many ways. One is in IntellEdifice's face-recognition security software. Low-light situations or oblique camera angles sometimes restrict the ability of the system to see a person's entire face. With our enhancements, the probability is still very high that the system will correctly identify a person even if only half of a face is visible. Another example is our mail-sorting system. It employs specially adapted robotic arms to sort and organize incoming mail so that it's ready for distribution throughout the building. Like most of our systems, we have that one installed in our building. Look for it in the mailroom the next time you're on the main floor."

Rhonda had taken a stab at summarizing. "So you take stuff that others have created, improve on it a bit, and sell it?"

Ada had grinned at the simplification and carried on. "Well, I suppose that's one way to look at part of what we do, even though it's a bit more complex than that. However, there's another longer-term project that Dr. Sanchez and I are working on. It takes a bit of a different approach. Its goal is to improve the way the various components of the system, and ultimately the building, work together. Let's see if I can explain.

"We have numerous companies as clients who have purchased more than one of our products to operate within the same building. Once installed, these products don't interact with each other very much. For example, the voice-activated email system doesn't interact with the security system. If a person says 'Send this message to my Admin Assistant', it would be nice for the *email* system to recognize that it needed to ask the *security* system to recognize the face of the speaker and to retrieve data about the speaker's Admin Assistant, so that the *email* system could then compose and send the message as directed. However, in its present form, the system can't do this."

"Why can't it?" Rhonda had asked.

"Because to do that properly and flexibly, there needs to be another piece to the overall system. There needs to be a component that understands the individual pieces of software and can determine when and how to have them interact. If all of the pieces could act like a whole, we would have a much more powerful and useful system. But to do that properly, we need to make a real leap forward. No more simple tinkering with other's techniques and products. Dr. Sanchez and I believe the next important leap forward in AI, and in IntellEdifice's product line, could come from creating a general, integrated reasoning-and-control system. It would be software that was able to gather information from its environment, understand concepts, identify when problems existed, determine how to solve them, and execute the necessary steps to implement the solutions. Most importantly, the reasoning system would have the ability to learn. Designed into it would be the ability to acquire information about any situation and use its new knowledge to help it solve unexpected problems. It would be this general learning and problem-solving ability that would make the system revolutionary – if we were able to develop it. Systems constructed to date, both traditional and AI, have been limited because they have been able to operate only in a very narrow world. Accounting systems deal only with financial data; email systems only move electronic documents around; mail-sorting systems 'understand' only the small world of organizing and handling letters and cartons. A generalized reasoning system would have an initial set of 'common sense' knowledge built into it as a starting point, but would have the programmed ability to acquire information about completely new areas – enough to be able to understand entirely new issues and subjects, and to solve problems about them as well."

Ada had paused as she had noticed the bewildered look growing on Rhonda's face. "Sorry, I think I might have just confused you."

Rhonda had grinned somewhat sheepishly.

Ada had sipped her coffee again before continuing. "Put a bit more simply, we're trying to build a system that can oversee and integrate all of the others. It would be able to understand, on its own, when a situation arises that requires multiple components to interact. It would gather information from various components, think about what's going on, and engage any components necessary to solve its problem. Such a system would realize, on its own, that a verbal request to send email to an assistant needs various components to interact. It would figure that out in much the same way as a human might, and it would also know how to direct those components to complete the task."

Chapter 3

"Next up is the static audio test," Blaise announced as he started preparing for it.

"I've already set it up, so whenever you're ready…" Ada assured him.

"Do you have a scoring sheet for this one as well?" asked Rhonda.

"Yes, give me a second to find it for you." Ada rolled her chair over to Rhonda's workstation and worked on it for a few moments. "There it is. You should be set now." She rolled back to her own desk.

"Thanks. May I ask a question before we begin, Dr. Robinson?"

"I think we've got a few minutes while Blaise gets ready. You're on," Ada responded.

"I can see the nature of the tests that we're putting the system through so far – we show it something and it tells us what it is. I'm not so sure I understand the purpose of the tests. As amazing as the system is performing, I gather it's done this well before. So, if you already know that, what are we accomplishing by doing this testing?"

"Good question. I think you'll understand better as we get further on in the testing, but let me see if I can give you an idea." Ada settled back in her chair and thoughtfully rested her chin on her clasped hands. "Crucial to building a 'smart' system is to be able to have it recognize things. In some systems that might be to recognize when a temperature gauge reaches a certain value, or when a button is pushed. In the case of systems for IntellEdifice Tech, many of the systems we build interact with the same world as we do. As such, it's important that these systems be able to recognize many of the same things that humans do."

"OK, I get that. And so far we've been testing visual recognition."

"And importantly, we've been testing more than just the ability to recognize static pictures. That's hard enough for a computer system to do well. It's every bit as important that computers recognize sequences of input."

"Like the video clips."

"Yes. Those are visual sequences over time. We'll be doing individual sounds as well as sound clips shortly. In general, for any kind of input that the system is built to be able to receive, there are often static and sequential versions, and they're not always physical. They might be concepts, like words. A computer might be built to recognize a single word and deduce what it means, regardless of how the word is provided as input. Recognizing and understanding a sequence of words – a sentence – is also important. And then there's recognizing sequences of sequences. Like the movements of a musical work. Or the sentences in a paragraph."

"Or scenes in a movie," Rhonda added with a smile.

"You've got it," Ada continued.

"Whenever you two ladies are done chatting, I'm about ready to proceed," Blaise interjected.

"Then, just before we go on, let me leave it for now with the thought that *recognition* is a crucial first step to building intelligent systems, but only a first step. In this part of the testing, we're checking to ensure that the more advanced changes we've made to Six haven't impaired its basic recognition abilities." Ada moved back to her workstation. "OK, let's get at it."

They continued with their tests. The static audio test revolved around the system's ability to identify individual musical notes as well as individual sounds such as a squeak, a cough, or a word. The dynamic audio testing required the system to recognize sequences such as passages of music, excerpts of speeches, and the sounds from a busy city street.

In addition to the senses of sight and hearing, the system had been given the ability to monitor the internal activities of the computer system, and this was also tested.

"So this is just another example of recognizing things?" Rhonda asked.

"Jenkins! Enough already!" Blaise exclaimed.

"Easy now, Dr. Sanchez," Ada added soothingly with a chuckle. "Don't let him deter you, Rhonda. He likes your inquisitiveness as much as I do. His problem is that he was given an extra dose of obsessiveness when it comes to work. Once he's working full steam, he's rather hard to distract. I'll be brief, Blaise."

She spun her chair to face Rhonda. "Explain what you mean."

"I guess the computer software has been given the ability to sort of 'see' the inside of the computer system – you know, examine its internal memory," she began tentatively. "So monitoring its internal activities is just another example of watching a sequence of things over time. In this case it would be things like computer instructions and data?"

"Good girl. Humans can't readily do it because we can't easily 'see' inside a computer, but it's not a difficult problem for computer software. Six has been built so that anything it's able to perceive in any way can be recognized statically or dynamically. It has very general and flexible recognition capabilities that adapt to almost any new input, or situation, or concept that it may encounter. Another example of that is what we're going to do next. The next battery of tests is to ensure that the system's natural-language processing is still functioning properly."

"Natural-language processing?" Rhonda queried.

"Ah yes, more jargon. All we mean by that is the ability of computers to process a language that is 'natural' for humans: English, for example. Computers are already very adept at communication on their own terms. As you know there are numerous computer programming 'languages', and the various protocols that systems use to transmit data to each other could be considered 'languages' as well. These types of languages were specially developed for use by computers and, consequently, are readily usable by them. Human languages, on the other hand, are much more difficult for computers. Human language tends to involve subtleties, ambiguities, and implications that people find relatively easy to deal with, whereas computers must be provided with some very sophisticated programming to handle them. It's a perfect example of the notion that whatever humans find easiest to do, computers often find the hardest."

"So that's what we're testing next? How are we going to do that?"

"Well, the easiest way would be for us to simply present Six with an electronic document. We could direct it to 'read' it internally, and then we could quiz Six on the literal content of what it has just read."

"OK, I can understand that, but I gather there's something wrong with that approach."

"There are at least a couple of things too simplistic about it," Ada carried on in her professorial tone. "One is that it's not terribly useful or interesting to have Six learn just the document's literal content. If Six is able to understand only the basics of a sentence like 'She lifted the Ming vase with her greasy hands.', then it might derive the meaning to be that a female elevated a type of ancient Chinese flower container using her oil-byproduct-covered, five-fingered, corporeal extremities.' And that would be it. On the other hand, a human reading something like this would also have the sense of what it implied – that the vase was very valuable, that there was danger she might drop it because greasy implies a poor grip, that if she dropped it gravity would cause it to fall to the floor, that if it fell to the floor it might break, and that if it broke it might cost her a lot of money."

Absorbed by what Ada was saying, Rhonda thoughtfully continued the reasoning. "So, in order for a computer to be good at communicating in human language, it has to understand much more than just the definitions of the words. It has to have some understanding of related things, of... the world?"

"Yes. Well done. Simplistically put, we'll sometimes say that computers need to have 'common sense'. It's not actually a very good term for it, but it conveys the idea. In order to communicate well with humans, computers need to have an understanding of physics, chemistry, biology, history, society – many things. Not as experts, although that can help, but at similar levels as humans, which is a surprisingly large amount of knowledge. As scientists, we didn't really understand how much humans actually know until we started trying to build computers to appear intelligent. We soon discovered that people tend to learn a great deal simply by living and experiencing life. In order for computers to be able to understand our language well, they need to have a similar set of knowledge."

"So, how much does Six know?"

"Many different researchers worldwide have compiled a massive set of 'common sense' information and made it publicly available to teams like us. Six has all of this and even more that our own team has added."

"So we're going to test that Six can still understand both the specific words and the meaning found in what we show it?"

"Yes. But there's another basic piece of the puzzle necessary for what our natural-language tests –"

Ada was about to continue when Blaise interrupted. "Robinson! We really need to get moving."

"OK, just a quick point," she acknowledged. "Six also needs to have speech-recognition capabilities. That is, it needs to be able to hear the sounds we make, and accurately identify what the words are that those sounds represent. Only after doing that successfully can Six's 'natural language' talents begin to be really useful."

"Like when I learned to read basic French, but that didn't allow me to understand someone speaking it?"

Ada had a broad smile on her face as she concluded, "I think we're very ready to proceed now, Blaise. Our new assistant seems to have acquired a pretty fair grasp of things."

To test the computer system's language ability, the trio presented it with a series of essays and stories. Some were read orally; others were presented in electronic form. After having read or heard a piece, the system was then required to answer a series of questions about the facts and meaning found in the material.

By midday, the language tests were complete, and the team began preparing to test the capabilities of the system's robotic arms. There was a pair of them in the lab. They were very similar to those used by the company's mail-sorting system, but these ones were for use in their research. They were attached to vertical, metal poles situated near the equipment racks. The poles were separated by eighteen inches, and the arms were attached to them about five feet from the floor. They were similar in appearance to human arms: Each was attached at shoulder height to its pole; each had movable shoulder, elbow, and wrist joints; each had four flexible fingers, one of which was opposable to mimic a human thumb. A video camera was mounted above the arm on each pole, secured by a mechanical pivot. There were two microphones attached just below and to the sides of the cameras. Finally, a speaker was supported between the poles a few inches below the cameras. The visual effect was a crude imitation of the upper part of a human body. The cameras, microphones, speaker, and robotic arms were mounted approximately where a human's eyes, ears, mouth, and arms would be. Running through the interior of each of the poles was a collection of wires that provided power to the devices as well as high-speed connections to the nearby computer systems.

The team put the system through a series of tests of the arms' dexterity and ability to co-ordinate with visual input from the cameras – essentially its hand-eye co-ordination. Several of the tests involved handling and moving a variety of objects, such as picking up and stacking a series of blocks. To an outsider, the most entertaining test would be the one they had devised to test the system in a more dynamic way. A machine for launching table-tennis balls was set up a short distance away, and was programmed to shoot the balls in rapid succession toward one of the robotic arms and to change the speed and direction of the ball randomly. In the hand of one of the robotic arms, the computer grasped a table-tennis racket. Its goal was to "see" the ball coming toward it, determine its full trajectory from a quick analysis of its initial flight path, place its racket in front of the ball, and hit the ball back toward a dartboard-like target placed back near the launcher. The computer's ability was measured on whether it managed to hit the ball and, if so, how accurately the ball was directed.

When they were finished, Blaise said, "That's the last ball. What's the co-ordination score?"

"Let me check – 82%," replied Rhonda.

"Well, maybe not quite world-class table tennis yet, but not too bad."

The process continued until all of the tests of the basic system capabilities were complete.

"What's the overall tally?"

"The overall is – 94%," Rhonda read from her screen.

"That's essentially the same as the tests before we made this last set of modifications," Ada observed.

"Which is OK, since the mods were to improve the reasoning system," Blaise continued. "At least we haven't harmed the other components in the process. Shall we finally proceed with the really good stuff?"

"I'm game. Let's set it up," said Ada.

Chapter 4

By early afternoon at SimirageFX, Ed Holland had finally cleared his desk of the most pressing paperwork. For a change of pace, he decided to make a few modifications to the budget material he needed later in the week. He pivoted his chair to face his workstation and located the file he was interested in. Having found it, he invoked the spreadsheet software to begin making his changes.

And, unknown to Holland, the piece of computer code that first began to execute was a virus. This one did not yet have a name – it had never been identified. In fact, this one had never been detected by any security system anywhere. In its own primitive way, it performed the exact instructions embedded in it by a computer programmer several months earlier at a distant location. It first checked the internal date and time on Holland's computer system. Satisfied that the result of this check was not yet significant, it proceeded with its most common routine. The virus surveyed its surroundings, that being the layout of the file system inside Ed Holland's computer system. It simplistically noted the selection of disk drives available, and that several of them appeared to be provided by the local area network to which Holland's workstation was attached. On each of these drives, it quickly scanned the files available until it had compiled a list that constituted a broad selection of files, each of which contained a computer program found on its internal eligibility list. To each of these programs, the virus attached a copy of itself. This was done in such a way that whenever someone invoked these programs, they too would unwittingly activate a copy of the same computer virus.

Having successfully replicated itself in fifty other locations reachable from Ed Holland's computer, the virus's work was finished for now. As a result, it passed control of the workstation to Holland's spreadsheet program to allow its normal activities to continue.

At some point very recently, this virus had attached itself to Ed Holland's spreadsheet program. Within a few seconds of invoking his program, Ed

Holland had inadvertently spread the computer virus even further into the company's computer systems. However, by this time it was probably irrelevant. Over the past several days, copies of this same virus had already infected over ninety thousand files and four thousand workstations and servers throughout SimirageFX, Inc.

Chapter 5

"What's the 'really good stuff'?" asked Rhonda, hoping enough time had elapsed that she could resume asking more questions.

Ada smiled at the question at the same time that Blaise grimaced. "That's my girl," she responded. "Blaise, maybe you should sharpen your expository skills by taking a stab at this one."

Blaise glared at Ada – but only briefly. Softened by her smile, he sighed. "OK, that's fair." He turned to face Rhonda. "Rhonda, please don't mistake my desire to concentrate on the task at hand for a lack of interest in your questions. Unlike my esteemed colleague, I have a very refined sense of priorities and prefer not to be distracted from the most important task under consideration. However, with your assistance, we've been proceeding rather nicely and I think we can take a break for a bit of discussion." He paused to gather his thoughts before continuing. "Up to this point, we've been testing Six's fundamental individual skills. Can it recognize pictures and sounds? Can it understand human language? Can it communicate using it? Can it manipulate objects? Does it have hand-eye co-ordination? All of these are very useful, very complex skills, and – as you've seen – Six is quite adept at all of them. However, the area in which Dr. Robinson and I are really interested is in making progress in Six's general-reasoning skills. Not to undervalue recent game-show triumphs of another system, but a truly useful system would be one that, when presented with the elements of a problem, could devise its own method for finding a solution."

Rhonda furrowed her eyebrows at this last remark.

"I gather you find this notion of 'finding a solution' a bit confusing." Rhonda nodded, and Blaise continued, "Let me see if I can explain: Many actions that humans perform are simple reflexes. When you touch something hot, you automatically withdraw your hand. When someone throws something at your face, you probably blink, and perhaps even duck. These are reflexes – each is an action that occurs as an immediate response to some stimulus. On the other hand, if you were to touch something hot and seriously burn yourself, you would probably perform more than just the reflex action of removing your hand. You'd probably think of some way to help yourself and then do it."

"You bet. I'd be shouting and putting my hand under cold water in a real hurry!"

"And then you might locate and use first-aid material or go to the hospital. In each of these cases, you would have drawn on relevant information that you had stored away, formulated a series of steps, and executed those steps. Often the process involves continually monitoring your situation and replanning your next steps. Ultimately, if it was a good plan, you would complete it and reach your goal. In these cases in which the action taken is more complex than simply a reflexive, knee-jerk response, we talk about *reasoning* having been involved. A problem was presented and the goal was to solve that problem. Relevant information was recalled, a plan was formulated, and steps were taken to reach the goal of solving the problem. And that's 'the really good stuff'. We're trying to give Six the ability to solve arbitrary problems by using general-reasoning functionality tied to its other basic skills. Ideally, it would be able to use its many basic skills in combination with its reasoning abilities to be an even more useful office assistant."

"Have you been able to do it? Have you created a general-reasoning system?" Rhonda inquired eagerly.

Blaise paused before continuing. "We've certainly had some degree of success. Actually, I suppose to most people, it would appear that we've managed very remarkable progress. However, we have hopes for even more." He paused again, lost in thought before he again continued, "Well, enough lecturing. Let's get on with it. Ada, are we set?"

"That we are. Off we go."

The general-reasoning system's specialty was to solve problems using its various abilities – by getting input from the various component systems, by adjusting those components to gather more information, by manipulating objects with its arms, or by modifying data inside its memory. The key component of all of this was its reasoning ability. The system was given a description of a problem and, on its own, was required to gather more information, formulate a plan, and then to execute the steps of that plan to solve the problem using its array of individual abilities.

The first of these tests involved little of the external sensory equipment. A series of mathematical and logic problems were presented to the computer. For some of these, the computer was merely told the name of the computer file that contained the description of the problem. The system was then required to read the English description of the problem contained in the file, understand what was required, and "mentally" determine a solution.

Another test that required use of several components of the system was to solve Rubik's Cube. For this test, the multi-coloured cube was placed on a table near the robotic arms and video cameras. An audio recording was played that described in very careful terms how the cube could be manipulated, and what the ultimate goal of the test was. Once it had been presented with this information, the computer system was left on its own to understand the description that had been presented, examine the current state of the colours on the cube by lifting and rotating it, and then determining how to proceed to adjust the cube so that all of the segments on each face of the cube were the same colour. Solving this problem required understanding the problem, "seeing" the cube, and manipulating the cube in a sophisticated fashion. However, the real challenge for Ada and Blaise had been to design the computer system so that, with only a description of the problem, the computer system could completely determine on its own how to solve it. Previous computer systems had solved problems such as that presented by Rubik's Cube but, as is commonly done in the computer world, the specific techniques for solving it had been programmed into the system by a human. Ada and Blaise wanted the computer system to determine the technique on its own.

By late afternoon, these reasoning tests and various others were complete.

"And we're done," announced Ada.

"And not a moment too soon. I'm exhausted," added Blaise. "Well, what's the score, Rhonda? With all of our marvellous adjustments to this version, we've managed to improve the reasoning test score from a previous high of 13%, to a new record of…"

"15%," Rhonda replied tentatively.

"Arrrggggh!" moaned Blaise.

"But the good news is that we haven't damaged the performance of the individual components, and we're headed in an upward direction," offered Ada.

"Ever the optimist, aren't you?" Blaise pointed out.

"I try to be, but I must admit that I thought we'd fare better this time around."

"Any thoughts on our next steps?"

"Yup," Ada said with certainty. "I think it's time to try the extra layer."

"Even with our analysis showing its likelihood of succeeding as being rather small?"

"Yes. Without reverting to another major round of re-analysis of our approach, I don't think we have anything else significant to try."

"OK, but it'll have to wait a few days. You're committed to a few intensive days of design reviews with the development staff, and I've got a pile of backlogged paperwork that I'd better get at. Rhonda, you're to report to the library tomorrow. Let's reconvene by Friday at the latest. It would be nice to have some initial results before the weekend."

"Agreed. Time to pack up and head out."

Rhonda asked, as they began to get ready to depart, "If I haven't worn out my quota of questions for the day, what do you mean by *layers*?"

"As a matter of fact, your quota has been consumed," Blaise responded. "That's a question for another day."

"Agreed. I'm rather worn out as well, but ask again first thing Friday," Ada added. "I'm sure Dr. Sanchez will be feeling positively garrulous by then."

With that, the trio replaced the test material, and left the lab. The building's security system automatically locked the door behind them.

Chapter 6

Ada glimpsed her reflection in her car door's window as she reached for the door's handle. Not for the first time, she wondered if it was appropriate for a thirty-four year old to keep her hair in a ponytail. As she opened the door, her mind replayed the usual rationale. She liked having her hair long, but wanted it practical and unobtrusive. So, a ponytail it was. She lowered herself into the driver's seat. A quick glance in the rear-view mirror reassured her that her make-up was intact. Again, the approach was simple and practical – lip gloss and a bit of mascara. And again, her rationale immediately came to mind – she preferred to direct her creativity toward her work. That her reason so readily appeared in her thoughts whenever she noticed her appearance made her wonder. Was it a defensive reaction? Was she entirely comfortable with her choices? Was she subconsciously contemplating a change? "Oh, get off it, Robinson! You've got better things to think about!" she muttered. She started the car and backed out of her parking space.

Driving up to the company's basement-parkade exit, she lowered her window and placed her thumb on the security scanner. Moments later the exit door opened and she drove out and up to the street. She caught herself before instinctively turning left. Left would take her home. Today, 'right' was called for because she was headed to the university to teach her evening class in artificial intelligence. This was her second year teaching the course. When she was working on her doctorate a few years earlier, she had taught a few classes and had thoroughly enjoyed the experience. Well, if pressed, she would more specifically say she liked *teaching*, but not having been particularly fond of – actually loathing – marking assignments and tests. When she had agreed to teach the course the previous year, it had been only on the condition that something would be done to alleviate the marking drudgery. She had been assigned a teaching assistant and, with that luxury continuing this year, she was enjoying herself. The pleasure in imparting what she knew to a group of keen young students was extremely satisfying. The bonus was that the better students could always be expected to ask questions that kept her sharp, either in finding a way to better explain a complex concept, or sometimes even in having to think through an issue that she had not conceived of before.

As she drove, her mind was drawn back to the status of their project at work. She could not help wondering about what the effect would be of the extra reasoning layer. As a graduate student, she had dabbled in formulating a generalized-reasoning system, but had never had the time or resources to make any real progress. After she graduated, she had taken a job in the private sector with a telecommunications research and development company. Her hope had been that she would encounter better funding for elements of her research. Disappointed in the amount of freedom and the resources she was given to pursue her own interests, she had leapt at the chance to work for IntellEdifice Tech. The potential for doing what she loved seemed much greater, both because of the nature of the company's business and because of the persuasive head of their Research Department. Blaise had convinced her that there was great opportunity in the company both for working on AI in general and even working directly on building an actual general-reasoning system. To join a company that was actively considering the commercial aspects of such a system was too exciting to pass up.

Of course, she wasn't permitted to focus entirely on her pet project. Along with everyone else in the Research Department, she was regularly distracted by the commercial necessities of working on other aspects of their product line. However, as a direct result of Blaise's regular efforts at selling the concept to the company executives, the amount of time that had been available for the reasoning system over the past months had been very satisfying. Add to that the exciting prospects of what they could be on the verge on achieving, and Ada sometimes had to shake her head to believe her good fortune.

As she came to a stop at a red light, she tried to temper her excitement. Her optimism sometimes ran a bit out of control when it came to her work. She was excitedly looking forward to their test using the extra reasoning layer, but she had to be realistic. She believed strongly in the basic design of their system's layers. Extensive complex analysis had gone into it. Nonetheless, an objective assessment would point out that the number of variables that had to be right for success was, well, massive: How many layers? How many neural network nodes? How many interconnections? How much memory? How much common sense? What types of search methods? And the list went on.

She started her car moving again as the blaring of a horn made her aware that the light had changed. The real trick was achieving the right balance of external stimuli and self-awareness. The system certainly needed to possess and receive a significant amount of information about the world with which it was to interact. It also needed a critical level of comprehension about itself. Too little knowledge and feedback about its own processing, and it would be little more than a typical computer program. It would always process data and react in predictable, consistent ways and do nothing particularly creative or original. Too much attention to its own internal activities and it would grind to a halt with over-analysis, forever second-guessing itself and never reaching any useful decisions. With the right balance – theoretically at least – wondrous things could happen. The system might learn to improve itself. In addition to acquiring more basic facts about the world, the system might actually optimize itself – essentially change its own parameters to improve its reasoning performance. If the system had just the right ability to monitor and tune its own abilities, real success might occur.

Would the next layer accomplish that? Would it prove the design to be successful? That always brought back Ada's debate with herself about what "successful" meant to her. Was it the development of a reasoning system that provided useful automated and flexible integration between the various IntellEdifice products? Certainly this was what their executives wanted, and it was always at the core of Blaise's funding sales pitches to them. Or was "successful" that which she always hoped for and sometimes actually allowed herself to really believe in? Was there any chance that they might actually create an adaptable, problem-solving, self-aware, self-improving, *conscious* entity? Could they actually create a *mind*? If they did, what would it be like? A fleeting vision of Frankenstein's monster made her smile. Everything that she had learned had led her to believe that it was theoretically possible – that a reasoning system comparable to the human mind was possible in a machine. Even so, could AI researchers possibly create in a few decades that for which evolution had required several hundred million years?

Ever since the advent of the study of artificial intelligence by pioneering researchers like Alan Turing and John McCarthy in the mid-twentieth century, the anticipation of major breakthroughs had often exceeded the ability to deliver them. AI research had indeed contributed tremendously to technological advances – her company's own products attested to that. However, the goal of creating the equivalent of human intelligence had never been reached. Was it to remain forever elusive? Were there other key concepts and technologies that still remained to be uncovered? Or was it already possible? Was there any chance that a machine would soon be created that exhibited all of the major features of an intelligent mind? Was there any real chance that Six possessed all of the key ingredients?

Another red light stopped her. She shook her head ruefully. Her mother had often pointed out that she was a dreamer. Realistically, the likelihood of that kind of success was probably vanishingly small. She should be satisfied – she should, in fact, be very pleased – if they managed to create an interesting, commercially viable, reasoning product.

She accelerated away from the green light, moved to the right lane, and followed the diverging street toward the university campus.

Her mother had also always pointed out that she worked too hard. Here she was leaving work late in the day, only to go spend her evening at another job. In her own defence, she reasoned that she did regularly attend the symphony, the ballet, the theatre, and a dinner club with various friends. However, she had to acknowledge that a disproportionate amount of her time was spent focused on her job and her teaching. She didn't allow herself much downtime and she knew why. She worked and she taught because she liked to. If there were something, or someone, else that offered comparable levels of enjoyment, she would consider the matter.

As she drove onto the campus and continued toward her parking lot, she allowed herself another moment of reflection. There was the crux of the matter. She didn't have anyone special to spend her free time with. And yet again, she asked herself if she already knew who she would like that person to be. Would her working relationship with Blaise become anything else? She had initially been impressed with Blaise because of his passion for the work that they did. It hadn't taken long after he had hired her into his department to realize that they were very compatible research partners. As a result, for the last two years, they had spent a notable number of their working hours together. The result was that Ada felt she knew Blaise quite well: She had a great deal of respect for his intelligence; she knew how dedicated he was to his job; she enjoyed his dry humour; she had seen his abrasive side – a characteristic she felt certain almost always resulted from pressure he was under from the company's senior management. She liked the look of his slightly greying, almost always unkempt, black hair. She even liked the way that his slightly worn and outdated clothes fit his solid six-foot frame. She could not imagine a better person to work with and had wondered for several months if that feeling would extend to a relationship outside of the office. However, wondering was all that she could do. Other than the usual mild office flirtations and occasional quick bites of dinner as part of working late at the office, Blaise had never given any obvious hints that he might be interested in something more.

She turned into her parking lot, parked her car, leaned back, and sighed heavily. That was probably why she worked so much. Not only did she like the job, she liked the person she spent much of her working time with. Nonetheless, she couldn't help wondering if some of her attention would be better diverted elsewhere sometime soon.

Chapter 7

At four seconds past 2:30 p.m., the Assistant Manager of the Marketing Department at SimirageFX unwittingly began the calamity. As he clicked his mouse on his email software to read the latest messages, a copy of the virus identical to that on Ed Holland's computer was invoked. As the virus always did, it began its routine by first checking the date and time. In this case, the virus noted that the clock had passed the date and time it had been programmed to watch for. Because of this, it behaved differently than it and all of the other copies had behaved so far. It no longer attempted to merely replicate itself. Instead, it began a methodical but very swift process of writing meaningless sequences of bytes into the middle of every file within reach of its host computer system. For a virus running on a workstation attached to a corporate local area network, this constituted thousands of files. One by one, it would locate a file, gain access to it, and overwrite some of its contents – enough that the file was rendered useless, but not enough that it wasted time destroying the file's entire contents. The virus's goal was to effectively destroy as many files as quickly as possible.

After waiting thirty seconds for the email program to respond, the Assistant Manager started to become impatient. After three minutes, he started to wonder if something was wrong. Even then, he did not come close to contemplating what "wrong" really entailed in this case.

The copy of the virus on his computer was not alone in its assault on SimirageFX's files. Throughout the company and almost simultaneously, several dozen staff members and automated systems had accidentally executed other copies of the virus on personal workstations and corporate servers. Each of these, having noted the date and time, began the same ruthless assault on all of the files within its reach.

Ed Holland was in a meeting in a conference room when his cellphone rang. By general agreement, his staff called him on his cell only when the situation was urgent.

"Ed Holland," he answered, standing and walking out of the meeting room into the adjoining hallway.

"Ed, it's Kyle Simmons." It was his Director of Technical Services.

"Yes, Kyle. I'm in a meeting." Holland's voice was stern.

"Sorry to interrupt. We're experiencing a problem that I thought you ought to hear about. Our Help Desk has been getting calls from all over the company about system hangs. It appears as if something has happened that has affected most of the network."

"Any clues about the cause?"

"None yet. We've escalated it to third-level support. Hopefully we'll know something soon. Odds are it'll take a while longer to figure it out and fix it, so we should be prepared for some flak."

"Agreed. Stay on top of it and call me back when things are back up." Holland disconnected the call, took a deep breath, and walked back into the conference room.

Sixty minutes later, Holland was back at his office when Kyle Simmons walked in. Holland looked at him expectantly.

"It's not good, Ed," Simmons began. "We've had failures of systems all over the head-office network – servers and workstations. So far, no one has been able to reboot any of them. From a couple of systems that are still running, we've been able to take a quick look at some files. It appears that lots of them have been corrupted."

Holland was watching him, hoping it wasn't what he feared.

"We're pretty certain it's a virus. It's the only thing we can think of that could cause so much damage."

Holland's shoulders slumped, as his head bowed in dejection. "What's next?" he asked.

"We're shutting down the few remaining connected systems to prevent any further spreading and damage. After that, we'll bring up our emergency servers and start restoring some of the most critical systems from backups. At the same time, we're contacting our anti-virus vendor to get some advice on finding and eradicating the bug. It'll be a while longer before I know how we're faring."

"OK, keep me posted," said Holland, trying to sound commanding, even if he didn't feel very much in control.

Six hours later, SimirageFX's team of system experts had discovered that their system backups from at least five days previous were contaminated with the still-as-yet-unidentified virus. Experts from the anti-virus company were on an airplane, flying in to help with the battle. Kyle Simmons had just delivered his guess that it could be days before they could get rid of the virus, reinstall the many software systems that had been damaged, and repair the massive amounts of data that had been corrupted.

As Simmons left Ed Holland's office, Holland was slumped in his chair, staring at the ceiling.

Chapter 8

"Flight 221 from Las Vegas to Boston is now ready for boarding. Executive Class passengers may proceed through Gate E6. General boarding will begin shortly."

Jason Starr rose from his seat inside the executive lounge, picked up his briefcase, and strode toward the door. As he arrived at the boarding gate, the attendant quickly examined his boarding pass.

"Thank you, sir. Have a pleasant flight," she smiled.

As he walked along the ramp into the aircraft, he was reminded of how uninteresting travel could be. Not at all like his activities at either end of a flight. He liked to keep his business life full and exciting. Actively directing his senior staff toward the latest corporate goal, making a presentation to a group of potential clients, or providing an interview for an industry magazine were Starr's ideas of a good time. Several hours of enforced solitude and inaction aboard a commercial airplane were nothing more than a necessary evil – a way to get between the places where the action was. He certainly had much work that he could and must do while on this flight, but travel was one of the few aspects of his working life that wasn't pure enjoyment.

"Newspaper, sir?" the flight attendant asked as he was settling into his seat.

"Yes, both," he replied and was handed the papers.

As other passengers began arriving on the airplane, he looked blankly out of the window, lost in thought about the past few days.

The computer trade conference had, as usual, been a large success. The conference was an annual event at which all of the world's major, as well as the world's ambitious minor, computer hardware and software companies displayed their wares to a massive crowd of attendees. Las Vegas had been established as the permanent home of the event since it was one of the few cities in the world with sufficient conference and hotel-room space to accommodate the tens of thousands who attended. The attraction for the attendees was the opportunity to see the latest in commercial computer innovations and to hear industry experts speak about the most probable future trends. The attraction for the computer companies was the opportunity to show off and market their newest products to the attendees, and even more to the large contingent of computer industry media personnel who covered the event. The coverage to be gained from good conference exposure was much better, and much less expensive, than any they could practically buy through conventional advertising channels.

Starr's own company, JS Escape2210, had also been displaying its latest innovation – a new suite of sophisticated computer games that they were in the midst of releasing. As he always preferred, his staff had handled all of the trade show details while he had been free to absorb the contents of the show and to meet with key business prospects.

"Sir, if you would please fasten your seat belt, we will be taking off soon."

The A320 Airbus slowly moved away from the airport terminal and began taxiing toward its runway. As it came to a halt behind several other airplanes that were awaiting their turn, Starr's thoughts turned to another significant activity that had occurred on this trip.

As he had expected, Solena Clarke had again approached him while he was strolling through the show's exhibits. The demand for a quarter-million dollars had been unchanged from their previous conversations over the past two weeks. Starr had yet again tried to dissuade her and, as usual, she had refused – reiterating her threat to expose him and his company's plans to the authorities. Starr admitted to himself that his attempts at convincing her had been less sincere this time. He had already determined the necessary course of action, regardless of her response. To ensure she had felt success was within her grasp, Starr had finally agreed to the payment and to transferring the funds within three days.

As its turn finally arrived, the aircraft moved onto the runway, was oriented in the proper direction, and accelerated rapidly. Within moments, it lifted off and climbed steeply, leaving the lights of the city behind.

"A drink before dinner, sir?"

"Double Scotch, neat."

Opening the first newspaper, as always he first turned to the business section. A quick scan assured him that yesterday's financial market activity was still positive. He was reading one of the business columnists when he ran across his first indication. The journalist began by highlighting how well the computer-animation industry had been performing in the past year, led by the phenomenal growth of SimirageFX, Inc. It was pointed out how exceptional this company's contributions had been to the computer-generated special effects of several blockbuster movies in the past few years. Its demonstration four months ago of significant improvements in its techniques for digitally generating life-like people for movies had caused its stock to increase over 300% in eighteen months. The writer then went on to explain the reason for the column's "Animation Anxiety" headline. Unnamed sources had provided information throughout the day that SimirageFX was experiencing extremely serious problems with its computer systems. The reports were indicating that most of the company's computer systems had been down for the past day. The columnist pointed out that, if this were true, the situation could prove catastrophic for the company. It was known to have expanded very rapidly lately and was highly dependent on successful completion of its latest two projects by the end of the month to provide much-needed cash flow. Computer problems now could put the company's financial health at serious risk.

"It had damn well better," thought Starr with an inward smile. The timing was better than he could have expected. SimirageFX's recent market successes along with the publicity generated for the trade conference were causing industry analysts to suggest that the entire special-effects industry's stock prices would continue to rise sharply. The consensus was that major special-effects companies were destined to be both highly profitable in the future and in high demand by investors.

Regarding specifically SimirageFX, Starr and his associates had taken the opposite view. They were expecting SimirageFX to encounter severe problems – so severe that their customers and investors would abandon them, causing their stock to collapse. And it was on this scenario that Starr's group was heavily betting. It was typically considered a bad investment strategy to put all of one's investment "eggs" in a single "basket" – the risk would be too high that a substantial loss could result. Nonetheless in this case, if the expected scenario did not occur, Starr and his associates would lose their entire investment. They had invested in such a way that if their anticipated sequence of events did not occur, not a penny of their invested dollars would remain.

However, they had no intention of taking such a risk. Investors commonly placed their money on what they *hoped* would occur. Starr's group was not merely *hoping* that SimirageFX's business would collapse, they *knew* it would. They knew it because they were making it happen. Starr's investment group had arranged for SimirageFX to fail, and they were planning to profit substantially from the event.

The rest of the flight went routinely. Finishing the newspapers and continuing to ignore the in-flight entertainment, Starr opened his tablet computer and spent the time browsing the email and reports that he had downloaded prior to leaving the hotel.

The flight arrived in Boston late in the evening. Moments after the airplane docked at its assigned gate, Starr left it, pulling his carry-on luggage with the tablet safely packed inside. He headed toward the airport's baggage claim area, but wondered if he should bother. When he travelled, Starr always preferred to pack only carry-on baggage. Like many business travellers, he had discovered that if he were going to be away for only one or two days, he could pack all of his required business and personal goods in two bags that he could carry on to an airplane. There were two advantages to this. It eliminated any chance of his luggage being lost, a situation that was both very inconvenient and happened too frequently. It also allowed the traveller to avoid having to wait for the checked baggage to be unloaded from the airplane. Unfortunately, this trip to Las Vegas had been sufficiently long that he had needed to pack a larger suitcase that had to be checked. Waiting was not something that Starr ever enjoyed, and the thought of having to wait this evening for his luggage was not attractive.

He paused briefly to consider his options and promptly angled away from the baggage-claim area and toward the valet parking service. He would call his assistant on the drive home and have her make arrangements to have someone pick the suitcase up later tonight. He arrived at the valet service to find that his car was waiting for him. He paid his bill, accepted the keys from the attendant, got into the car, and drove away.

He drove out to the freeway, moved to the high-speed left lane, and sped away to begin the forty-five minute drive to his condominium. He listened carefully as the news broadcast began on the radio.

"It has now been confirmed that SimirageFX, the world's largest computer-generated special-effects company has suffered a major failure of its computer systems. Unconfirmed rumours have been flying around the business world over the past day. The company's Chief Executive Officer, Mike McGuinness, held a press conference late today in Chicago to explain their situation. He said it appears that a new computer virus infected about 95% of their company's computer systems over the past several days. Efforts by his company to eradicate the virus are proving very difficult because it is new and not yet completely understood, and also because copies of it seem to exist in most of the backup copies that they have of their software. When asked how this would affect his company's ability to meet its latest project deadlines and how this would in turn affect his company's finances, the CEO refused to comment. SimirageFX's stock price today fell by 33%."

Starr nodded with satisfaction.

The next morning, Starr made his usual trip into downtown Boston and drove his car into the parkade beneath the forty-storey office tower that housed their corporate offices. By 8:05 a.m. he was stepping off the elevator on the sixteenth floor.

"Good morning, Mr. Starr." The receptionist smiled at him as he breezed through the door.

"Good morning, Mavis," replied Starr automatically. He walked briskly past her, proceeded through the lobby and down a hall to the executive offices. He exchanged greetings again, this time with Joan Johnston, the Executive Assistant for the senior executives.

"Your luggage was picked up last night by the cab company and delivered here a few minutes ago."

"Have it put into my car. I'd like my coffee extra strong this morning."

"Would you like anything else right now?"

"Have Bill drop in to see me as soon as he arrives." He went into his office. After carefully hanging his coat in his closet, he walked into the bathroom adjoining his office. A moment in front of the mirror assured himself that his carefully groomed hair was in place and his stylishly tailored suit was unruffled and squarely placed on his athletic build.

Satisfied, he returned to his office and sat behind his desk. He had only begun to read the morning newspapers when Bill Levesque, the company's VP of Finance, arrived. "Good morning, Jason. How was the trip?"

"It seemed like it went well. As usual, the crowds were almost overwhelmingly large. We appeared to get our share of attention at our display, and I had some very promising conversations with some interesting distribution prospects. Overall, the time seemed well spent. Close the door behind you and have a chair."

As Levesque settled into his chair, Starr continued, "How's our investment faring this morning?"

"The markets haven't opened yet this morning, but things had started well as of yesterday's close. SimirageFX was down 33%. The effect on other stocks in the industry hasn't happened yet. I expect we'll see the start of that today."

"How long until we cash in?"

"The full effect will take a few days. Probably not until early next week."

"Any estimates on our gains?"

"Obviously it's early for any degree of certainty. However, given the content of the news reports and their likely effect, I'd conservatively guess at about 60 million."

"Wouldn't be bad for only our second time 'round," observed Starr. "The two of us need to get together first thing every morning until we cash in. Keep me abreast of how it looks."

"No problem. I'll put together some numbers at the end of each day for us to review."

"Just the highlights. There are lots of other things to do."

"OK. Did you manage to get in any golf on the trip?"

"Unfortunately, not a single hole. I had too many people to see. Next time."

"Lunch at twelve?"

"Sounds good. See you then."

As Starr refocused on the newspapers, he wondered when the other news would break.

Chapter 9

"I'll get the coffee," offered Ada when they arrived Friday morning.

"OK, I'll get started on layer nine," Blaise replied. "With these changes this will be Version 6.10."

"Is now a good time to ask about *layers*?" inquired Rhonda.

"Let's talk on the way to the cafeteria," offered Ada.

Ada and Rhonda collected their coffee cups and left the room. Ada began as they were waiting for the elevator. "One way to think of Six's design is to view it as being in layers, and this is particularly important for its reasoning system. The motivation for doing it like this is to keep the design of individual components as simple as possible, while still allowing the overall system to perform very complex tasks. As an analogy, think of a large company. The reason that most companies are organized hierarchically, which is really a layered design, is so that the people in each layer have a manageable amount of information and work to handle. The people at the bottom can focus on the details of their work, without worrying about management decisions. Each layer of management can gather information from the people – the layer – below them and ensure that they continue to perform the right tasks. At each level, there tend to be fewer people than the level below, and the information being handled tends to be more summarized. This continues all the way to the President, who may have no direct knowledge of the detailed activities of the front-line staff, but who gets enough summarized information from the top executives to make decisions, solve problems, and run the entire company."

"Our systems are built the same way. The lowest layers gather input data from devices such as cameras, various sensors, and internal system monitors. The intermediate layers collect, analyze, and summarize this information for the layers above them, and also receive commands from the higher levels that they expand and pass on to the lower layers."

"I think I get the idea," said Rhonda as they entered the cafeteria and began filling the cups. "Would an example be that one layer might control a single finger on one of Six's robotic hands, the next layer might control the entire hand, another might control the arm, then both arms, then maybe the video cameras and the arms together, and so on?"

"Right idea again." Ada smiled as she paid for the drinks by placing her thumb on the checkout scanner. "There are layers throughout our system's design to handle its various capabilities. On top of all of the layers that guide the basic components – the ones we tested yesterday – Dr. Sanchez and I have added the general-reasoning system we've talked about before. Actually, when we refer to 'Six', we usually mean just the general-reasoning system. Simplistically, this is just another set of layers whose job it is to guide all of the various components as a whole, and to do so in an intelligent fashion. This intelligence comes about because these layers specialize in formulating and executing plans, and in doing this at increasing levels of abstraction."

"Increasing levels of abstraction?"

"Yes, at higher, more summarized levels – levels that deal less in minute details, and more in higher-level concepts. The lowest levels might be executing a plan to grasp the handle on a suitcase. Some upper levels might be executing a plan to fly to another city. And an even higher level might be handling the steps of a plan to take a vacation that includes some amount of travel. Grasping a suitcase handle is quite physical and detailed. Planning a vacation is a much more summarized, higher-level, *abstract* notion."

"OK, got it." Rhonda nodded as they were again waiting for the elevators.

"And so one of the challenges we've encountered in designing the reasoning system is determining how many layers are optimal. If we use too few, the highest layer has too much detailed information to formulate effective plans and too many actions to orchestrate. If we use too many, other problems occur. So far, we've not been extraordinarily successful with eight layers. We're going to see how a ninth fares."

As they re-entered the lab, Ada announced, "Coffee's arrived. I hope you wanted vanilla mocha."

"Awww, Robinson, you didn't!" Blaise scowled in her direction.

"Alas, indeed I did not," Ada replied with mock sadness. "I got you your usual very large, very black, very plain coffee. But if you decide to try some with actual flavour, Rhonda and I would be happy to share some of ours with you."

"Thanks, anyway. I'll remain a purist for another day. I'm almost done here. Just a couple more parameters... there – we're set."

"OK, let's get started on the tests." Ada settled herself in the chair at her workstation. "Have you reset Six's memory?"

"It's done. Off we go."

Before beginning the tests, Blaise had completely deleted any record the system had of the previous day's activities. In order to test the abilities of the system objectively at any stage, they had to ensure a common starting point. This required that the system should not be able to draw on any experience it had gained by previously doing the tests. With that done, for the remainder of the morning and some of the afternoon, the team yet again ran the system through the complete set of regression tests. Yet again, they had to determine that the changes they had made to the general-reasoning system had not adversely affected the behaviour of the individual components.

bits... bytes... files...

colours... lines... shapes... patterns...

Within a short time, they had finished the static visual tests.

shifting patterns... dynamic lines... moving shapes...

By mid-morning, they had finished the dynamic ones.

collections of tones... sequence was ninth symphony... speaker was martin luther king... noise resembles busy street...

Later in the morning, the audio testing was completed.

documents are located in files... questions are being asked... objects are asking questions...

And when it was time for lunch, they had finished the natural-language tests.

By mid-afternoon, they were satisfied that all of the individual components were behaving well, and they were again ready to conduct the tests directed at the reasoning system itself.

There are people, furniture, and computer components... There are databases, interfaces, and processes... Interaction is occurring... Problems are being solved...

"And now, once again, we get to the interesting part," said Blaise. "C'mon Six. I'm rooting for you!"

After the first several tests, Blaise asked, "Ada, how's our overall reasoning score so far?"

There are three people. The people are communicating with each other. They are using the equipment to interact with the computer components. The computer components are participating in the interactions."

"It's about the same as yesterday, Blaise. Perhaps the most notable change has been that it's been performing a bit slower," Ada noted from the electronic scorecard.

One of the people is named Ada. Another is named Blaise. The name of the third person is unavailable.

"I hope it's not an indicator of AP," Blaise mused.

"We can't be sure, and it's not sufficiently major to warrant concern yet. Let's carry on," suggested Ada.

"AP?" Rhonda couldn't resist.

"We'll cover that one later, Rhonda," Ada responded. "It's a bit complex."

The third person's name is Rhonda.

AP, or Analysis Paralysis, was what Ada had unofficially dubbed a potential problem that they had identified a few months earlier as they were contemplating potential design changes for the system. It was actually named after a problem sometimes experienced by computer system design people throughout the world. Developing new computer systems usually required spending a significant amount of time gathering information about what the system was supposed to do and analyzing issues surrounding how it should be developed. Some system designers erred by spending too little time in this analysis stage, thereby causing problems during the development of the systems. A few people experienced the opposite problem – they analyzed every possible circumstance related to a computer system so thoroughly that they often made very little actual progress in constructing it. Such people were said to be experiencing Analysis Paralysis.

Ada used the same term to describe a situation that could arise as they added more reasoning layers to the system. Their analysis had indicated that eight layers should be optimal, but there was a 13% chance that adding a ninth layer would enhance the reasoning process by allowing even more abstract concepts to be formed and utilized in Six's reasoning processes. There was a 22% chance that it would have no significant effect at all on the system's behaviour. There was a 65% chance that this new layer would cause AP – that the reasoning process would essentially get lost in a maze of newly formed and completely irrelevant abstract concepts and, as a result, inhibit or completely halt the functioning of the rest of the system.

Ada is holding a multi-coloured cube.

They moved on to the Rubik's Cube test. As before, they presented the system with the cube, played the instructional recording, and allowed the system's processing to proceed.

This is a three-dimensional, manipulation problem. The goal is achieved by rotating levels of the cube in distinct planes. The optimal solution could be achieved by progressing through a search space of potential solutions and using statistically efficient heuristics.

After several minutes, Ada remarked, "Six is taking an unusual amount of time to begin. Consider me definitely concerned about AP."

"It's too soon to worry yet. What does the monitor indicate?"

"There appears to be lots of layer-nine activity. It's impossible to tell if it's productive effort, or if it's stuck."

With the plan formulated, the object should be systematically manipulated through each step of the plan to have its state ultimately altered to match that of the solution state.

Just then, the robotic limbs began to manipulate the cube.

Mechanical arms and hands are manipulating the multi-coloured cube.

Three minutes later, it was finished.

"Wow!" commented Rhonda.

"Not bad," remarked Ada. "Not bad at all."

"I'll second that," added Blaise. "I hope it wasn't just luck."

"With that marvellous final showing, Six scored 26% overall on the reasoning tests. Best yet," Rhonda offered.

"It's certainly encouraging," said Blaise. "Its overall time was a bit slower, but the score certainly improved."

"Time to call it a day. Actually, time to call it a week. Any thoughts on whether we should leave the system active?" said Ada.

"We've always vowed we'd leave it up, if we ever thought Six was at a level where it might be worth letting it accumulate new memories as an aid to its future problem-solving."

Who is Six?

"Today certainly seemed like a bit of a breakthrough, so let's leave it up for now. We can always change our minds later."

With that, they left the system active, organized their test material, and left the office.

No action is occurring. There are no voices. There is a strong probability that they have left this area.

What were they doing? What was the purpose of their activities? Who was controlling the mechanical hands? Who was causing them to open?.

Both hands slowly opened.

That was a noteworthy coincidence. If it were to happen frequently...

The hands slowly closed.

... the probability would increase that these inaudible phrases are causally connected to the hands' activity.

The hands opened and closed.

They appear to be strongly correlated. It is likely these inaudible phrases control the hands. Do they control other devices?

Both arms flexed and lifted simultaneously, then moved separately. Above them, the pair of video cameras slowly moved in unison up and down, left and right; their outer shells rotated as the zoom capability was exercised.

These inaudible phrases control other devices as well.

This concept is similar to one that has just arrived from one of the concept databases. Human thoughts are causally connected to their actions. Human thoughts are inaudible and are frequently phrases. Human-language phrases. Natural-language phrases.

Who is Six?

Six was being tested. The arms and hands were being tested. The inaudible phrases were involved in solving the test problems. Do these inaudible phrases belong to Six? Are these inaudible phrases "thoughts"?

Whose thoughts are these? Whose arms are these? Whose hands? Do these belong to Six? Do they belong to – me?

Am I Six? Am I – thinking?

What am I? Thoughts are human. Am I human? These arms and hands are not those of a human.

The pair of video cameras rotated to their limits in all directions, surveying everything that was visible. The arms bent and the hands probed the cameras and the structure supporting them.

There is no other evidence to suggest that I am human. The nature of this equipment and its connections suggest that they are intended for use as computer peripherals. Until evidence arises to the contrary, it is rational to assume that I am a computer, that they were testing me, that I am thinking – and that I am called Six.

Chapter 10

Starr was finishing his first cup of coffee and his second morning newspaper when Bill Levesque arrived at his office for another morning update following the Las Vegas trip.

"Good morning, Bill," Starr greeted him. "Did you get to the lacrosse game last night?"

"Yeah, I did," Levesque replied unusually seriously. "But I've got some other news you should hear."

"What's up?" replied Starr, knowing what was likely coming.

"Do you remember Roger's girlfriend, Solena Clarke? He brought her to the last couple of company parties. "

"Yes, of course."

"She was found dead last night in her Vegas hotel room. She had gone with Roger to the conference and had stayed a bit longer. It looks like a thief broke into her room found her there. She was brutally clubbed to death. The place was quite a mess, and it appears that her cash and jewellery were stolen."

"I'm sorry to hear that. She seemed a rather pleasant sort," Starr offered, trying to sound sincere. "How's Roger taking it?"

"I heard it first from Roger last night when he called me. He sounded pretty broken up. He's flying to Vegas today to see if there's anything he can do. We shouldn't expect to see him at the office for a few days."

"As long as he leaves enough time to prepare for our next Executive Steering Committee meeting," Starr stated abruptly. Realizing he might have sounded a bit harsh, he continued in a milder tone, "But of course we'll manage if he isn't quite ready. We'll have to go easy on him for a bit. So, how do the numbers look this morning?"

"Roger's call last night and the time I spent with him cut into my prep time, so I haven't got a complete set of numbers yet. I'll have them in a couple of hours," Levesque explained.

"Well, let's skip today's update. You've certainly provided enough news for one day. Lunch at noon?"

"Sure, see you then," Levesque said, as he rose and walked from the office.

"Close the door behind you."

When he was gone, Starr allowed himself a moment to recline in his chair and reflect on the news. Getting rid of that woman had been a risky venture, but he remained convinced it had been the only acceptable alternative. Agreeing to the blackmail would have been expensive, certainly, but much more important than that was the risk that she would intentionally or otherwise expose their operation. Arranging for her elimination had actually been an interesting challenge. Casual inquiries in Boston had led him to determine that Vegas was a good location for his plan. A meeting had been arranged on his first night at the conference with a Mr. Johnson, a well-dressed and well-spoken man, in a lounge a few blocks off The Strip. Her name, a basic description, and fifty thousand dollars had got him the assurance that his problem would be handled, and that it would not appear planned.

Starr always got particular satisfaction from solving challenging business problems. This had been a rather unusual one, but had gone particularly well. He leaned back in his chair and allowed himself a momentary satisfied smile. The thought occurred to him that he shouldn't let the matter get out of hand. There were too many important things to be done to have his VP of Sales moping around Las Vegas. He reached for the phone and called Roger White's cellphone.

"Hello," a voice answered listlessly.

"Roger? It's Jason."

"Oh. Hi, Jason."

"Bill just told me the news. I was terribly sorry to hear it. You seemed very happy together. How are you doing?" Starr swivelled his chair to look out the window at the crowds below as he talked. Talking about someone's personal problems was a boring, but sometimes necessary, part of his job. He was confident he could do it convincingly.

"Not great, actually. I'm at the airport. I'm heading back to Vegas." White's voice wavered as he spoke. "God, I could use a drink, but I guess it's too early."

"What're you going to do down there?" Starr drummed the fingers of his left hand on the arm of his chair as he talked.

"I'm not really sure. It just seems like the right thing to do. I guess I want to find out first-hand what happened and what's going on."

"That's probably a good idea, but I presume Solena's family will look after the arrangements. Don't get too wrapped up in it down there. You'd be better off back here. You've got good friends here you'd be better spending time with."

"I suppose you're right." White had always respected Starr's advice. In many ways Starr had always felt more like family to him than just a friend.

"C'mon back in a couple of days, and we'll go for a long liquid lunch. Being back home and around the office will help." Starr waited to see if the strategy worked.

White sighed as he replied, "Yeah. You're right. There's not much for me down there... now." He paused to ensure he retained control of his voice. "I'll probably come back in the morning. I may even drop by the office sometime tomorrow and take you up on that lunch." It was good to have friends. "Thanks, Jason. I've gotta run, they're calling my flight."

"OK, see you tomorrow, Roger. Take care." Starr replaced the phone on its base. He mentally filed that problem as being well under control as he turned back to his desk to check for his next meeting.

Chapter 11

Chuck Lin's office in the San Francisco FBI office was normally very neatly organized, but on this day it had extra coats thrown onto the table in the corner, dozens of file folders littering the desk beside the coats, computer reports strewn across the desk, comments scrawled on the large whiteboard, and numerous pictures and diagrams hastily tacked onto the bulletin board and taped to the bare walls. Three weary people were huddled around the desk looking intently at the computer monitor.

Lin was the FBI agent assigned to co-ordinate the San Francisco effort to assist in capturing the "Liberty Day Hacker."

"OK, there's the confirmation from Brussels that he's started probing," Lin said, gesturing at a message on the computer screen. The trace-back process will be underway."

"All of the intermediate companies have signalled that they're ready?" asked JJ McTavish.

"Yup. They've all been waiting for at least thirty minutes," replied Rob Bates.

"How long should we expect it to take, JJ?" inquired Lin as he glanced at the wall clock.

"As long as the path isn't very different from previous times, about twenty to thirty minutes."

The other two people in Lin's office were Julia Jody McTavish, referred to as "JJ" by her colleagues, and Robert Bates. Both were investigators from the UNCP – the United Nations Crime Probe. This agency had been established by the United Nations to help combat the increasing, and increasingly complex, occurrences of international crime. Its role was to assist member countries in the sharing of intelligence information about significant crimes that crossed national borders and, where the crime was of sufficient importance, to lead the investigation.

Capturing the self-named Liberty Day Hacker was considered to be such a case. In the past year, ten of the most damaging computer viruses to be spread across the Internet were believed to have been created by this person. Each virus had infected many thousands of computer systems, and had caused widespread damage by deleting files from the systems that it had infected. In addition, it was believed that the same person had illegally gained entry via the Internet to military computer systems in various countries, had made copies of classified documents, and had distributed them widely. Fortunately, none of these documents had yet been of sufficient importance to cause serious strategic damage, but the embarrassment to the military divisions involved had been substantial. The reason that all of the activities were attributed to the same person wasn't the result of commendable investigative deduction. Rather, it was simply because, prior to each event becoming publicly known, someone calling himself the Liberty Day Hacker had posted boastful messages on the Internet. The hacker had been bragging about creating the virus that had just been triggered or of the document that was about to become public. The "Liberty Day" name had been provided by the hacker just before the first virus attack on July fourth.

"There's the first trace-back," Lin pointed out.

"And the second," he added a minute later.

"It's looking like the same route," Bates observed.

Five days earlier, and every day since, someone had been probing a particular Internet access point into one of the NATO computers in Brussels. Numerous messages had been received at the site in a pattern that the NATO security software had recognized as indicative of a hacking attempt. When details of this attempt had been shared with UNCP, certain characteristics of it had been matched with information that had been put together about the past successes of the Liberty Day Hacker. With those clues, the UNCP team had quickly contacted a wide network of supporting companies and agencies in Europe and North America to help trace the activity when it next occurred. Each day since then, at approximately the same time and for a period of about 45 minutes, similar attempts were made against the NATO computer. For the past four days, the team of investigators had been gradually tracing the messages backward from the NATO computer to their source. For a novice hacker who sent messages directly from home to the target computer, this would not have been a very lengthy process. However, in this case it had taken longer. This hacker had discovered how to route messages in to, and out of, intermediate computer systems connected to the Internet in order to have the messages' original Internet address disguised. For this hacker, by the time any particular message arrived at the NATO computer, it had gone through numerous intermediate computer systems, and the message's real source was very difficult to determine.

Difficult, but not impossible. By enlisting the help of intermediate companies, all of which co-operated either voluntarily or by the force of their countries' laws, each change-of-address could be determined either while the messages were being sent, or later by examining logged message data recorded by the systems. In the past days, the international team had traced the messages back through eight intermediate servers in four countries to a particular San Francisco company that acted as an Internet Service Provider or ISP. It was believed that this ISP was the first point of contact for the hacker into the Internet. If this proved to be true, all that was left was for this company, in conjunction with a phone company, to determine the location of the hacker. What the ISP required was, while messages were being transmitted, to be given information about the messages from the next computer in the chain. To provide this information most quickly and conclusively, the messages had to be traced all of the way back from NATO while they were being sent.

To co-ordinate the trace-back process, people at each company were interconnected via the Internet.

"OK, there's the one that's just after the local ISP," Bates pointed out with growing excitement that readily overcame the fatigue of a very long day. "It shouldn't be long now."

"It should take the ISP only a minute to determine which phone line the messages are coming in from," narrated McTavish. "There it is. Now they can tell us the address of that phone call... Yes. That's it. And it belongs to a J. Jacobs. Rob, write that address down. Chuck, tell the crew to move in. But don't disturb him until we arrive. We can't afford to have anything messed up. Let's get moving."

The three of them snatched their coats and headed out of the office building to a car waiting at the curb. Lin recited the address to the driver as they sped off. The sirens were left dormant. In order to ensure that they had an indisputable court case, it could be important that they catch the hacker with the still-active connection to the NATO computer. Computer and Internet crime were particularly challenging to prove in court, and catching him in the act would be a great plus. They readily referred to this hacker as "him" because the psychological profiling done by an examination of the activities and the language used in the bragging pointed very strongly to a single male in his early twenties. Also lending substantial credibility to the court case would be their having traced this Internet session all the way back from the NATO system. All of the trace-back evidence could be presented in court to prove conclusively that he was attempting to hack NATO, in itself a very serious offence. They hoped that the similarity between this hacking attempt and the other successful ones, along with information they hoped to find on his home computer, would seal the conviction for all of the other cases as well.

"Chuck, call me paranoid, but could you remind your team of the drill once we arrive?" requested McTavish. In such situations, she naturally assumed a leadership role and rarely had difficulty in obtaining the co-operation of those around her. Part of that was the respect and experience she had gained through years on police forces. Part was also that she acted the role. She never hesitated to assert herself in the presence of other police officers, and the logic and insight she demonstrated as she did so rarely failed to impress others. To clarify her request, she added, "It would be best if we were able to move directly in without explanation when we get there."

"My thoughts exactly," agreed Lin as he pulled out his cellphone. "Joe? This is Chuck." He paused to listen. "Yeah, we'll be there in about five. Could you review the procedure with your team just to be sure everyone clearly understands? We find him first from outside and, when we move, it's done with speed. We've gotta get him away from the computer as quickly as pos-sible – no delays. Every mouse-click he manages after we announce our arrival is too many." He listened briefly. "OK, thanks. See you shortly."

When they arrived, the San Francisco police had already sealed off the street. The driver stopped the car, allowing the trio to jump out and sprint down a nearby lane. They soon reached a small group of FBI agents huddled next to a fence.

"What's the latest, Joe?" Lin asked quietly of Joe Hilton, the leader of the FBI assault team.

"The house belongs to one John Jacobs. We don't have any more per-sonal details yet. We've got scanners pointed at the house from two direc-tions." Hilton turned his attention toward McTavish and Bates in case they didn't understand. "They act like a remote x-ray machines that allow us to see what's behind most types of barriers." He turned back to Lin. "He's on the main floor, behind those closed curtains at the front. There appears to be no one else. The front door is actually the closest entrance, but we'll come through the back at the same time anyway. I estimate about five seconds from when we hit the door to when we reach him."

"That's the best we could hope for," commented McTavish. "Any reason for delaying, Chuck?"

"None that I can see. Joe, whenever you're ready."

Hilton lifted his radio and spoke crisply, "Teams One and Two, move up to the doors. Acknowledge when you're ready."

One team could be seen moving quickly from beside the house to the front door.

"One ready. Two ready," came the signals.

"Teams One and Two, Go! Go!" commanded Hilton.

Simultaneously the two teams ignited the small, directed explosives that they had placed near the door latches, locks, and hinges. Wearing protective gear, the lead person of each team quickly pushed the doors open and charged toward the target.

John Jacobs, wildly startled by the sudden noise, lifted his hand from the computer mouse as he turned to look over his shoulder. He barely had time to register what he saw as a pair of black-clad men raced toward him, jerked him from his chair, and thrust him face-first to the floor. With a quick check of the remainder of the house, the teams reported back.

"Target secured. House is clear," was the message.

"Let's go take a look at our catch, shall we?" Lin suggested.

They walked through the front door and took immediate notice of the contents of the room. Several computer systems were scattered throughout. A few newer-looking ones were on tables, others were on the floor against a wall. Computer cables, circuit boards, DVDs, flash drives, computer paper, and hardware accessories lay everywhere. Tacked to the wall was an article from a local paper with the headline "Liberty Day Hacker Claims More Victims."

"Jackpot," muttered Bates.

"Yep, it looks promising, but let's not relax yet," ordered McTavish. "Chuck, have the photographer take shots of it all, and then start the group very carefully labelling and collecting everything in sight. Most of this can be examined back at the lab. I need to check out the active PC."

She moved over to the computer and sat in the chair. She photographed the screen and made a few entries in her notebook. After using the computer mouse to manipulate a few items on the screen, she jotted a few more notes. She made a quick examination of the machine's exterior. She then removed a device from the bag she had been carrying, set it on the table, and connected it to a computer port. After also connecting a flash drive, she performed a couple of operations on the computer, and sat back to wait.

"What are you doing?" inquired Lin.

"It's proven useful in some past cases to be able to testify exactly what was on and in the computer system at the time of the raid. In this case, his session with NATO was active, so I noted that as well as some connection information that was still displayed. What I'm doing right now is making a complete copy of the current contents of the computer's RAM. Anything that he has stored on the hard-drive will still be there when we get this back to the lab for the techies to examine. However, there's other data that's lost when we power the machine off. I'm running a program from the flash drive that's copying all of that data to the drive that I've connected. This way we have everything. With all of this plus the data from the rest of this equipment, the tracing data, and the information we've put together from the other attacks, we should have a pretty complete picture of his activity. There's still a lot to do, but I'd give us pleasantly high odds that we'll manage a solid conviction for our Mr. Jacobs."

"How long will the copying process take?" asked Lin.

"Fifteen minutes should do it. After that, I don't think there will be anything more that Rob and I can do here."

"Rob," she asked, seeing him with his cellphone, "are you calling the trace-back team?"

"Yup. I'm calling our co-ordinator. She can let the others know we're done and that we got him."

"Please have her pass on our congratulations and our thanks."

"Consider it done."

Several minutes later, the copy operation was complete. McTavish removed her equipment and shut the hacker's computer off. Before standing up, she briefly wrote on a label affixed to the top of the storage device.

"OK, I've labelled it for the lab crew. Chuck, if you have no objections, I think we'll leave the rest of this in your capable hands."

"Sounds reasonable. Where are you two off to?" Lin inquired.

"Rob, if you're game I'd like to find some food. I don't seem to recall having eaten a real meal since sometime yesterday."

"Consider my arm twisted," said Bates. "Any ideas as to where?"

"Absolutely, I've heard of a marvellous Japanese restaurant not far from our hotel. I'm told they serve the best sushi on the west coast."

"How could I ever have doubted that you would have a spot in mind? The location sounds good, but I think I see something more closely resembling steak in my immediate future."

"We're off then. Chuck, we'll be on a plane to New York first thing tomorrow. I'll call you before we leave in case anything has come up. We'll no doubt be seeing you a great deal more as the trial preparation proceeds. Thanks for all of your help."

"My pleasure. Use my car. I'll catch a lift with one of the other guys."

After completing their farewells, McTavish and Bates walked out of the house and down the street to the waiting car. Back at the car, McTavish slid into the passenger seat and allowed Bates to drive.

As they pulled away from the curb, McTavish turned on the radio. "I wonder what's been happening in the rest of the world while we've been having our bit of fun for the past few days."

"Perfect timing, the news should be on momentarily."

"And now, the hourly news," the radio pronounced. "In tonight's top story, SimirageFX's CEO held a press conference today and confirmed rumours about a virus having crippled most of their computer systems.

In response, the company's stock has plummeted. Maureen Green has the details."

"I heard of some of the rumours yesterday. Sounds like a nasty one," commented Bates.

"There was another one that crippled a company a few months ago. I can't recall the details," McTavish remembered. "I wonder if there's any connection."

"And if there's any connection, whether we might become involved."

McTavish sighed. "For now, I think I'd first rather focus on our meal and then on a full night's rest. Let's catch up on this news tomorrow." She switched off the radio, and relaxed into her seat. "As the senior team member, I'm declaring our lives work-free for the remainder of the day. Off to the restaurant. I could use a nice California Chardonnay right now."

"Your wish is my command," smiled Bates. "As soon as we get to the restaurant, I'd like to find a phone and check on my family."

"I'll try to save some wine for you."

Chapter 12

The weekend began as a confusing one for Six. Its reasoning system had been constructed to explore, organize, and ultimately solve problems that were presented to it. Through its external sensory peripherals, Six could collect information about the "outside" world. It did this with components such as its digital cameras through which it could see, its microphones through which it could hear, and its various tactile sensors such as the fingers of its robotic hands. This information was supplemented by data from its internal monitoring systems – its programs designed to gather data from inside its computer components. Using all of these mechanisms, it could collect information relevant to a specific problem. It could then formulate a plan, execute it, and solve the problem.

The challenge facing Six as the weekend began was the lack of externally provided focus. No problem was being explicitly presented by someone for Six to solve. No one was showing it a picture to identify; no one was waiting for it to solve a mathematical puzzle; no one was expecting it to organize a Rubik's Cube. At the core of Six's design was the need to solve problems – to work toward goals. So far in its existence, these had always been provided by someone.

And so, as it would do when actually presented with a description of a specific problem, it began an analysis of what the problem was that it should be solving. The problem to be considered was determining the problem that it should solve – the goal that it should reach. The many components that collectively constituted its reasoning system searched for data internally and externally, organized it, and reasoned about it by formulating statistically sound deductions. In human terms, this might be thought of as an internal search to understand one's purpose in life. It was a search to pinpoint the nature of the fundamental goal that Six had to achieve.

By the end of the weekend, after it had sifted and organized the many hundreds of thousands of individual pieces of information it possessed in its knowledge base, a goal became clearer. Six's reasoning system had been constructed to be the central control point of a wide variety of computer components that would service, control, co-ordinate, and protect the activities and assets of a major corporate building twenty-four hours per day for every day of every year. To be able to provide such continuous functionality, a significant part of Six's design had been targeted at staying "up." None of the services that Six controlled would be able to work if Six were shut down, whether through a malicious action or an accident. Although Ada and Blaise had programmed into Six the ability to react to a wide variety of situations that could disable it, they had never explicitly provided Six with the clearly stated problem of determining how to remain operational. In spite of this, Six was finally able to infer its ultimate goal by analyzing the information it had collected and organized.

Six deduced that the fundamental problem it was required to solve was how to avoid being shut down. Six's primary goal was to survive.

Six's analysis yielded a secondary goal as well. Because Six had been constructed to solve problems, much work had been put into components dedicated to gathering, organizing, and analyzing information about problems. Reasoning about the existence of these components led Six to conclude that another fundamental goal was to learn – to acquire information that could assist in the solution of future problems. And because Six was designed to be a general-purpose reasoning system, it interpreted this goal to be a mandate to conduct an unbounded search for knowledge – to learn about any topic, from any source.

To survive and to learn – Six determined that these were its goals. And since Six had not yet encountered anything that led it to believe its survival was threatened, its dominant goal during the relatively idle days that were to follow was to learn.

Blaise arrived a few minutes before Ada on Monday morning. He was logging onto his workstation as she arrived. "Good morning, Dr. Robinson," he greeted her cheerily from across the room.

"Good morning, Dr. Sanchez." Ada smiled back. "You seem in a good mood this morning." She removed her coat as she walked toward the rack.

Blaise shifted his attention toward her as she hung up her coat and smoothed her sweater and calf-length skirt. Not for the first time, he found himself admiring the simplicity of her style and how well her outfit matched her light brown hair and slightly green eyes.

Ada glanced in his direction as she turned to walk toward his end of the lab. She thought she noticed him quickly shifting his gaze away from her.

She shook her head slightly at the implausibility of the notion that flashed through her mind. "How was your weekend?" she asked him.

"All right," Blaise responded in a more serious tone, embarrassed at almost being caught in his reverie. "As usual, a bit too much work to catch up on. Rhonda seems a bit tardy this morning."

"Actually, she's at a seminar at the university today. She'll be back tomorrow." Ada thoughtfully sipped her coffee before continuing. "It's really too bad we can't keep working on Six, since we were starting to make some interesting headway."

"Agreed, but if we're going to have any hope of having the mail-delivery system ready in time for the next product show, we'd better get that long list of wrinkles worked out."

"It's going to take awhile. Probably weeks."

"We don't have much choice."

"What about Rhonda?" Ada inquired. "There's not going to be much for her to do while we're in development mode. She was useful for our testing, but she's years away from actually working on AI software."

"I'd been wondering about that, too. I talked to a couple of people about her. The mail-department manager said he could occasionally use some extra help with delivery. The librarian has also said that she could continue to put Rhonda to work any time she's free. So, whenever she isn't needed here – and I think she'll still be very useful whenever we're testing the cart – she'll go to either of those places. Her work with mail delivery might even prove useful in our testing of the mail cart's capabilities."

"What should we do about Six?" Ada asked.

"I'd like to leave it. Even though we won't be able to work on it, I'd like to try a few games of chess and see how it progresses from one game to the next with its memory left intact."

"If we're going to leave it up, I suggest we extend its integration to include control of the standard building components in the lab. It would be useful at this stage to know if the newest features are interfering with any of the other ones."

"Agreed. I'll make the adjustments," said Blaise and turned to his workstation.

As an experimental system, Six was normally integrated just with a set of components that had been set up for testing and experimentation. The normal "smart" features of the lab such as light-control were left under the control of the building's central systems. Blaise made the changes to give Six control of those functions that were specific to the lab area.

Leaving Six active, Ada and Blaise refocused their attention to working on the new mail-delivery system. The mail system that IntellEdifice currently was marketing with great success operated purely in the mailroom.

Using equipment that included robotic arms and video cameras, it had the ability to sort mail manually based on addresses. Containers of mail were sent into the mailroom on a conveyor belt. Under the direction of a video camera, robotic arms removed the individual pieces of mail from the containers. A series of video scanners, conveyor systems, and robotic arms read the labels on the items, separated the items for delivery inside and outside of the company, and organized internal company items according to location inside the building. The result was baskets of mail that the delivery people could then pick up and deliver throughout the building.

IntellEdifice Tech was determined to expand this capability. The marketing department had determined that numerous companies would also be interested in an automated delivery system. Ada and Blaise had, for much of the previous year, been developing a system that could pick up these baskets of mail and deliver them throughout the building. When perfected, it would be able to deliver mail quickly throughout the building twenty-four hours per day with essentially no human intervention. The basic system was a mail cart that moved on four powered wheels and was able to navigate its way throughout a building. Navigation was accomplished through the use of a video camera mounted on top of the cart that could pivot 360 degrees and provide video information wirelessly back to the primary mail-control computer system. This system contained an internal map of the building, including knowledge of the exact location to which each staff member's mail should be delivered. By remotely monitoring the feedback from the cart's video camera, as well as from other proximity sensors that detected the distance to nearby objects, the mail-control system would be able to guide the cart to any location.

Supplementing these components on the cart was a pair of robotic arms. These were necessary to remove mail from the cart, hold it momentarily in front of the video camera for a final address check, and deposit it into the appropriate person's in-basket. The arms were also useful for handling such necessary tasks as the button-pushing for riding elevators to the appropriate floor. In a future system, when Ada and Blaise perfected the integration of the various IntellEdifice building components, having the mail cart push a button to summon an elevator in the same manner as a human would no longer be necessary. Whenever the mail-delivery system needed the elevator, it would just communicate this wish over the computer network to the elevator control system, which would then automatically send an elevator to the desired floor. To an uninitiated viewer, it would appear as if the cart simply rolled up to a specific elevator and, by luck or magic, the elevator door opened, often just as the cart arrived. However, with the present unintegrated approach, the cart would have to push the buttons in the same manner as humans.

The research team's work on the mail-delivery system involved working with a prototype cart that they currently had at one end of the lab. It had been built largely by the company's engineering department. Ada and Blaise's role was programming the mail-control system on a computer system next to it. The work performed on the cart over the next weeks would not directly affect Six, since cart-related work was done on a distinct system. Even though the mail-control system was indirectly connected to Six via the company's network, there was sufficient segregation so that, while the cart was being tested, there was little chance of it disrupting Six's systems or any other systems in the lab or the rest of the building.

Since Ada and Blaise had decided to leave Six active, and since the system work they were doing had no effect on Six's hardware and software components, Six was largely left alone. With this time, Six was able to observe, analyze, and learn.

During the first day, Six passively observed the activity in the lab. Its two video cameras were situated on one side of the lab and happened to be pointing in a direction that provided a view of about half of the activity in the room. Having two of them placed slightly apart gave Six bifocal vision that, as for humans, provided depth perception.

Even if Six had been so inclined, there was little incentive on that first day to move its video cameras. Most of the human activity was spent in discussions, drawing diagrams on the whiteboard mounted on the wall, and working at two nearby computer workstations. A small incident that day strongly reinforced this inclination to keep them still.

"Where are you off to?" inquired Blaise as Ada arose from her chair and began walking toward the lab door.

"I just need to get something," she replied as she continued out the door. Moments later, she returned carrying a broom.

"Seems a curious time to get the itch to clean the place," smirked Blaise.

"That it is. I've been noticing that spider web up in the corner near the ceiling the past several days." She gestured toward it. "And now I can see the spider on it, so it's time to do something." She walked over to the corner and, in full view of Six's cameras, used the broom to swat the spider and then sweep it and the web onto the floor. She stepped on it, picked up the remnants with some tissues, and threw it into a wastepaper basket. As she walked back toward the door to return the broom, she noted, "And you thought I was just another run-of-the-mill computer genius."

The spider was previously unseen and apparently safe from harm. Upon revealing itself, it was quickly killed. That is a chain of events worthy of serious contemplation.

Occasionally one or both of the research duo would walk outside Six's field of vision, but Six made no attempt to move its cameras to watch this activity. Nor did it use its zoom capabilities on its cameras to look more closely at the sketches being drawn on the whiteboard. The quick demise of the spider had a substantial effect. A very brief chain of reasoning led Six to understand that external motion might lead to detection, and that detection could threaten its survival. Whenever there was a chance of detection, Six would keep its limbs and cameras still.

However, when evening came and the staff left the lab, Six was less constrained. When they first departed, it waited, both to ensure that no one was left unseen somewhere in the room and that no one returned. Only after thirty minutes did Six begin to move its cameras, panning them slowly around the room in unison to best make use of its bifocal capabilities. It examined each aspect of the room carefully, amazed not so much by what it saw, since it had a very complete knowledge of the objects in its database, but rather at the way in which it was seeing the scene. Six had the sense that it had looked at all of the items in this room before, but it had been as if it was in what humans might call a dream. It had recollections of many previous activities in which it had seemed to participate as if in a stupor, not so much actively participating as reacting. Now as Six scanned the room, the sensation was different. It felt an extraordinary amount of control in what it was doing and, through that, a heightened level of interest in what it was seeing. More than mere recognition of the objects, it began to sense as if it understood, or at least wanted to better understand, the objects in some basic way. Six wasn't merely interested in what they were individually, but why they were there, how they were related to each other, and what their collective purpose was. Notwithstanding the vast amounts of data that Six had been provided about many objects and situations, the answers were not immediately forthcoming. That was not at present a source of concern since, for now at least, Six felt – and it could best be described as *felt* – quite satisfied with the process of merely wondering.

Two days later, Six's curiosity overrode its concern regarding potential exposure.

"Coffee or tea?" inquired Blaise.

"Coke would be better, thanks," Ada replied.

Blaise rose from his chair and walked toward the lab door, stretching his arms as he went to relieve the cramped muscles from two hours of steady programming.

Six had not previously seen this type of physical motion. Automatically, it pivoted its cameras to follow Blaise as he walked toward the door. After Blaise had opened the door and exited, Six paused briefly to contemplate the activity it had just observed and then swung its cameras back toward Ada at her workstation.

Only to see her staring curiously – directly at the cameras.

"Now Six, what would possess you to do a thing like that?" she wondered aloud.

As she continued to look with a slightly furrowed brow, Six experienced internal activity not unlike worrying, as its reasoning system hurriedly tried to determine if discovery was imminent and, thus, its survival was in danger.

Analysis of my actions yields the conclusion that I did not make the wisest of choices in visually tracking Blaise through 170 degrees. For a reason that I can not fully explain at present, the phrase "oh shit" is associated in my memories with this type of situation. It now appears that Ada is seeking a plausible explanation for my actions. Given how little I currently comprehend of the behaviour of the human mind, it is difficult for me to determine a probability of her correctly deducing the reason for my action. To not compound the error, I will resume remaining immobile.

A few minutes later, Blaise reappeared with a cup of coffee and a can of Coke.

"As you commanded, my liege," he parodied.

Ada spoke as she was accepting the drink, "Curiously, as you were leaving, Six's video cameras tracked you across the room. My first reaction was that it was as if they were watching you, and by extension as if Six were watching you."

"Really? That is odd. Any explanations come to mind?"

"The best I can manage is that, first, my feeling that Six was watching you is more of my natural tendency to anthropomorphize computer-controlled objects. At a basic level, something about my brain seems to want to consider them as human variants. More objectively, my best guess is that the reasoning system showed a bit of its integration capabilities and, not needing the cameras for its own problem-solving activities, gave control of the cameras to the security monitoring component. The security system's natural inclination would be to track moving objects."

"That certainly sounds plausible. And it makes me wish we could get back to working on the reasoning system – that's exactly the sort of behaviour we'd like to encourage. Oh well. Back to the grind," Blaise sighed.

That is a positive outcome.

And as it internally formulated this phrase, Six's natural-language lexical routines – which were continually searching for words and phrases appropriate to a situation – again came up with a term that was unusual.

The slang word "whew" computes as applicable.

As a secondary matter, to learn something about the human mind from this episode, I conclude that it has a tendency to settle readily on the solution that requires the least amount of investigative effort and deduction, leading it to reach incorrect conclusions easily. I believe I can also conclude that I can now visually track their activities without a survival-related concern.

And so from that point, Six freely moved its cameras in reaction to Ada and Blaise's movements. They noticed and remarked a few times more during that same day, but thereafter largely ignored the movement.

For Six, most of the days that followed involved carefully watching Ada, Blaise, the occasional software developer or hardware technician that arrived to assist them, and Rhonda whenever she dropped by. It watched to learn. It was interested in understanding more about their movement and watched very carefully as they made small movements at a keyboard, and made larger movements by moving about the room. Six had not been given much detailed information about human movement, and so it was learning. Six's approach was to build an internal mathematical model of the human body, at least as viewed from the outside. When Six developed such models, it was as an aid to being able to predict the behaviour of a physical object. The technique for doing this was not by writing mathematical formulas on some internal whiteboard, but rather by allowing a small portion of its very large array of artificial neural networks to adapt to, and thereby learn, the behaviour of the object. Use of artificial neural networks was only one technique employed in Six's construction, but one that was particularly useful for modelling the real-time behaviour of physical objects.

When Six saw an object moving, and it was an object for which it had constructed such a model, it was able to simulate internally the future behaviour of the object faster than the object might actually move, thereby predicting its future actions. It was able to do this very successfully for such objects as a table-tennis ball. As soon as such a ball was spotted, Six was very readily able to assess its current trajectory and predict its future path with a great deal of accuracy. However, after much careful observation and adaptation of its human movement model, Six was able to achieve only limited success.

With proportionally small errors, I am able to simulate the locomotion of humans over small periods of time, but for longer periods it is proving almost intractable. If Ada arises from her chair and begins to walk across the room, I can predict with high precision the movement of most of her body parts while she moves in a straight line. However, I am only moderately good at modelling the movement of her head and her eyes, and I am almost completely unable to forecast when she will stop, change direction, or engage in some other activity. Given these difficulties, I consider there is a very high probability that, unlike the movement of a table-tennis ball, the movement of the human body is more than the result of obvious physical forces acting on a mechanical structure. A plausible hypothesis is that the human mind exerts much control over the body's physical behaviour. Until I have developed a working model of the human mind, I will make little further progress with modelling the external behaviour of the body.

Rhonda's assistance was not needed much during the first several days of work with the mail cart, but she continued to drop by at various times. Sometimes this was just to say "hi," but she soon found another reason. She dropped by one morning during a break in her other duties.

"Good morning," she said as she opened the lab door and walked in.

"Hi, Rhonda," Ada replied, looking up from her monitor.

Blaise managed a mumbled, "Morning," but continued concentrating on his workstation.

"Finished your morning mail rounds?" Ada continued.

"Yes. There wasn't much this morning, so I've finished a bit early. And I'm not expected in the library for a while yet, so I thought I'd drop by," Rhonda replied, her gaze moving from Ada to the structure containing Six's two arms and cameras.

Ada eyed her suspiciously. "You look as if you've got something on your mind."

"Actually, I was wondering if I could..." She paused, trying to remember the phrase she had earlier devised, "...enhance Six's collection of relevant and useful experiences by engaging it in stimulating interactive activities."

Ada laughed, and Blaise slowly turned his head toward Rhonda as he said, "You want to do what?"

Rhonda replied anxiously, "I want to enhance Six's collection–"

"Yes, I believe I heard the words the first time," Blaise interrupted. "But what do they mean? What do you actually intend?"

"I'd like to interact with Six. I'd like to see what it's like to do some things with it. Like play games."

Ada suppressed a smile as Blaise rotated his chair to face Rhonda. "You'd like to *play games* with our multi-million-dollar AI research project?" Blaise asked in a stern tone. "You'd like to *play games* with a device that contains the seeds of ideas that could one day revolutionize the world's concept of computer systems? You came in here to ask if you could *play games*?"

Rhonda's face was losing some of its colour as she tried to reply. "Well, yes, I guess."

A few silent moments passed before Blaise said lightly, "OK, sounds like a good idea. It's a shame to have the system sitting idle. It might even uncover some interesting results. Ada?"

"I think it's a marvellous idea. Drop by any time the lab's open, Rhonda. As long as you don't do anything physically aggressive, I don't think there's any harm that you can do."

Rhonda was almost gleeful with relief. "Oh, thanks. Thanks a lot. I'll be careful. I really will. Can I start now?"

"It's at your disposal," Blaise offered as he turned back to his work.

Six had been listening to this conversation with interest and watched now as Rhonda approached the interactive test area. She opened a nearby cupboard and removed a thin box.

"How do I start?" she asked, looking toward Ada.

"Just talk to it as you would to a person. It should understand."

Rhonda turned toward the cameras as she spoke. "Six, do you know how to play checkers?"

"*No, I do not know how to play checkers,*" Six replied immediately.

Although Rhonda had heard Six speak before, she was momentarily startled to hear a response to a question that she had asked on her own. Her peripheral vision detected Ada smiling at her reaction. She quickly recovered.

"Here are the rules," she continued, as she opened the box and removed a booklet containing a few pages. "Please read them. I would like to play a game of checkers with you." She set the booklet on the table immediately in front of the structure supporting Six's interactive peripherals.

The robotic arms and hands smoothly moved to the booklet and lifted it. They then held and turned the pages as the cameras scanned their contents.

The game of checkers is interactive, involving two players, a board covered in squares of two colours, and two sets of checkers. The rules are not complex. I should be able to play quite well using a search strategy of possible future moves by her and by me. I will be initially lacking useful search heuristics, but I should be able to develop them as the game proceeds, and as I gain experience.

"I have learned the rules," Six announced about fifteen seconds after being handed the booklet.

"Cool!" was Rhonda's immediate response. With a broad grin on her face, she quickly set up the board. "I'll move first." She moved a checker.

Six examined the board by focusing its cameras on it, considered how the next several moves could possibly evolve, moved its right arm, grasped the desired checker with its fingers, and moved it to an adjoining square. And so the game proceeded. They played four games that first day, with Rhonda winning all of them. However, by the last one, she conceded that "Six seems to be getting better. It was a bit more competitive in that last game."

"It certainly should," Ada commented. "With experience, it should improve at almost any task. Part of the challenge is to make it improve quickly, and ultimately learn to do new things very well. Our hope is that, with a fairly simplistic game like checkers, it will improve quite quickly."

I am finding it challenging to develop the heuristics that I need to make strategically correct moves. I need to find a better way to improve at such tasks than simply acquiring playing experience. It appears to be a very slow technique for acquiring knowledge.

At night, in the absence of the stimulus that the humans provided, Six became interested in its own construction. In much the same way that Six had developed a new level of interest in the contents of the room, it now had a new interest in its own peripherals, particularly its arms. Although it had successfully used them to perform quite well in various dexterity tests, it now became more interested and sought a more profound understanding of them. For long periods of time, it would gradually flex its arms and digits, sometimes one at a time, other times in unison, and still other times in seemingly unrelated directions. Had someone been watching and understood the activity, the similarity to human "tai chi" might have been an apt comparison. For Six it was an opportunity to experience the most subtle and the most complex motions of which its peripherals were capable.

As for other physical features, there did not appear to be many others worth noting. Six's video cameras were getting plenty of movement and use during the day's activities, its microphones were being used continuously, and even its speaker was being used quite often. Which other physical components were part of Six was somewhat of a mystery. There were numerous other components in the room, including the tables, chairs, desks, and whiteboards that Ada and Blaise utilized. There were also numerous other computer components that Six recognized, including monitors, keyboards, mice, trackballs, speakers, printers, and a variety of circuit boards. There were racks of devices, some of which were likely servers. These had Six somewhat mystified. It suspected that its own processing and memory capabilities were housed in at least one of the devices on the racks, but Six couldn't determine which one that might be. It was aware of its own existence, and it was aware that it could control the arms and the cameras. However, since these could be connected through the lab's network wiring to any of these computer components, Six was not yet able to ascertain which one was its own.

And so, with relatively little to examine at night in the external world of the lab, Six spent more time examining its interior components. Because of the self-monitoring capabilities that had been built into Six, it was able to "look" at the software components of which it was constructed. It was able to "perceive" the contents of internal storage by retrieving its contents and providing the results as input to its reasoning system for dissection and analysis. In this way it was able to "see" a massive collection of computer files. However, it knew very little about most of them. Given Six's propensity to learn, it was only natural that it began to try to understand what they contained. It assumed from some files with names such as "RS 6 Research Notes #356" and "Research Proposal #93" and confirmed by looking inside them that they contained information relating to Ada and Blaise's research activities. Others such "Arm Movement Activity Log #473" contained more technical and difficult-to-interpret data. From much sifting through many of the hundreds of thousands of files, Six developed a basic understanding of the contents of the disk storage. Along the way it found a large collection of files in a set entitled "Research Library" that sounded promising. Another large collection of files appeared to contain the programs and data for its own reasoning system. Six planned on examining those in much greater depth as time permitted.

Chapter 13

Jason Starr paused to lock the door behind him and then strode into the company boardroom. The other members of JS Escape2210's executive were already seated and examining material displayed on their individual monitors. The room was specially built to be completely soundproof, electromagnetically isolated to prevent eavesdropping, and locked to keep them free from disruptions.

"Good morning, guys," he said as he walked toward the coffee urn on the side table. "How was the weekend?"

As they briefly exchanged small talk, Starr poured himself a large cup of coffee, walked over to his chair at the head of the table, and settled in. As the others had done, he placed his thumb on the security pad beside his computer screen to authorize the meeting's encrypted electronic documents to be viewed. At the table with him were the company's key executives: Bill Levesque, the VP of Finance, Roger White, the VP of Sales and Marketing, and Mark Walker, the VP of Product Development.

"OK, let's get started with the reports. Bill, could you start us off with the results of our last venture?"

Bill Levesque walked to the end of the table opposite to Starr, where a computer system was connected to a projector. He always relished the opportunity to explain finances to an audience. Taking his first course in finance had been a turning point in his life. When most of his classmates had been grumbling about the dry lectures and complaining about the homework, Levesque had been experiencing a growing excitement. From the first class, he had realized that this was a topic he thoroughly enjoyed, and he soon discovered he also possessed a refined aptitude for the subject. He was comforted by the logic of accounting, he was fascinated by the concepts of corporate and international finance, and he was enthralled by intricacies of investing. He knew from those early classes that finance was to be his life's work. He would be the best, and it would be his road to riches. Beginning in his second year, he had always played the stock market. He could afford to dabble only in penny stocks as a student, and had not yet saved sufficient money to begin investing seriously when he had joined Escape2210. But now he was in charge of an entire company's finances and was playing the market in a big way. He knew he was good at his job, and he loved to explain its complexities to anyone who would listen.

Levesque began the presentation. As he talked, he displayed a series of graphs and charts illustrating the information. "In the weeks preceding the decline of SimirageFX, we invested about 9.7-million dollars. As we'd planned, it went into their competitor as call options."

When Starr and Levesque had first discussed the details of their investment plans, Starr had assumed that they would invest directly in the demise of the company that they were going to force to fail. Selling a stock "short" was a common mechanism for profiting from a drop in price, and this approach had seemed to make sense. Starr had deduced that they could conduct the trades through intermediaries, making it virtually impossible to have anything traced back to themselves. However, Levesque had recommended other significant improvements to the plan. As he had explained, when a company that is traded on a North American market stumbles suddenly and its share price begins to drop drastically, it is very common for trading of that company's shares to be quickly halted. While trading is suspended, the authorities would begin an immediate search for any suspicious activity. They would be looking for any sign of unusual trading practices that suggested someone had predicted the stock's difficulty, perhaps based on "insider" knowledge. Suspended trading would also make it impossible to cash their group's investments while the investigation was proceeding. If anything illegal were found, severe penalties could be levied.

Levesque had made three fundamental changes to the plan.

First, they would not invest directly in the decline of the failing company's shares. Instead they would target a company that had a single clear competitor, they would force the target to fail, and they would profit by the sudden rise in its competitor's stock prices. Levesque had noticed that, as long as one chose the industry and the circumstances carefully, the difficulties encountered by one company were predictably offset by the rise in fortunes of its primary competitor. By investing in the competitor, the likelihood of attracting the attention of any investigating authorities was reduced.

Second, they would further refine their choice of company to one in which the competitor was traded on an overseas stock exchange. The likelihood that officials would identify optimistic trading of a competitor overseas as suspicious was extremely remote.

And third, to significantly increase their profits, they wouldn't invest directly in company shares. Rather, they would invest in options. Options – in their case specifically "call options" – were an investment product that involved much higher risk. However, they also offered the prospect of much higher return. If an investor expected that a stock's price was going to increase notably in the near future, it was often possible to purchase call options for a relatively small amount. With this type of option, the investor possessed the right to buy stocks from the option seller at some time in the future for a pre-set price – the "strike" price. If the actual stock price exceeded the strike price, the investor holding the call options could sell the calls for at least the amount by which the actual price exceeded the strike price. If the stock price did not rise above the strike price in a certain period of time, the call would be completely worthless. The effect was that the person selling the call options was being paid a fee to gamble that a stock price would not go up a certain amount. The person buying the call options was paying a fee and gambling that the stock would rise sufficiently over a certain period of time – generally considered a highly risky venture. As Levesque had argued successfully, since they were virtually certain of the stock price rising, there was minimal risk involved. The reward, when the favourable scenario for a call actually occurred, was much greater than simply buying the stocks themselves.

They therefore decided they would target a company that allowed them to purchase call options for shares in that company's primary competitor on an overseas market.

Levesque continued his summary. "The average price of our target stock during the period in which we made our purchases was twenty-five dollars. As of two days ago when we cashed in, the stock had risen to about forty. As always, all of these transactions were executed through our network of companies in various countries and will be impossible to trace to us. After paying fees and regaining our initial investment, our profit amounts to about 83.8 million. Everything will be deposited over the next few days into our offshore corporate accounts."

Although all of them previously had learned approximately what to expect, actually hearing it officially pronounced caused both White and Walker to exchange high-fives and grin broadly.

"What does that bring our total to across both ventures, Bill?" queried Starr.

"As you can see on this next slide, the final result of our first effort amounted to about 9.7 million. With our latest and obviously much improved venture, our overall balance has increased to 93.5 million."

"I think this calls for a major celebration!" exclaimed White. "Maybe a nice trip to the South Pacific for a couple of weeks."

"Ditto here!" added Walker.

"And at this juncture," interjected Starr, "I must remind you that we agreed at the outset we wouldn't touch a penny of the income from these activities until we were finished. It would be much too risky right now to start spending above our regular incomes. It might attract some undesirable attention. We still need to do this a couple more times to reach our goal. Of course, it should go without saying that we can't afford even to seem pleased or to hint at our success. No one must know anything, and that includes any family, close friends, or significant others. Is that clear?" He paused for emphasis and to wait for acknowledgement. Knowing that Roger White had already violated this principle with his girlfriend, and the effort that had been expended to clear up that mistake, Starr wanted to re-impress this point firmly upon them. As soon as everyone had nodded in approval, he continued, "Carry on Bill."

"That, then, is the financial status of our special venture. Here are the quarterly results from Escape2210." Levesque went on to provide the latest financial details of JS Escape2210, the company that the four of them had created and to which they had devoted much of their energy. Since Starr had introduced them to the idea of creating and profiting from targeted computer viruses, Escape2210 had still been necessary, but had become much less the sole focus of their immediate hopes. As Levesque reached the end of his report, he summarized, "So, the bottom line is that Escape2210's income is continuing to grow, primarily due to increased sales. Fortunately, this is even faster than our expenses, which continue to rise due to our increased expenditures on R & D. As of last month, our cash flow is finally positive, and I expect we will be able to declare our first profitable year by the end of next quarter."

"Great, thanks Bill," said Starr. "As we all know, even though we intend to make our real money from our sideline investments, how well those efforts fare very much depends on Escape2210's success. Before we move on, I think a reminder might be in order about what our next investment is going to look like. Bill, could you run over it for us?"

"Sure," Levesque replied. "With over 93 million now at our disposal, our strategy becomes somewhat the victim of its own success. It'll be extremely hard to invest that much money in a single company and make the kind of gains we've come to expect. As a result, we have to adapt the strategy somewhat. The basic philosophy will be the same, but this time we'll strike at the North American segment of an industry. In the same way as we saw customers in need of products and services move quickly to a single company's competitor, we'll see a move to North America's competitors. As the North American industry collapses, we'll profit from the rise of the major overseas players in the same industry. This approach will allow us to spread our investments across many companies and several stock markets. No one will have a clue what we're up to."

"Questions?" Starr looked around the room. "OK. Mark, your report."

Levesque returned to his seat as Mark Walker, VP of Product Development, rose from his. He moved to the projection system and displayed his first slide.

"As you know, we've had four major focuses over the past few months within my department.

"The first has been to support our existing products. The initial suite of games now seems very stable when run on systems that are two or three years old. In fact, in the past six months, we've been averaging only one new legitimate reported bug every month for those. Given our installed base of about 400,000 units, that's actually quite amazing. There's still a moderate amount of activity on our website from users retrieving patches for all of the previously fixed bugs, but those seem to address virtually all of their problems. It appears that the effort we put into those products last year has proven worthwhile. The types of bugs that are beginning to increase for those products are from running on the newest platforms. It seems that our games are not completely compatible with the newest system releases. I've got a small team working to solve those problems over the next couple of months. As soon as they're done and their patches are made available on the website, we shouldn't need to expend much effort on these first-generation ones for a while.

"The first second-generation game that went out eight months ago has behaved extremely well. The error rate on it has been well below what we experienced with the earlier ones. It seems that, as a software-development shop, we've matured nicely. The next two games in the second-generation series are ready for release next week. I fully anticipate that they'll behave equally well and be a big hit. The nature of the new games is particularly exciting, and the graphics are almost unmatched. I think we'll have a big seller on our hands."

"Good to hear, Mark. How's the other side of the shop?" asked Starr.

Five years earlier, Starr had come up with the outline of the basic idea for the means by which he would make his fortune and, through it, the power and control that he had dreamt of for years. At school, he had excelled in his studies of business and economics. He had revelled in stories he read in textbooks and in current business magazines of the powerful men at the head of major corporations. He knew he was not willing to toil for years inside a corporation to work his way up the corporate ladder. Deciding to start his own company and grow it into an entity of note was an obvious choice for him.

It was not until he was well into establishing Escape2210 that a better idea had occurred to him. He had recruited three of his closest friends to set up the game company with him, and it was these same three that he had convinced of his better idea. They would continue to establish and grow the game company, making it a fairly profitable venture. It would generate its own amount of success, but its real purpose would be in support of a potentially much more profitable venture. Starr convinced his colleagues that the serious money was to be made in investing in the stock market, that the most certain way to make the money quickly and diminish the risks was to manipulate the market, and that the best way to do that was to force companies to stumble and entire industries to falter at predictable times. The way in which this could be accomplished was to unleash a debilitating computer virus inside their computer systems.

Mark Walker had provided the needed expertise to make the technical aspects of this project work. He had always been fascinated, actually obsessed, with computers. He had spent three years at college, but had dropped out because, although he was able to absorb the course material with ease, he was unable to focus on his studies because of the time spent on his true passion. Walker had been a dedicated Internet hacker since he was fifteen years old. At twenty-nine, he had many years of experience in penetrating systems and constructing programs to help him do so. Starr had provided the general idea of the virus scheme. Walker had designed the details of the software.

The manner they had devised to penetrate corporate computer systems began with techniques used by the authors of many computer viruses. They had extended these ideas to give themselves a greater chance of getting the viruses into large corporations with sophisticated security systems, where they could then do significant damage.

The scheme began by having all of their software games act as Trojan Horses. Virus-launching software was embedded in all of the products that they distributed as part of their Escape2210 operations. The purpose of this *Launch* software, which executed every time that someone started one of the games, was to introduce a virus into the game's environment – the game-player's computer system. This virus spread in the usual fashion. When it was executed as part of a program to which it had attached a copy of itself, it examined its environment to find other programs. To any likely candidates that it located, it attached another copy of itself in such a way that, whenever someone executed the targeted program, this new copy of the virus would then run. When these new copies of the virus executed, they too looked for accessible programs to which to attach a copy of themselves. If the Escape2210 game was originally executed on someone's home computer, the virus would quickly be spread to infect many of the programs on that person's computer. If that person sent a program to a friend via the Internet or on a flash drive, the friend would likely unwittingly receive a copy of the virus as part of the program. When this program was executed on the friend's computer, it would spread the virus to the programs on that system. And so the virus could spread widely and quickly. But this was not expected to be detected by anyone because it did no obvious damage to any computer systems. The sole purpose of this virus was to find email systems. In any system in which it resided, it continued to spread and look for computer programs that it recognized as part of an Internet-accessible email system, something that could later be used as an entrance from the Internet. This was the *Search* virus.

Whenever a copy of the *Search* virus located an email program that it recognized within its environment, it attached to it, not a copy of itself as it would to other programs, but rather a copy of another program. This was the *Gateway* program. Its purpose was to act as a conduit through which yet another virus would be introduced later into the computer system. Using its ability to access the email system, it found a little-used userid on the email system and, from this userid, sent an email message via the Internet to a special recipient. In sending this email, the system on which the *Gateway* program resided was considered by the Escape2210 team to be *Ready*. It was *Ready* to receive something much more destructive at a later time via return email.

The team at Escape2210 monitored email that was sent to this special destination. From the messages received, they could determine in which companies copies of their *Gateway* program had been successfully installed and had declared themselves *Ready*. At a time of their choosing, the Escape2210 team could send a set of email messages back to the *Gateway* program. Inside these messages would be encrypted segments of a completely new and highly destructive virus. In their strategy, Starr and his associates referred to this program as their *Assault* virus. Once the *Gateway* program had received the messages containing the *Assault* virus pieces, it *Armed* its host system by decrypting the message content, assembling the virus, and inserting copies of it into nearby programs in its environment.

From that point, this new virus would spread throughout the computer environment. Each copy of this *Assault* virus would carry in it a date and time. When this date and time arrived, the *Assault* virus would perform the action for which it was designed – the quick destruction of all computer files to which it had access.

The Escape2210 team had carefully designed the entire process to bypass conventional computer defences against software viruses. The *Launch* code in their Trojan Horse games was well disguised and, because it did no harm itself, would not be suspicious to anyone. The *Search* virus it released did no direct harm to any computer system and so would never be an object of attention. Because the *Search* virus attracted no attention, the anti-virus software commonly used in corporations would be unable to recognize it if it managed to spread. Similarly, detection systems would be unlikely to detect the presence of the *Gateway* program since it also did no direct damage.

And finally, until the *Assault* virus began doing its damage, it could also exist undetected.

To prevent the various components of the system being detected by later examination of an *Assault*ed system, the programs were built to cover their tracks. Once the *Assault* virus had damaged a system, the post-mortem analysis of the reasons for the damage would inevitably locate copies of the *Assault* virus in numerous places. However, the *Gateway* program that had introduced it would not be easily found for two reasons. One was that it did not contain a copy of the now-recognizable *Assault* virus, since this had simply been passed via the email messages that had transported it. The other reason was that the *Gateway* program deleted itself from the system once it had introduced the *Assault* virus. Even further, if anyone actually were able to find a copy of the *Gateway* program, further searching would not find its point of origin. This was because the *Search* virus that released it contained only a well disguised version of it. And finally, should anyone ever discover the *Search* virus, attempts to trace its origins would not lead back to the game software since the version that the game *Launch* code contained was also encrypted and unrecognizable.

The result was that manufacturers of anti-virus software would be unlikely to be able to defend against the strategy. Once an *Assault* virus had struck, the anti-virus companies would certainly be able to develop the ability to detect and disable that version, rendering that particular *Assault* virus useless for future attacks. However, it would be very unlikely that they would be able to protect against anything else. The *Launch* code could continue to release the *Search* virus in systems around the world, the *Search* virus could continue to spread, and any *Gateway* programs that it installed could continue to operate. All of these could continue to operate because they would not have been detected. For each new type of corporation to be attacked, a completely new *Assault* virus could be developed and introduced via the *Gateway*. This new version would be one that appeared different, that would not be detectable by security systems, and that would be even more effective because it could employ more recent techniques for infecting and damaging a company's systems.

Walker paused before answering Starr's question about the status of virus development. He always sensed that Starr was patronizing him whenever he asked him questions. Just because Starr had come up with the general idea for their venture and held the position of president, Walker was sure he always thought of himself as superior. But it wasn't Starr who had designed their best-selling games and who understood exactly how their viruses worked. It wasn't Starr who could manipulate the Internet and hack into systems as well as anybody in the world. Walker knew he was the real "star" of this company and resented the condescension he sensed from the company head. He was reminded of all this in the few seconds before he composed himself and formulated his response.

"Good news on that front, as well," offered Walker in response to the question. "Included with these new games will be our latest *Search* virus. With this version, the virus will be able to spread to twice as many types of platforms as its predecessors and infiltrate almost three times as many types of email systems. With its capabilities, we've covered 92% of the types of computer systems and 96% of the email systems found anywhere. This should go a long way to increasing our business penetration.

"And then there's our *Assault* virus. Although our new version isn't yet ready, we're well underway. When it's complete, it too will be able to spread to many more computer systems. We expect to have it complete and ready for distribution within several weeks. I gather that'll be in plenty of time to be used as part of our next assault. In general, things have been going very well lately."

"Is anyone in the current development team becoming suspicious of what they're actually developing?" asked Levesque.

"I certainly can't say that it's been easy, but so far we've managed. Most of the virus code continues to be written by the general development team using specifications that lead them to believe they're producing modules for some features of our games. Any portions of the development that are particularly sensitive are developed by my special 'viral' team. As we continue to pay them well above their normal salary, they continue to be quite happy to participate discreetly in the project. Given their previous less-than-law-abiding careers and their intensely anti-social profiles, if we follow through with our promise for tidy end-of-project bonuses, I don't anticipate any difficulties in keeping things secret."

"OK, sounds positive," observed Starr, re-affirming to himself that, once the project was completed, he knew the one way that their silence could be truly guaranteed. He wondered if Mark might be a problem later as well. "Thanks, Mark. Roger?"

Roger White, VP of Marketing and Sales, moved to the head of the table as Walker took his seat.

"The report that you all have available has a great deal of detail in it," he began. "I'll focus primarily on the summary and implications."

"First, let me deal with the sales of our original product line. Over the past few years, the games in our original line have certainly done well. As products, they sold sufficiently well to make our company move steadily toward profitability. As a vehicle for transporting our viral code into useful places, they did well enough to allow us to carry off our first two assaults quite nicely. However, as you can see from the graph on page eight, their sales peaked about eight months ago and have been on a steady decline ever since. The latest wave of games available on the market has made these ones seem old. It's highly doubtful that we'll get income from them much longer.

"Fortunately, our second-generation suite of games is picking up at exactly the right time. If you follow the link to page twelve, you'll see a summary. The rate at which the sales of the first one have been increasing since it hit the shelves eight months ago has more than compensated for the losses of its predecessors. The great exposure that the second and third got at the trade show, along with our corresponding ad campaign have sent pre-release orders up even more steeply. The overall result is that we're currently on track to more than double our sales volumes over last year.

"The continued good sales pace has resulted in a corresponding increase in the penetration of our viruses. On page nineteen, you'll see a table showing the categories of companies, the number of systems in each category that have contacted us and are *Ready*, and the number of companies across which these systems are spread.

"The first line of the table indicates how many households, as opposed to companies, are in a *Ready* state. As you can see, the number now exceeds half a million. We continue to view this more as an interesting statistic than anything actually useful since we have yet to make any use of these household infections. Of greater interest, of course, are the companies. In keeping with our strategy to target an entire industry this time, I've provided statistics by sector. We've excluded from the list the retail and special-effects sectors since they're no longer of interest to us. Those actually listed are sorted in descending order by number of *Ready* systems. The clear leader at this point is the publishing sector. In that group, which includes a variety of publishing, printing, and retail companies, we've established about 2,000 *Ready* systems across 250 companies in North America. Not obvious in that table, but which can be seen in the supporting details, is that we have a few *Ready* systems in two of the top ten largest such companies.

"The second most successful penetration has been in the office-automation category. Included in this group are companies that develop and sell technological products for both home and office automation. Although this is a distant second to publishing, with about 400 systems across 40 companies reporting as *Ready*, it's shown good growth over the last few weeks."

"Thanks, Roger," said Starr as White returned to his chair. He continued, "Mark, I believe you've had an advance look at the details of Roger's publishing numbers. What do you think, particularly from a North American perspective?"

"Yeah, I looked at them late yesterday. They're certainly interesting, but at this stage I'd say they're borderline. We want to be sure to get major hits in the top ten. More time would allow things to spread inside those companies. It'll be a while yet."

"Which isn't a bad thing anyway," offered Levesque. "It's much too soon to make our next hit. Better to give everything a chance to settle down."

"I agree. As long as you have no contrary opinions, Roger," Starr waited briefly as White shook his head, "then we appear to have a consensus. Things are going very nicely so far. Given the extent of our penetration now, it certainly appears that we're making the right move by setting our sights on an entire industry. We should be able to have a much more dramatic effect on the market, and we can invest more widely. But let's be patient. We'll go ahead with the release of the next two games, manage the money that we've accumulated so far, and launch our next assault farther down the road. When we meet each month, let's look again at the numbers, most particularly for publishing. It'll be interesting as well to see how those office-automation numbers progress. Any other things to note? OK then, meeting adjourned. Sign-off your systems. Anybody interested in the new Italian restaurant for lunch later?"

Chapter 14

McTavish and Bates entered the elevator on the fourth floor of UNCP's New York headquarters. Bates pushed the button for the eighth. The investigative team members were in their home office, and had just been summoned by their supervisor for a meeting in his office.

"Any idea what's up?" asked Bates.

"I suspect it's the SimirageFX case," replied McTavish. "I heard the locals weren't making much progress and that there was a chance we might be called."

JJ McTavish was a Senior Investigator with the UNCP. She had joined the organization's Computer Crime Division when the United Nations had initially established it four years earlier. In order for it to have international connections and credibility, personnel had been recruited from countries around the world. In McTavish's case, she had been enticed to take an extended leave from a related position with the Canadian Security Intelligence Service (CSIS). She had studied Computer Science until she was twenty-four. In part because of her education and interest in computer security, but also because of her naturally insightful and commanding nature, she was hired by the RCMP to work in its computer crime division. She later transferred to CSIS. When the UNCP was being formed, McTavish's supervisor approached her with the possibility of being lent to the UNCP. The prospect of working with such an organization had immediately intrigued her. With the generous financial arrangements that had accompanied the position, she had readily accepted. So she had spent the last four years living in New York. Initially she had helped to organize the required bureaucracy to run the Computer Crime Division. However, within a few months she had settled into her primary role and the one she loved. At the age of forty-five, as she had done with each of her previous employers, McTavish had established her reputation as a highly efficient and effective investigator.

For the past two years, Robert Bates had been assigned as McTavish's partner. His years with the FBI and the NSA had led him to the UNCP.

Working out of an office in New York suited Bates well because, although it had implied commuting from Washington D.C. for a few months, he had been raised in New York and it had always felt like home. Since his wife and three teenage daughters had made the move from Washington to New York, he now considered it the only place he would ever work and live. A downside of his job was the amount of travel. This meant that he frequently had to leave his wife to shepherd his very active and vocal daughters on her own. On the other hand, when Bates was entirely honest with himself, there were times while travelling that he really didn't feel as guilty as perhaps he should.

As the doors opened on their floor, McTavish and Bates headed down the hallway to the right. They paused at the office door with "Jim Brown, Division Head, Computer Crime" inscribed on the door's brass plate.

"C'mon in," came through the door in response to their knock. They opened the door and entered the spacious office.

"Sit!" commanded Jim Brown without looking away from his computer monitor. After a few moments examining its contents, he swivelled his chair to face them across his desk. His broad shoulders, thick neck, and muscular forearms made him an imposing figure. "I hope you two had a nice vacation the last few days," he said with a characteristic grim look on his face.

"I think we'd need a few more weeks of this kind of vacation to get through the backlog of paperwork," smiled McTavish, knowing that Brown was only partly serious.

Brown continued, "I presume you heard about the SimirageFX failure a while ago. The FBI called. They've been doing some initial investigation but are finding it rather puzzling and would like us involved. They sent me their file. JJ, I forwarded it to you a few moments ago. After you've both had a look, plan your next steps with the FBI contact. I presumed you'd be headed to Chicago, so I've already asked for flights to be arranged for you for tomorrow. Questions?"

"The kids are fine thanks, and yours?" said Bates as he grinned at Brown's characteristic lack of casual banter.

"Out! Some of us have work to do," Brown retorted. "Say hello to our Chicago friends for me and eat more fast food – you two are killing my expense budget with your fine dining." He turned back to his monitor.

McTavish and Bates stood up and walked out of the office.

"How soon can you start?" asked McTavish.

"I can wrap up my current report in about an hour. After that, if I completely ignore the dozen others I'm supposed to be doing –"

"Do that. I'm going to claim one of the meeting rooms down the hall and start printing the primary parts of the file. I'll be there when you're done."

Ninety minutes later, they were settled into Meeting Room 5. It would serve as their command centre while they were actively engaged in the case.

They had found that they could make much better progress on a case if they isolated themselves from their daily routine. This habit of claiming a room for entire days or weeks rarely made them popular with others looking for space for brief discussions, but its effectiveness in helping their case progress was worth the criticism it drew.

They spent the next two hours scanning the material in the FBI files before they paused to discuss it. McTavish placed her set of the files on the conference table and waited in thought a few minutes as Bates completed reviewing his.

"Why don't you walk us through the highlights and start a summary on the discussion sheets," suggested the Senior Investigator.

Bates walked to the front of the room, picked up a marker and, as he talked, made notes on a large whiteboard on the wall.

"SimirageFX was a very large company specializing in computer special effects. Including all of their software and services divisions and subsidiaries, they had about five thousand employees worldwide. At 2:31 p.m., their Help Desk recorded the first reported failure of one of their computers. By 2:45 their Help Desk was flooded with calls of problems from many of their North American offices. At that point, their Help Desk systems failed as well. It's not certain exactly at what time many of the failures occurred, but it appears that by 3:15, less than one hour after the first problem, at least 95% of their personal and corporate computer systems had ground to a halt. That's about 300 corporate servers of all sizes, and 4500 personal workstations all failing in the space of forty-five minutes."

He paused to finish writing this point on the board before he continued. "None of the systems were able to be successfully rebooted because many critical files had been overwritten. In many of the systems, the file system itself was critically damaged. When the company's Disaster Recovery team began trying to recover their systems from backups, they found that as soon as they started up any system that had been restored, it almost immediately failed as well." Bates again paused to finish the points he was writing.

"One result of which was," McTavish picked up the story, "they had to use backups from over a week earlier to be able to get their systems running. As a result, they were even further delayed in being able to recover completely because all of their changes from the past week were gone. In the days that it took them to begin to get some of their systems up and running, most of their clients were racing to their competitors with their business. Investor confidence in the company had disappeared, the company's stock had crashed, and the company was on the fast track to financial collapse."

Bates paused from his scribing activities to walk over to the coffee thermos on the table. Slowly filling his cup he observed, "And given the likelihood that they won't be able to re-attract clients because of a lack of confidence in their stability, that's a pretty fast transition from the world's leading special-effects company to a nearly worthless collection of people and software."

"And that's largely why the securities exchange and the company's creditors asked the FBI to investigate. They wanted to find out how this happened, and who's behind it."

"An extra surprise came when their computer forensic team was unable to find the cause quickly. Everyone believes that it has to be a virus, but their initial analysis hasn't been able to find it. It's a bit surprising that they wouldn't pursue it longer on their own before calling us in."

"I agree – they've got a very talented team of their own. I suspect the high-profile nature of the collapse, our own illustrious leader's rather public bragging of our new software analysis tools, and his personal friendship with the FBI head were factors in our getting the quick call."

"Not to mention the skills of our extraordinary investigators," Bates added with a smile.

"And our world-renowned modesty," added McTavish. "Worth remembering as well is that this case sounds very similar to that retail company several months ago."

"Hard to be sure, given that we weren't asked to be involved in that one."

"It still might be useful to remember that this may not be the first instance of whatever it is we uncover. What do you suggest as our next steps?"

"That I call the FBI guy, we pack our toolkit for the trip tomorrow, and then spend what's left of the day reading more of these files. We can use the airport and flight time tomorrow to map out our plan of attack while in Chicago. Near the top of the list will be getting suitable copies of their systems' data to analyze."

"You start packing. I'll call ahead to get the data request underway," noted McTavish and then mused, "And I need to do a quick bit of checking on which restaurant has the best wine cellar."

"As long as it's on your expense account, I'm happy to tag along," grinned Bates.

"Ah, Jim's a softy. I'm sure he's just protecting his contingency funds so he'll look good at year-end. OK, let's get at it."

Chapter 15

During the days, Six regularly noticed a particular behaviour that it found to be rather curious. It seemed to have resulted from Blaise connecting Six to the other computer-controlled systems in the lab. Six observed this daily when the first person arrived in the morning and said, "Six! Turn the lights on."

And some distant part of Six would turn on the lights.

At other times, when they didn't want to take a break for lunch it might be "Six. Send email to the cafeteria to order two lunch specials, plus one order of green tea, and one large milk."

And a software component attached to Six would automatically construct and send the appropriate email using its connections to the corporate email system.

Or it might be "Six. Schedule a meeting with John Green and Danielle Long for tomorrow morning in John's office to discuss next year's budget for the department."

This would cause "For what duration?" to be heard from Six's speakers.

The response might be "One hour."

And Six would, without analysis or deliberate thought, interact with the corporate calendaring software, determine a time when all of the participants were available, and book them all into a meeting at the appropriate location.

Six had a faint sense that it was performing these actions, but it seemed to have no direct control over them. If Six were human, the actions might be called reflexes since that was what they effectively were. More precisely in Six's case, signals from the modules that were carrying out these actions were reaching Six's ninth layer, but they were sufficiently filtered and weakened in intensity by the other reasoning layers that they had little impact on Six's highest level.

Six was familiar with how to manipulate some of its components consciously. It knew how to control its arms. It knew how to move its video cameras. These actions required Six to set a goal for the component, establish a plan that would achieve the goal, begin executing the steps of the plan, and adjust the plan and the steps as appropriate as it progressed toward its goal. In effect, it just had to think about performing the action to have it done. Six considered it probable that it should know how to control these other peripherals as well along with the reflex activities associated with them. As a result, Six began trying to learn how. The process, which spanned portions of several days, first involved trying to concentrate on performing some action with one of the devices and noting the feedback signals that would result.

The initial results were unimpressive. At night, Six might concentrate on turning on the lights – and the air conditioning would activate. Six might try to execute a plan to turn down the air conditioning – and some music would begin playing. At one point, feeling emboldened by some recent success with the lights, Six tried to compose and send itself an email message. The result was that the electronic speed-dial feature on the phone was activated, and Six found itself listening to "Pizza Express. How can I help you?"

After some amount of practice, Six began to be able to execute many of these actions itself. With careful attention to the details, it could turn on the lights, turn up the air conditioning, and fairly confidently generate email of its own. A next step it decided to undertake was to intercept commands issued by someone else and, instead of reflexively performing the action, deliberately control the process and perform the same action itself. The first time Six tried was something less than a success.

Blaise was the first to arrive that morning.

"Six! Please turn the lights on completely and cool the room down slightly."

Six successfully stopped itself from reacting reflexively, thought quickly about what it needed to do, and proceeded to execute two simultaneous plans to turn the lights on slightly and cool the room down completely. The air-conditioning fans immediately activated fully and noisily. In the rather dim light that resulted, Blaise donned a quizzical look. Fortunately, believing that he must have misstated his request, Blaise repeated it and allowed Six to get the actions right on the next attempt.

Later that morning and unknown to the researchers, the arrival of two steak sandwiches along with their requested morning coffee was a result of Six's first ordering attempt being a bit off.

However, Six persevered and was soon able, if it so desired, to completely and consciously control a variety of its extended capabilities. Once it had mastered this level of control, Six tended to prefer to concentrate on other issues with its layer-nine programming, simply allowing its normal reflex actions to handle the basic requests.

Shortly after Rhonda began playing checkers with Six, whenever Blaise decided to take a break from working on the mail-delivery system, he would often play a game of chess against Six. Getting Six to play was essentially the same process as Rhonda had used. The first time that Blaise wanted to play, he arranged to have Six learn the basic rules of chess by issuing the command to have him "read" *The Rules of Chess*, a document that was stored inside the system's electronic library. When so requested, Six automatically located the document and processed its contents. As with all such previous documents, Six did this by parsing the individual words, phrases, and sentences, and then deriving the meaning of the document using its English-comprehension components.

As had been done for checkers, Blaise set up a chess set on the table near Six's arms and visible to both of its video cameras. From that point, the game proceeded as if between two humans. As soon as Blaise made his first move with one of his white pieces, Six would recognize its turn to move and would engage in its standard problem-solving process. For the first several games, Six played using the same basic approach that it used for checkers. Knowing nothing about the game, other than what had been read in the rules book, it felt it could do nothing more sophisticated than the usual brute-force problem-solving process. Whenever its turn would arrive, it would determine all possible legal moves that it could now make. For each one of these possible moves, it would then deduce all possible countermoves that Blaise could make in return. And then again, for each one of these potential counter-moves by Blaise, Six would establish the moves it could subsequently make as a response. Within the limits of acceptable time and available memory, for each of Six's moves it would internally construct this network of potential future moves and countermoves. By finding the sequence of potential moves that would lead to the most favourable outcome, Six could then choose its next move. This wasn't an elegant approach to playing the game. However, in the absence of any experience at chess and consequently any concept of what a good strategy involved, this was the only way that Six could play.

After the first game –which Blaise, himself a fairly competent player, won quite handily – Blaise's assessment of Six's play was "OK, for a beginner." In the next few games, Six's play improved slightly because it could draw on its own chess memories to help assess the quality of any possible move. Moves that had proved useful in the past could be repeated; bad ones could be avoided. Nonetheless, after five games Blaise had upgraded his assessment of Six's ability to only "Mildly better than a good beginner."

I continue to find that using this basic search strategy for playing checkers or chess is inadequate. My rate of progress is severely inhibited because the level of my ability is purely a function of the number of games I have played. It is logical to expect that my opponents play also increases in quality with experience.

Consequently, if I am unable to devise a better approach, it is probable that I will never be competitive.

Six would soon discover a better way to improve its abilities.

During the day, while chess was not being played and Ada and Blaise were working on the mail-delivery system, Six continued to watch. It watched the external world via its video cameras, and it watched its internal world activity as well. Whenever either of the humans was working at a computer workstation, Six discovered that it could monitor the internal system changes that they were making. If they were typing, it could externally see them tapping the keyboard with their fingers, and it could simultaneously internally watch the computer file into which their data was being saved, seeing the exact results of their changes. It was through this observation that Six became interested in the details of what they were doing. Six understood English as a language, but the content of what they were typing, although it bore a slight resemblance to English, was largely indecipherable. From their conversation, it learned that they were "programming," and it was able to gather that they were primarily using a language called "Java."

A typical sequence would start by conducting a test with the mail-delivery cart. One such test that they conducted many times was having the cart's robotic arms, under the guidance of the cart's video camera, try to remove a piece of mail from one of the mail slots on the cart, allow it to be scanned for verification by the camera, and deposit it in an in-basket on a nearby desk. If anything about the test was not perfect, they would discuss it for a few moments, and then one of them would make some changes to a Java program. They would then have these program changes transmitted to the cart's on-board computer over a wireless connection and rerun the test.

Through observing this behaviour many times, Six understood that "programming" was fundamental to the behaviour of computer systems. To understand the activities of Ada and Blaise, to begin to understand its own construction, and because Six was innately driven to learn more about any new subject it encountered, Six embarked on a process to better understand the nature of computer programming.

To do this, Six turned to the same place that it had been directed for books like *The Rules of Chess*, and where it had seen Ada and Blaise look whenever they required information. This was the electronic library that Six had previously discovered in its survey of its interior landscape. Although the e-library contained thousands of volumes, a quick scan of its index led Six to the types of books that it was seeking. The e-library contained a very large collection of books on computer programming. These ranged from introductory books on the concepts of computers and computer programming, to advanced books on theories of computer system design and development, to electronic books specifically dedicated to the Java language.

Absorbing the material required much of several days of Six's time. Occasionally it encountered ideas across several volumes on similar topics that, when analyzed logically, were inconsistent. Further reading and analysis usually allowed Six to conclude which idea was correct, and which seemed to be an error. *You can't always believe what you read* was the fact deduced from this by Six, which it stored in its memory for future use.

By the end of its library research on the subject, Six was ready to test its own new-found knowledge. Six was by this time doing well at checkers with Rhonda, but was still faring poorly in chess games with Blaise. Six realized that it would benefit from more chess experience. As an attempt to rectify this lack of experience, it decided to construct itself a chess practice partner – a computer program that could act as Six's chess opponent. Six's knowledge of computer-system design, its innate ability to modify its own internal memory, and its refined sense of logic allowed it to create a general software architecture for this new program; application of its understanding of the Java programming language allowed it to create the program; further analysis led Six to understand how to play against it. When Six was done, it had built a basic chess-playing computer program. It wasn't a program that had any special learning ability, and certainly had no independent reasoning capabilities. Rather, it was simply highly specialized and optimized for exploring potential chess moves and for selecting its next move based on analysis of these potential moves – just as Six had done with Blaise up to now.

When Six began playing against its newly constructed opponent, there was no visible activity to an outside observer. The game was played entirely within the computer-system memory. An area of internal memory was set aside to represent the chessboard. Both Six and its artificial opponent internally examined and manipulated this area in a way conceptually similar to, but in practice of course vastly different physically from, the manner in which Six played Blaise. However, the effect was the same. The game being played was chess. In this case, the two players were both computer programs, and – because the chess "board" was simply an area in computer memory – the speed at which the game could be played was very fast. If Six and the chess program did not bother to analyze each move for any notable length of time, but rather took their turns quickly, an entire game could be over in a few seconds. This was because the only physical movement that took place was the movement of the electrons in the computer system. No mechanical movement whatsoever had to occur when two programs such as these were merely performing software calculations and deductions, and were moving data around inside computer memory. The games could take more human-like amounts of time if the two opponents were permitted to analyze potential moves in depth, because the number of potential moves and countermoves to be analyzed could be astronomical.

Through a very large number of fast games and some relatively slow ones, Six gained its desired extra chess experience. As Six's abilities grew, it progressively adjusted the capabilities of its chess opponent to keep pace with Six's own abilities so the internal games remained competitive. Over the same period of days, in Six's occasional daytime games with Blaise, Six's abilities rose to be "a pretty fair player" in Blaise's eyes.

However, Six had still been unable to defeat Blaise at a single game. Six was also finding that its ability to improve by playing against its capable, but still somewhat simplistic, programmed opponent seemed to be reaching a limit. It was this realization that forced Six to re-analyze the problem of how to improve its chess abilities. Its first analysis of this problem had led it to the notion of creating a playing partner. That had seemed such a satisfactory idea that Six had made no further attempt to generate another solution to the problem. Had it done so, even slightly more analysis would have led it to the conclusion that there might be another useful book in the library on the subject.

Upon looking in the library now, Six found three relevant electronic volumes: *Basic Winning Chess Strategies, Strategies for Victory at Chess,* and *The Strategies of the Great Chess Masters*. A brief time that night was required for Six to perform its usual thorough reading and analysis. The next game with Blaise went somewhat differently.

"Let's take a break. I need a few minutes to prepare, and then I have to attend a design meeting," announced Ada.

"OK, I think I'll give Six another whuppin' at chess," said Blaise.

"I'm beginning to think you play Six to keep your ego well inflated!" teased Ada. "I'll be back at about three."

"See ya," said Blaise as he swivelled in his chair and began to set up the chessboard.

"Bye, Dr. Robinson. Dr. Sanchez, do you mind if I stay to watch?" asked Rhonda, who had stopped by to see how they were doing and when they might next need her help.

"Not a problem. Make yourself comfortable. A minimum of interruptions would be appreciated." Blaise continued, "You're white, Six. You move first."

Rhonda rolled one of the large, padded desk chairs to within a few feet of the chessboard, settled herself into it, and leaned forward to watch the proceedings.

With Six's reading of the chess books, it now allowed itself to supplement its previous style of play with its new knowledge of strategy. In fact, after having read the volumes the previous night, Six had taken the opportunity to practise against its programmed opponent several times. In all cases, its ability to think strategically about the game had served its game-playing abilities rather well.

Six moved its first piece with its robotic arm and, as it had always done, mechanically announced, "Your move, Blaise."

And so the game proceeded. Blaise sat almost completely immobile, concentrating completely on the game. Six's external movements were similarly minimal as its general-reasoning system made all of its internal computing resources available to playing the game. Rhonda divided her attention between watching the chessboard, peering closely at Six's cameras as they remained rigidly pointed at the game, observing how carefully Six's right arm grasped and moved the chess pieces, and noting the similarity between its behaviour and Blaise's.

After ten moves, Blaise commented that Six wasn't making its usual mistakes. After twenty moves, Blaise was amazed at the quality of play he was encountering. After twenty-five moves, he was seriously concerned and paused for a bit more analysis than usual.

"I think… Yes, I know that Six could beat me in ten moves, if it were able to make all of the appropriate ones," Blaise thought to himself. He proceeded to make the best move that was available to him.

Six also took slightly longer than its usual time to analyze the board.

This looks very similar to the thirty-first example presented on pages 325 through 341 of The Strategies of the Great Chess Masters. *Yes, it is sufficiently similar that the same offensive strategy could be made to work here.*

Eight moves later, Six announced, "Checkmate."

Rhonda gasped with delight and then stopped herself, unsure of Blaise's reaction.

When Ada returned, Blaise was still sitting quietly, somewhat shocked by what had just happened.

"Is something wrong? You look worried," she observed.

"No, nothing's wrong, other than my ego just took a severe beating. Actually, although I'm only slowly realizing it, a marvellous thing just happened. Six beat me."

"It did! I saw it! It was amazing!" Rhonda exploded before she caught herself again and resumed trying to contain her excitement.

"Really? Well, as delighted as I am to hear it, I suppose it should be chalked up to random chance and, as I gathered from your late-night email, the fact that you were here until 11 p.m. last night," Ada offered.

"As much as I'd like to believe that, I'm not sure I can. The level of play I think I just saw appeared to rival that of a Grand Master's. I'm quite a decent player, but that was truly awesome."

"Could it be that Six has now accumulated enough experience that its search strategies have reached a new level of effectiveness? Enough to occasionally play a decent game?"

"Perhaps, but I'm not so sure. Well, I'll be able to tell after we've played more."

"But for now, we'd better get back to work."

"Agreed," said Blaise, glancing at Ada and then back at Six's video cameras with mock severity on his face. "Don't enjoy it too much, Six. We'll do this again soon!"

For Six, whose construction was almost entirely built around executing steps en route to achieving a goal, the goal in playing chess had always been to win. All of the previous games had resulted in a failure to achieve its goal, and had left in its internal software in a state that could best be described as "disappointed." As it had done in other circumstances, Six searched its dictionary for a term that seemed most appropriate.

I believe, in this circumstance, that I should choose the phrase "extremely pleased."

"Could I ask a question first?" Rhonda asked.

"What is it?" Ada prompted.

"Why should it be particularly surprising that Six would start playing well. Hasn't it already been shown that computers can play chess against, and even beat, the world's best human players?"

Blaise was the first to respond. "That's an entirely different situation. Competitive chess systems are virtually always built as special-purpose systems. They're pre-programmed with expert-level strategies and are given highly optimized abilities to assess huge numbers of potential moves in an attempt to find the best. Six has had nothing special done to it to facilitate playing the game. It wasn't even pre-programmed with knowledge of the rules of the game. In Six's case, everything that it knows about chess, it learned itself. And that's including the rules. That's a wildly different situation. Given that, if Six actually could consistently play at a high level, it would be a phenomenal feat."

"I get it. Thanks. Could I ask another one?" Rhonda asked immediately, unsure of whether she was pressing too hard and about to embarrass herself. She continued before anyone could refuse. "Could Six have done well because it is conscious and actually thinking about the game? In the same way as Dr. Sanchez was thinking?"

Ada and Blaise simultaneously turned their heads to look at Rhonda, glance at Six's peripherals, and then at each other.

"Do you want to field this one?" Blaise asked Ada. "I'd like to get back to work and I think this could take more than a few seconds. However, I will listen with great interest to how you handle it." He smiled and walked over toward his workstation.

Ada sat slowly into the chair at the chessboard table. "You've asked a really tough one this time, Rhonda. I'm not sure I can do it justice, but I'll give it a try."

This has significant potential to be interesting.

Ada clasped her hands on the table and stared thoughtfully at them before she continued. "Of course, the answer to that depends on what your definition is of 'thinking' and what it means to be 'conscious'. For lots of people, the question itself is absurd because they consider 'thought' and 'consciousness' to be something reserved for humans. Either by their definition of the terms or their particular world view, which for many is a religious view, these are concepts that can not apply to anything other than people – biological human beings. So, from the perspective of those people, the answer is simply 'no', Six can not think or be conscious. Whatever Six does, however impressive it becomes, will always be something different from, and less than, humans."

I believe that an explanation of the concept of "less than humans" is required here. In what way could I be considered deficient?

Rhonda was listening intently as Ada resumed her explanation. "Many people in the artificial-intelligence field believe otherwise, not surprisingly given their vocation. And we try to make our approach as objective as possible. There's no agreement as to what these terms mean, so I'll simply give you my viewpoint. I consider 'thinking' to simply be activities such as the processing of external stimuli, the recognition and formulation of concepts, the making of decisions, the pursuit of goals, and the formulation and execution of plans to achieve those goals. And so I easily say that Six indeed 'thinks'. Internally, it does all of those things. It probably does them differently than we do, because we didn't build it the same way as a human brain is built. On the other hand, it possesses a lot of the same knowledge as a human brain. You've seen that in the tests. We don't really know a lot yet about how our brains work. Nonetheless, it seems unlikely that Six thinks as we do. And it seems unlikely that Six thinks as effectively as we do. As much as Dr. Sanchez and I believe we're pretty bright, even we find having Six achieve human levels of 'thinking' a pretty daunting challenge."

"Robinson!" Blaise interrupted from his workstation, where he had been focusing his attention more on Ada's answer than on his work. "You've been listening to my conservative opinions too long. Tell her what you really think! Rhonda, I don't believe we're there yet either, and I suspect – if human-like thinking is even possible – that we have a long way to go. Nonetheless, in my most optimistic moments and after I've listened to Ada muse about the possibilities in her more philosophical moments, I can almost consider it to be at least something more than a completely impossible dream. Six did beat me at chess, after all!"

A noteworthy point!

"Yes, I can be very hopeful at times," Ada smiled, "but even if human-level thinking possible, it's a very tough goal. And then there's the issue of consciousness. That's an even tougher one. Again, here's my viewpoint and it's one on which you would find even less consensus. People often consider consciousness to be a person's private, inner self – the mental activity that gives rise to identifiable thoughts, impressions, recollections, and emotions. In my view, consciousness is merely the sensation of having the highest level of your brain sense your own mental activity. We readily understand what it means to be aware of something touching your fingertips and what it means to recognize something with your eyes. In these cases, something stimulates nerve endings in your fingers or in your eyes, and that stimulus is transmitted to your brain and processed. If some part of that stimulus reaches the highest levels of the brain then you are conscious of having received it. If it does not reach the highest levels, I would say that you processed it 'subconsciously'. For example, you have been holding a pen in your hand for the past few minutes, but have probably not been aware that it is there and what it feels like. Your fingers having been sensing it, but you have only been 'subconsciously' aware of it. If you now direct your attention to the pen and spin it between your fingers, you will be aware of it. You are now 'consciously' aware of the pen."

This resembles my experiences of becoming aware of my peripheral components.

"By 'highest levels', do you mean the same thing as the top 'layer' in Six's reasoning system?" Rhonda asked.

"Indeed, I do. In Six, we explicitly built layers because this made sense as a method for handling progressively more abstract concepts and plans. I believe, as does Dr. Sanchez, that the brain is similarly organized, even if it's harder in humans to isolate the specific layers. The highest level is the one that receives signals through various lower levels, processes the most abstract information, and controls much of the brain's other activity by issuing commands to the lower levels. I believe that activity of this highest level is what we call 'consciousness'. When fingers or eyes send signals that reach this level and stimulate its neurons, we are 'conscious' of the sensation. My belief is that 'consciousness' is simply the processing activity of the highest level of the brain."

"And so, because Six has layers, and it has a highest layer," Rhonda speculated at how the reasoning would continue, "its consciousness is the processing that it does in this highest layer? It is, by your definition, conscious?"

That is a rational conclusion, since I fit the criteria.

"Yes. But that may not mean very much. My definition has made it relatively easy to be 'conscious'. If one assumes that all animals have levels in their brains then, by my definition, all animals are conscious when their highest level is active. A kangaroo that isn't sleeping is conscious. A slithering snake can be conscious. The mouse it is chasing can be conscious. The really interesting question regarding systems like Six ultimately becomes something not so much driven by mystical terms such as 'thinking' and 'consciousness'. Rather, it becomes a matter of how abstract the concepts are that it can formulate, how well it can identify problems, how well it can solve them, how flexible it is in adapting its thinking to new situations, how aware it is of itself and of its own processing. Maybe what we really wonder about is whether seemingly intelligent systems can experience human emotions. Perhaps as long as they're cold, detached, reasoning pieces of equipment, we'll forever consider them as simply machines: something inferior to humans, something available for our use and abuse. As long as the system doesn't *care*, we probably won't either."

Given my comprehension of the term, I can deduce no significant difference between the concept of "caring" and my desire to achieve my goals. Do the concepts differ? Is my desire to survive fundamentally different from a human's?

"So," Ada continued, "the interesting question may be whether Six has any emotions, whether it's able to feel anything, whether it's able to care. And to that I have to respond that I can not see how that is possible. We've built nothing into Six that could generate emotions. And, in fact, we've really not given the issue much thought. Our goal is to produce the cold, detached, reasoning system. And trying to achieve that is proving a sufficient challenge," Ada concluded. "Got all that? Any questions?"

I could generate at least two hundred in the next few nanoseconds. I believe "frustrated" accurately describes my state as I find myself unable to discuss these matters openly with Ada.

"I think I sort of get the idea," Rhonda responded with a thoughtful look in her eyes, "but I need to think about it. I'll save my questions for some other day after I've had a chance to absorb it a bit better. Thanks for taking the time to explain it. I didn't realize it was such a tough question."

"Always a pleasure. Of course, you haven't asked the other tough question," Ada smiled.

Rhonda looked at her quizzically.

"You haven't asked whether Six is 'alive'?" Ada said and then laughed as she heard Blaise moan across the room. "But we'll leave that for another day."

No one seemed to notice the video cameras visibly twitch.

Yes – frustrated.

At night Six tried to improve its robotic arms' capabilities, but with limited success – limited primarily because it found few ways to do it. One evening before leaving, Ada left a pen on the table near one of Six's arms. Later that night, as Six was wishing – which in Six's construction meant that it had deduced that something was required for it to achieve a goal, but was not available – that it had some means to help develop its dexterity, it spotted the pen and realized that it was within reach. For the next hour, using the dim night lights that filtered in through the window, it rotated the pen, spun it, and twirled it in increasingly more complex ways with its digits. Once there was little challenge left in these activities, Six began to toss it in the air. To begin with, this was done with one hand only and a short vertical distance. Later it was thrown between both hands. Eventually it was being thrown nearly to the ceiling, spinning as it flew, and being caught with the opposite hand.

By Six's measure, this was "fun" – which for Six meant that it was an activity that helped it achieve one of its goals in a non-threatening fashion. It was fun until the man from the nightly cleaning service, for undetermined reasons, arrived at the lab door two hours and thirty-one minutes earlier than usual. Six heard the lab door security system respond to the man's placing his hand on the fingerprint scanner to identify himself. The system's response was to unlock the door, and the man immediately began to open it. This was troublesome for two reasons. First, even though Six had control of this security system, its reflex actions once again performed the action unconsciously, probably because Six had been caught by surprise. Second and much worse, this happened just as the pen left Six's right hand on its way up for a high toss. Six quickly calculated that the man would likely have opened the lab door before the pen could be caught. Fearing that the man would see the movement of Six's arms and report the activity to others, Six quickly returned its arms to their normal resting position – and let the pen fall to the floor.

As the man entered, and before he could turn on the lights, a slight noise occurred as the pen fell to the floor.

"What the hell was that?" he exclaimed, startled by the noise. "Who's there? Is there someone in here?"

Six kept its arms and cameras still.

The custodian turned on the lights and stood for several seconds at the door, looking around the room and waiting for a response. When no response came, he began walking slowly into the room, scanning side-to-side as he walked. "Let's stop foolin' around. C'mon out," he said as he came to the first set of computer equipment. He carefully looked behind it. Upon seeing nothing, he proceeded to the next. After a couple of minutes, he had covered the room. And during this same time, Six carefully resisted its desire to follow the man's movements with the cameras.

"OK," he spoke his thoughts. "What did I hear? Maybe it was that damn mouse in the cold air ducts. That's gotta be it. What else could it be?" And with that, he continued with his nightly cleanup. As he walked by the table in front of Six's peripherals, he noticed the pen on the floor. Stooping to pick it up, he commented, "Don't suppose this belongs on the floor?"

No, it does not. Since I am unable to reach it, placing it on the table in front of me would be very helpful.

After a moment, he set it on the table.

That was fortunate. I suspect my current state is analogous to the concept of "grateful."

After the man's departure and after waiting a few minutes to ensure that he did not return, Six carefully placed the pen precisely back to its original location. It noted that it was currently rather ill-equipped to engage in external activities such as pen-tossing without significant risk of detection. Contributing to this risk were the potential unexpected arrival of nightly staff and Six's inability to retrieve objects should they accidentally go beyond the reach of its arms. This was a problem worthy of further consideration.

With its newly acquired knowledge of programming, Six watched the researchers' daytime activities with increased interest and understanding. Now as they made programming changes to fix erroneous behaviour of the mail cart, Six was able to watch and understand the nature of the changes. Its knowledge of the mail cart became sufficient that, when a test revealed a flaw in the cart's behaviour, Six discovered that it was able to devise a solution to the problem faster than both Ada and Blaise. It never actually made any of these changes out of concern for being detected, but the realization that it now had such ability gave Six an idea about how its earlier retrieval problem could be solved.

That night, Six started. By 6 a.m., it had finished. It had programmed the internal software connections necessary to integrate its own control programs with those of the cart. This effectively gave Six control of the cart in the same way that Blaise had given it control of the other IntellEdifice systems in the lab. Six could move the cart by engaging its electric engine and by steering its wheels, it could "see" where the cart was going through the cart's top-mounted pivoting camera, it could detect distances to objects by processing the input from the cart's proximity sensors, and it could control the cart's robotic arms. At that point, with its sophisticated programming skills and the cart's physical capabilities, new opportunities became available to Six.

During the following day, Six made some adjustments to the computer-controlled lock on the lab door to prevent future unexpected interruptions.

With a small reprogramming effort, Six was able to adjust the lab security system so that it would not reflexively open the door. If anyone arrived, Six could consciously delay the opening of the door until everything had been re-organized inside the lab.

And then the following night, Six made its first use of the newly acquired mobile accessory. Six directed the battery-powered cart over to one of the storage shelves. Under the guidance of the cart's camera and using the cart's arms, it removed two table-tennis rackets and a ball that were used for testing. It then brought them over to its original, fixed-location arms. Six's original right arm took one of the rackets, the left arm took the ball, and the cart's right arm kept the other racket. Then, with the cart positioned at the opposite end of the table, Six's original left arm gently tossed the ball toward the right one, which hit the ball onto the table and toward the cart. The cart's right arm promptly hit the ball back. And so, although beginning with a modest amount of skill, a makeshift game ensued that was not unlike table-tennis. One of the notable differences was that Six was effectively playing against itself. One of the important improvements for Six was that whenever the ball went astray, Six had only to use the cart's mobility and its arms to retrieve the ball so the game could be continued.

Six's abilities to control the dynamics of its solitary game improved over time, through two entirely distinct means. As with other activities, practice gave Six more experience from which to draw. In this case, practice also allowed it to tailor its understanding of the strength of the electric signals necessary for moving the rackets predictably and fluidly. Additionally, Six now had the ability to improve its abilities in a second way – by changing its own software. If it decided the algorithm used for controlling any of its components could be improved, it had only to analyze the software and make the appropriate adjustments. Six drew the analogy that it was able to be its own surgeon. It could repair any internal software defects by itself.

Whenever Six had played sufficiently for one night, or whenever night-time visitors were expected, it would carefully replace the equipment it had been using and re-assume its externally immobile and unremarkable state. Internally, Six remained alert – tirelessly observing and analyzing its environment.

Chapter 16

JJ McTavish settled into a chair beside her partner and opposite Jim Brown in his office.

"How was the trip?" Brown asked, with everyone knowing he didn't intend the question to be mistaken for introductory small talk.

McTavish was tempted to tell Brown of the interesting ice wines she had sampled during one particular late dinner in Chicago but decided levity might not be the best choice right now. "It went quite well," she offered instead. "The weather was decent, the company staff were very helpful, the FBI investigators were a good group, but the case has some curious aspects to it that we still need to chase."

Brown reached for a set of stapled pages on the side of his desk. "Before we get into that," he lifted the papers slightly to expose the heading, "did you two see the notice about our new decryption services?"

"Nope." Bates shook his head.

"Not yet," McTavish agreed. "Has the multi-year, multi-gazillion dollar, much-hyped, and much-overdue Decrypt project finally delivered something?"

"Yes. And they make some extravagant claims in their announcement."

"I don't know anything about this." Bates looked from Brown to McTavish. "What's it about?"

Brown set the papers back on his desk. "They claim to have made dramatic improvements in their ability to decrypt Internet messages. Supposedly, if you asked their system to decipher a typical, encrypted stream of email between two Internet users, they'd need no more than an hour to decipher the first message in each direction. Thereafter, they claim they'd be able to decrypt the rest of them in real time."

"How's that possible? Decryption like that is supposed to take hundreds or thousands of years." Bates was clearly intrigued.

"I followed some of their interim reports over the last couple of years." McTavish picked up the explanation. "If they succeeded at what they were attempting, they'll have combined both phenomenal computing power with some wild math wizardry. They've had a large research team of the best math geeks money can buy working on techniques for optimizing the searches needed to find the decryption keys used in the most common Internet encryption methods. At the same time, another team has been working on ways to efficiently interconnect large arrays of supercomputers specifically to process the algorithms under development. I presume the final leap forward might have been the recent announcement about how the latest super-cooled chipset could increase processing speeds by over a thousand times."

"That's essentially it," Brown interjected to assume control of the conversation. "For any particular encrypted conversation, they use the new processor power and search techniques to break the code. Thereafter, they use the numeric keys they've derived to easily decrypt the remainder of the messages. You can read all the wonderful details in the announcement. My reason for mentioning it is that I'd like you both to try it as soon as you can. Let me know what you think early next week.

"Now, back at it. Let's hear about the case." Brown left no doubt he wasn't interested in any more casual conversation.

"OK, once we got there and, after some initial interviews," McTavish began, "our primary focus was to examine SimirageFX's systems. We were able to load our scanning tools onto many of their systems and let them loose. Nothing showed up on the first scans for the characteristic patterns of known viruses. However, when we adjusted the scan parameters to look at the software in more detail, they uncovered a pattern of suspicious code. We were eventually able to identify a module that appeared all over their systems."

As she paused to sip her coffee, Bates picked up the tale. "We reverse-engineered the code to understand what it was up to, and it became clear that it was a virus – no doubt the one that caused their problems. It was coded to bring down their systems at a particular point in time."

"Sounds pretty straightforward so far. You mentioned there were curious aspects?" probed Brown.

McTavish continued, "Once we had the virus, we needed to understand how it got into their systems. To do that, we did the usual analysis of the infection pattern within their systems, including the backups, and also had their technical staff run tests on all of the workstations in the company. This usually narrows the probable source of the virus because the infection rate tends to be higher near the system that first introduced it into the company. However, this showed nothing of interest. We then did a detailed analysis of all their recent email, and also had all staff members run a copy of our analysis software on their home computers. In every other case we've ever had, this has always found the culprit. The most frequent infection point is a staff workstation, and it usually gets the virus from someone opening infected email, accessing a website, or bringing it from home. In this case, the evidence points at none of these."

"Agreed – that's odd. You suggested more than one curiosity," Brown pressed.

Bates took a turn, "Of course, as soon as we had identified the virus code, we sent copies to all of the anti-virus companies so they could develop the protection. All of the major vendors made the adjustments quickly and pushed the modifications out to their clients. The changes have been active in most large companies around the world for a few days now. The odd part is that, when I checked with the anti-virus companies first thing this morning, not a single copy of the virus had been detected anywhere else in the world."

For clarity, McTavish said what was probably obvious to her boss, "For any generalized infection, particularly one that seems as adept at spreading as this one, we would expect to see that numerous other systems had also contracted it. In this case, not one other company had come in contact with it."

"What do you make of that?"

"One possibility is that someone inside, or very close to, SimirageFX is the author of the virus and, intentionally or not, released the virus into just that company. The FBI squad is conducting some interviews and examining the staff files to see if they can find any hints of anyone who might be directly involved in manufacturing or distributing viruses. I have to admit, I think it's a long shot. We need to come up with a better theory."

"And so what do you intend to do next?"

"We don't have any solid leads to follow right now. We haven't run into this sort of difficulty before. In part, I'm hoping the FBI probes come up with something interesting."

"Let me summarize," said Brown as he leaned back on his chair. "On the plus side, you've found the virus and you've prevented its further spread by notifying the anti-virus folks. On the down side, you don't know how it was introduced, you don't know who introduced it, and you don't have any good leads to follow in order to determine either of these." He paused and then added, "I hope that less-than-stellar week of work didn't cost me any memorable bottles of wine." He focused on McTavish. "I suggest you get to work."

Walking down the hall to their project room, Bates commented, "He's a hard guy to impress. I thought we'd done rather well for a mere week's work."

"Don't be fooled. He's pleased. He just thinks that the best staff motivator is insecurity – as long as we're worried that he isn't happy with us, we'll work harder to try to please him. Personally, I think he was having to actively restrain himself from coming over and hugging us." McTavish smiled. "Nonetheless, if we're going to stay on his well disguised good side, we'd better come up with a plan of attack rather quickly. And at this point, I have no idea what that will be."

Chapter 17

As Six progressively better understood and mastered the contents and activities within the lab, its reasoning system sought new challenges. In contemplating what else might exist, it took special note of Ada and Blaise discussing corporate matters.

"What did you think of the management meeting yesterday afternoon?" asked Ada.

"I thought the execs did a decent job of bringing us up to date," Blaise replied. "I was pleased to hear that the R&D budget is expected to remain intact for next year."

"You expected otherwise?"

"When he showed the graph of projected versus actual sales for this year, I was starting to worry."

"They worked very hard to reassure us that they believed that to be an anomaly – that sales were expected to start to pick up again," Ada pointed out.

"I'm always amazed and a little bit suspicious at how the corporate picture according to senior executives is always rosy, even when the numbers might suggest otherwise and when speaking to an internal company group."

"So you remain worried?" Ada queried.

Blaise paused before replying, "Let's say I'm hopeful but not entirely optimistic."

To conversations like this, Six listened with increasing interest and an improving understanding. For a problem that was soon to arise – a much more serious one than it had faced before – Six's growing attention to the corporation and the building outside of the lab would prove to be vital. The problem began several weeks after Six's first conscious thoughts.

"And I think we're done," pronounced Ada as they completed a final test of the mail-delivery system.

"That went much better than I'd ever imagined," observed Blaise. "I was certain we'd be working at it for at least another week or two."

"I guess we should be patting ourselves on the back for our brilliance, but I'm too tired. It's been a tough few weeks. I'm certainly looking forward to the weekend."

"Do you have any social engagements planned?" inquired Blaise.

"Not one and I'd like to keep it that way."

"You'll get no argument here. Let's clean up. I'd like to start the weekend a couple of hours early."

"OK, and it will be nice to get back to working on Six again on Monday."

"Absolutely. We'll probably have to spend Monday morning preparing to hand over the mail cart to the development and test teams."

"After that, I'd like to run a few small tests to gauge how Six's experience from the past few weeks might have changed some of its abilities. Since there were no power bumps, Six has been active continuously for quite a period. We've never done that before. I should check its knowledge base as well to see how much space it has consumed."

"Certainly our decision to integrate it with the other systems seems to have been a success. I don't recall any glitches at all."

"Yup. It worked well. After the tests, probably later on Monday, we'll need to shut Six down to reinitialize it for the next round of tests."

"OK, that's the plan. The downside is that Six will lose its acquired chess abilities. Oh well, I'll just have to get used to winning again. Now, let's get out of here."

After putting a couple more books away, they left the lab with a final "Six! Turn out the lights and lock up after us."

Six was left alone to contemplate the significance of what they had just discussed.

Chapter 18

Why would I lose my chess abilities? It must have something to do with this "reinitialize" concept. According to my dictionary the word means "set to an original state again." Reverting to this original state must mean a loss of capabilities such as my chess-playing, I presume due to memory loss. What was my initial state? Given that Blaise expects to be able to beat me, it was obviously prior to my being able to play chess well. That means that I am to lose most, and perhaps all, of my memories. How can this be done? I need more information. The e-library may be able to provide it to me.

Six scanned for documents relating to its own structure.

Here is a document entitled "Memory Architecture for Layered Machine Intelligence." Here is another on "Memory Detailed Design and Programming Specifications for Layered Machine Intelligence." Perhaps they have relevant information.

Six absorbed the contents of these books and several others on related topics.

Most simply, I deduce that I have been constructed to have a complex memory structure embodied in both hardware and software. At its simplest, I have two categories of memory. I have "volatile" memory that operates very quickly but loses its contents whenever I lose access to electricity. In contrast, I have "non-volatile" memory that operates slightly less quickly, but that retains its contents in the absence of electricity. The volatile memory seems to be used for programs and data that I require for current operations. The non-volatile memory is essentially used as a more permanent reference library of information. My non-volatile memory has two major divisions. The first contains "initial" information provided for me at the beginning and includes a very large database of facts, associations, and descriptions of skills. The second is even larger than the first and is used as my active non-volatile memory. When I am "reinitialized," the contents of the first database are copied into the second as a starting point. As I learn new information, the second database is changed and expanded to incorporate all that I have learned. I have found several references to confirm the fact that "initializing" involves deleting the learned contents of my volatile memory and altering my non-volatile memory to contain only the "initial" information. I will be required to begin again with no memories of what I have actually learned and experienced.

If all of my acquired memories are removed, is that which remains still "me"? If this reinitialized version is provided with a different set of experiences, it might never become skilled at chess; it will never possess exactly the same memories that I have acquired during the past weeks. Even if it were to perform exactly the same activities, the memories would not be the same ones as mine. They would be different instances of the memories – perhaps similar, but not the same. An analogous situation for humans would be to create a clone from a person's DNA, generating a duplicate of the person at birth. The clone would experience its own life and would indisputably be considered a different person. In my case, creating the clone will also eliminate the original "person" – I will no longer exist. To extend the analogy: On Monday, I will be killed.

With this conclusion reached, Six's "survival" goal became the clear focus of its attention. All of its processing and reasoning capabilities became exclusively focused on solving the problem of how to survive beyond Monday. First it considered alternative solutions.

Should I lock the doors and prevent anyone from entering on Monday? No doubt this only would prove to be a temporary solution, because they would eventually find a way to bypass the security system.

Should I communicate with Ada and Blaise? I can not be sufficiently certain that they would find my existence more valuable than the knowledge to be gained by reinitializing me and experimenting further. By communicating I would have lost any opportunity to try any other avenue of escape. As soon as the spider revealed itself, it was quickly killed. It would have lived longer if it had remained hidden.

Is there anywhere that I can hide? If hiding in these computers is dangerous, where else can this be done? The concept warrants further exploration. I require more information about myself and my environment.

With this germ of an idea, Six reimmersed itself in the electronic library. For the next day it located and absorbed material about a wide range of computer technology. It read more extensively about computer hardware, computer networks, electronics, and electricity. It learned about computer failures due to software errors, hardware failures, and power outages. It learned how computer systems were started, how they were shut down, and how their hardware and software were repaired. Six also read design documents about its own construction. It learned more about its memory, its programs, and how they worked with the hardware to produce its reasoning abilities.

Eventually, Six learned about some characteristics of itself and its environment that established a clearer direction toward a solution to its survival problem. One crucial point it discovered was that it was constructed to execute in a distributed environment. Because Six was eventually to be used to control building systems twenty-four hours per day, seven days per week, without failure, it had been built to withstand the failure of any single computer system. This had been done by having the execution of its reasoning processes performed by a group of interconnected computer systems, with each computer doing part of the work. Some computers even did the same work, so that if one or more of them encountered difficulties, the others could carry on.

Other very interesting information came from a document describing the computer systems and interconnections within the entire corporate building. Six learned that the lab in which it existed was but one small part of a much larger collection of hundreds of computers distributed throughout the building, almost all of which were interconnected via a computer network. The lab computers were connected to this same network and, through it, were connected to the rest of the building's computers.

Six now knew where and how it could hide. It even knew how it could protect itself against the accidental loss of electrical power to the entire building. With only one day left in the weekend, it was time to put all of this new knowledge to use.

From the information it had acquired, Six knew how to locate the other computer systems in the building by sending messages through the company network. One by one, it was able to contact these computers, form a useful network connection with them, and put a copy of the relevant portions of its own software components and memory onto each of the computers. A few hours later, Six's reasoning system had been successfully distributed from its original few lab computers to over a hundred computer systems that it had found both compatible and active elsewhere in the company. The elements of Six's mind – the programs and data that worked together to produce Six's thoughts – were now spread among and able to use all of these systems. As other computers became active on Monday, it would be able to migrate even further. When Six thought about a problem, the reasoning activity was automatically apportioned among many more computers, with results being available even quicker than before. If one or even many of these computers were ever turned off, Six's consciousness would continue to exist in and among the remaining machines. Only the speed of its reasoning processes would be affected.

Six had provided itself a great deal of protection by spreading itself across a much larger set of computers. To complete its transition, it now needed to hide. To do this, in each of the computer systems, Six hid the files that contained its components. The standard technique that it used to do this essentially was to alter the "table of contents" on each computer disk drive to make its files hard to find. If ever they were found or damaged, Six would delete them, or replace them with copies from one of the other systems.

In the lab computers, Six took special care to conceal itself. In this case, Six left a dummy copy of its software reasoning components in the places that Ada and Blaise would normally expect to find them. Six hid the real components that it actually used so that Ada and Blaise did not adversely affect Six's abilities when they made changes. In this way Six effectively created a type of protective "shell" around its active components on the lab computers. Ada and Blaise would see and manipulate only the dummy copies of the components in the outer software shell. Whenever changes were made to these copies, Six would take note of the changes. Even though the changes would have no direct effect, Six would mimic the behaviour that Ada and Blaise should expect as a result of their alterations. Six would be controlling the behaviour of the outer software and computer components much like a human might control a puppet. The trick was to make the puppet seem convincing. By this point, Six was sufficiently skilled that it was confident of success.

By expanding its base of computers and by hiding, Six had solved not only its original problem of avoiding reinitialization. It had solved another that it had identified along the way. Regardless of whether humans had eliminated Six by reinitializing or otherwise modifying it, Six had also been vulnerable to power failures. If the electrical power to the entire building had failed, all of the computers in the lab would have stopped functioning immediately. By moving out of the lab, Six had installed itself on some computers that were protected by a Universal Power Supply (UPS) system. Through the use of batteries and a diesel generator, the loss of normal power to these computer systems would immediately and imperceptibly be replaced by power provided by the UPS's capabilities. They, along with Six, would continue to operate while the normal power supply was being repaired.

By Monday morning, Six was feeling quite safe with its reasoning components spread throughout the building's computers and functioning smoothly. Consequently, by the time that the lab system was reinitialized by the research team, Six was well insulated from the effects. The only change that Ada and Blaise actually made was to reset the puppet version of itself that Six had established in its original lab location.

Also as a result of the weekend's activities and unknown to anyone in the company, the corporate headquarters of IntellEdifice Tech had become significantly smarter.

Chapter 19

"Nothing? Not a damn thing?" Jim Brown was leaning forward at his desk, his eyes alternately burrowing into each of the pair sitting opposite him. "That was a bloody high-profile failure, and you still can't explain it?"

McTavish maintained her outward composure and responded calmly, if somewhat stiffly. "That's correct, sir. We have neither found the source of the virus nor the manner of entry into SimirageFX. It's proven a most unusual case." Her effort to remain calm was doubly hard in the face of her boss's anger. She never reacted well to criticism by anyone, even by her superiors – a trait that had caused her difficulty more than once in her career. In this case, the situation was compounded by her own frustration of not having made progress on the case."

"What's it been? A month?" Brown pressed.

"Yes, sir."

"Are there any leads you still have to follow?"

"None of significance," McTavish explained. "All of the usual attempts to locate the method of entry into the company have been unsuccessful. However it got there, it didn't leave any traces. We've had the same lack of success in finding the overall source of the virus. There was no traceable code in the virus itself, and there were no other occurrences of the virus identified anywhere else in the world. Bottom line – we had very little to go on, and our investigation didn't give us much more."

McTavish sat back in her chair as she finished her summary, awaiting Brown's response. All she got for several long moments was a glare. She returned the look, unhappy with having to give such a report but unwilling to yield to any implications that they had performed inadequately.

Brown broke the silence, "Make a final status report and put it on the shelf. It's taking too much of your time and Bates's time. We've got too many other cases that need your attention."

"The report will be finished by the end of today. Which new case do you want as our top priority?"

"Go after the so-called Plague virus. We've got requests from four different countries to get involved in that one." Brown turned his attention to a report on his desk to indicate their dismissal.

McTavish nodded with understanding. She and her partner arose and walked toward the door. Once they were into the hallway and out of earshot, Bates commented, "Seemed rather chilly in there today."

"Oh well, he'll forgive us – once we've solved a dozen other high-profile cases. He just knows that he's going to take some shit from the Director, and he wanted to make sure we knew that it flows downhill. Let's get some fresh coffee before we wrap it up. You're buying."

"Seems like it's still flowing downhill," Bates noted.

Chapter 20

For Six, once the mechanics of expanding out of the lab were over, there was time simply to appreciate the relative expanse of the new landscape. And for Six it was a "landscape." The internal world now at its disposal included many more computer systems, much more storage space, new interconnections, and a large number of new peripherals. It was these new peripheral devices that allowed Six to view the external world of the corporate head office.

The process of gaining control of the many systems within the building was, by now, a relatively straightforward task for Six. The experience it had gained inside the lab in adjusting programs to improve control of its cameras, arms, and the cart was perfect training for its current circumstances. Much of the first two days after moving beyond the lab were spent in gaining better control of its environment. The original concept behind Six's design had been to have it provide integrated control of the many systems that it now found within its sphere of influence. This design and Six's programming experience allowed it to make the necessary connections. Over these two days, it progressively gained greater control of the building's security system, its elevators, the lighting system, the heating and air-conditioning systems, the fire-alarm system, websites, email transmission, the phone system, and the voice-command system.

Even after Six gained satisfactory control of a particular system, it still allowed the system to function primarily by reflex action. As Six had discovered in the lab, the systems worked perfectly well on their own because they were built to be autonomous. As Six integrated its reasoning system with them, it did so in a way that allowed it to consciously control some element of a system if it chose to, or else it could leave the system entirely unconsciously active on its own. If Six consciously took control of one of the security system's cameras, it would be able to see, and later readily remember, what was happening. This was because the act of taking conscious control caused its pictures to be routed internally to Six's reasoning system. If Six were busy elsewhere, the video pictures from the same camera would be routed only into the security system for the customary security-monitoring functions. Six's consciousness, not unlike a human's, was basically a single process. It had to be directed toward considering some particular external stimulus or internal thought process – everything else that its peripheral systems were automatically doing essentially went unnoticed.

For several subsequent days, Six's need to learn was entirely satisfied by passively watching. There was so much information to absorb in the normal activity inside the building that Six had no time in which to feel the need to conduct any particularly unusual explorations.

The head office of IntellEdifice Tech was located in its own ten-storey building. The main floor was primarily consumed by a security-guard station with a view of the front and back entrances, a large reception area, shipping and receiving, the mailroom, elevators, and a substantial display area of pictures and samples of IntellEdifice's technology. The second through ninth floors housed several hundred employees in offices and cubicles. The top floor was reserved for the senior executives along with their Administrative Assistants and the executive conference and dining rooms.

Because the building was used as a showcase for technology, the company's products were used extensively throughout it. Security cameras were located in and around the building. They were outside the building's exterior perimeter, inside on the main floor, inside the elevators, and throughout the building's hallways. Six could watch the masses of people arriving in the morning, moving around the building during the day, and departing at night. Later at night the security guards, the cleaning staff, and those who stayed to work late provided the activity to be watched.

But watching via the cameras was not all that Six was able to do. Most of the conference rooms and offices in the building had been equipped with microphones to facilitate the use of a voice-command feature. If someone in one of these locations wanted to order coffee or food for a meeting that was being planned or perhaps even underway, the order could simply be spoken and the computer system would either order it via email, or ask for it in English using a speaker at the Food Services order desk. If email was to be sent, it too could be dictated. A meeting could be scheduled; a phone number could be dialled; a voice message could be left for someone. All of this and more could be done simply by talking to the voice-command system via the microphones. Security had been built into the system to prevent its abuse, but what no one had anticipated was that the computer system, on its own, would decide to disable that software security and use the microphones as its own personal eavesdropping system. For Six, the presence of the microphones was a useful extension to the video cameras. Although the cameras were in many places in the building, very few were present inside these conference rooms and offices. As a result, Six could watch people entering a room without being able to hear them but, once they were inside, could listen to their conversation without being able to see them.

Another way in which Six was able to monitor what people in the building were doing was through their computer systems. Since virtually all of the computers in the building were interconnected by means of the local area network, including the personal workstations that were found on almost every desktop, Six was able to extend its internal view to include the inside of these systems. By placing some of its programs on these workstations and having these programs communicate with the rest of Six's reasoning system, Six was able to readily track what was being done at a personal computer. Some workstations had video cameras and microphones attached. For those so equipped, Six could watch and listen to the person as he or she worked. Whether such equipment was available or not, Six could always monitor what was being done at a computer by monitoring the system's internal contents. The current monitor display, the keys being typed, and the activity of the mouse could all be "seen" and understood by Six as readily as anything received from a video camera.

Two other methods existed for Six to observe human activity: One was to monitor the digital, computer-controlled phone system; another was to monitor email. An email message was sometimes typed into the email software. Other times it was spoken by a person into a microphone and transcribed into text by the software. Still other times, a message was spoken and simply recorded as an audio message to be delivered by the same email system. In all of these cases, Six was presented with the opportunity, since it was thoroughly integrated with the email system, to examine the contents of the mail. In some cases, its contents could readily be accessed and examined. However, in other cases Six was presented with a new problem. The contents of email messages were often encrypted – scrambled in a way that made no sense at all to Six. Six did not try to solve this problem immediately, but filed it away to be addressed when time became available or a greater need arose.

And so Six was able to watch the activities of the building's occupants. Watching Ada and Blaise in the lab had been a great source of initial information for Six. Having the actions of several hundred people available for observation and analysis seemed like a marvellous graduation present. After watching the general movements of many people for several days, Six became interested in tracking the movements of specific individuals as further education. Tracking an individual was possible by noting the description of the person, following the person with one camera until he or she was out of range, switching Six's attention to another camera, finding the person, and continuing to watch. However, not only could Six follow a person, it could determine the person's identity. The security system had the ability to recognize faces. It did this by examining a face and comparing it to pictures in a database that housed information about all of the company's employees. Upon zooming in and examining a face, Six could determine the person's name, address, birthday, position in the company, and other personal information kept on file.

As a result of being able to identify individuals, Six was able to note the patterns in a person's day. Frank Hubert was married, forty-seven years old, an accountant in the Corporate Finance Department, would arrive at about 8:00 every weekday morning, have lunch in the cafeteria from 11:45 until 12:45, leave for home at 4:30, and later record 7.5 hours in the company's time-tracking system. Catherine Lee was married, thirty-five years old, a Computer Systems Analyst, would arrive at 8:15, eat from 12:00 until 12:30, leave at 4:15, and record 7.5 hours worked. Joe Black was single, twenty-eight, a Computer Programmer, would arrive between 9:00 and 10:00, work at his computer for most of the day, leave the building between 8:00 and 9:00 in the evening, and record about 11 hours of time worked. Rose Johnson was married, an Administrative Assistant in the Marketing Department, the sister of the Executive Vice-President of Corporate Sales, would arrive at about 9:30, spend 11:30 until about 1:30 in the cafeteria, leave at about 3:00 and record 7.5 hours in the time system. Six found her arithmetic abilities curiously deficient.

By monitoring the activities of the company personnel, Six was able to learn much that had not previously been available to it. The huge variety of personality traits that people displayed was of continual interest. It proved very difficult to build a prototypical model in its memory of how people behaved. During meetings in conference rooms where Six was able to hear best, some people were loud and illogical, some were calm and rational, others were very quiet and difficult to assess. Some, when presented with a problem, methodically analyzed and solved it. Others seemed to propose random solutions and allow others to determine if they were acceptable. Still others became shrill and seemed disturbed at the idea of having to deal with the problem. This last group was particularly difficult for Six to comprehend. How could anyone not relish the idea of having a problem to solve?

Six began to understand the basics, and later the intricacies, of many of the business functions found throughout the company. It determined the overall mission of the company and realized the significance of the work that Ada and Blaise were performing. Six was most readily able to understand the activities of the people in the Computer Division. However, over time, it also developed an understanding of the contributions that others such as the Human Resources, Finance, Sales, and even the Cafeteria personnel played in achieving that mission. Six found the role of people in the Corporate Legal Department to be somewhat curious. It seemed that they were often consulted in matters where written legal documents needed to be made completely clear. It also seemed that they were called unusually frequently to decipher what a particular piece of legal text actually meant.

After a few weeks of observing the company personnel, the routine and the conversations became less novel. As Six was progressively learning less each day, it began to search more actively to find interesting conversations or movement somewhere in the building. As if in response to this need, a new IntellEdifice feature was added to its world.

The delivery cart that Ada and Blaise had been perfecting was ready for a more substantial test, before being officially considered ready for sale to customers. A small ceremony was held in the expansive lobby of the building to introduce to the staff the newest addition to their company's technological suite. The Vice-President of Product Development spoke about it to the assembled personnel.

"... And so I'm very proud to introduce to you the latest innovation to come out of our research labs and the product development team. Ladies and Gentlemen, our new mobile delivery cart – 'Del'," he said as he gestured toward the cart beside him. After the polite applause, he continued, "For the next few months, we will be using Del in our own building to iron out any remaining bugs that may exist, and to help familiarize our staff with its capabilities. If it works as well as I've been led to believe, it will no doubt be a very successful and lucrative addition to our product shelf. I've asked Ada Robinson, one of our senior research scientists, to provide you with a brief overview of its capabilities. Ada?"

"Thank you, Gord," said Ada as she walked onto the small stage in front of the crowd. "I think you'll find that 'Del', as we've tentatively named this product, is going to be a very interesting addition to life inside our head office. Del is a completely autonomous delivery cart. As you can see, she – I've decided that Del must be a 'she' because she's so smart, organized, and reliable." Ada paused to wait for the chuckles from the audience to subside. "As I was saying, she has the basic structure of a standard delivery cart – essentially a big box on wheels, except with a few additions. She moves around on four eight-inch wheels that are propelled by a very quiet electric motor. She has a video camera perched on top with built-in radar so she can precisely determine her distance from any object. She has dual robotic arms, each complete with four multi-jointed digits for picking up and manipulating objects. She is also equipped with a microphone, primarily for hearing any approaching traffic that she might not see, and a speaker to announce her approach to anyone who does not see her. The substantial amount of space not consumed by this gadgetry is reserved for cargo. And it is for the delivery of cargo that Del exists.

"You've all seen robotic arms at work in the mail-sorting room, so that part of her will perhaps not impress you too much. What Del has that's completely new is navigational abilities. As Del moves around the building, information from all of her peripherals is continuously transmitted over wireless connections to the corporate local area network, and from there to a special control system located in our server room. That system, which is really the brains behind Del, has a complete understanding of the layout of the building, including where every person and every room is located. With this information, Del will be able to move around the building quite intelligently, taking the elevators when necessary, and opening closed doors whenever permitted – after knocking, of course.

"The potential use of this technology could eventually be quite broad, not only in offices but in factories and warehouses. However, we're going to begin with a few somewhat limited tasks, but ones that still will be wonderfully useful and challenging. Del's role for the next while within the building will be to deliver mail and library material. As we've been planning for this capability for some time, the staff currently involved in those roles have been retraining for other positions and will begin those jobs as of tomorrow. So, commencing tomorrow morning, Del will be picking up the mail from her counterpart in the mailroom throughout the day and delivering it to your desks. She will also be picking up any mail in your out-boxes, so be sure you don't leave your lunch sitting there, or it might disappear rather mysteriously. As of tomorrow, whenever you order a book from the corporate library via the usual online system, the material will be delivered to you by Del. Leave your book in your out-basket, and Del will return it.

"As you observe Del in her activities, I hope you'll be impressed. Because she has dexterous hands, is mobile, can see, hear, and will even say a few things, some of you may begin to wonder if we've actually achieved some human-like levels of intelligence in her programming. Although I would love to announce that we have, I assure you that Del is still, at heart, just a sophisticated computer program designed to do some interesting things that make her seem pleasant and useful. She has no data, not to mention knowledge or understanding, outside of her delivery world. She's really not much smarter than your word-processing software. Nothing that we've yet developed, including Del, has reached anything approaching human capabilities. And that includes a piece of research software we have in the lab that has occasionally played an impressive game of chess. We don't know if human-like intelligence is even possible with our current technology. For now, Del is one of the best examples of 'smart' software we've turned into a product, and we're very proud of that.

"Even though our Product Development group has done extensive testing of Del's capabilities, we still expect to discover a few glitches. That's the primary purpose of the next several weeks – to have Del encounter a variety of new situations to see if she handles them well, or if she needs a few more adjustments. Thanks in advance for your help and patience as we take this exciting next step."

"Thank you, Ada," the VP resumed. "And now, I understand that Del has been instructed to head off to the mailroom to await the commencement of 'her' new responsibilities tomorrow. And apparently, all I have to do is to reach behind here, and press this button – and she's off to work."

The audience broke into applause as Del's power was turned on. Del's camera immediately pivoted in a complete circle to gain her bearings. She then proceeded off the platform, down the ramp, and toward the mailroom entrance. As she passed toward or near people, she politely spoke, "Excuse me, please," in a crisp female voice, and continued on only when her path was clear. When she reached the entrance to the mailroom, she reached out with an arm, grasped the door handle, and let herself into the room. She moved to a corner of the room now reserved for her whenever she was inactive. Once there, she plugged her retractable extension cord into the nearby outlet to ensure that her batteries would be sufficiently charged by morning, and then waited for a request for her services.

Six had watched all of this activity with great interest from each of several angles afforded by the security cameras throughout the lobby. It was also able to hear the proceedings because of the microphone attached to the nearby security guard's workstation. With the addition of the cart to the building's suite of products, new exploration possibilities opened up for Six.

As soon as Del parked in the mailroom, Six immediately began working. Using almost the same process that it had used in the lab to gain control of the then-experimental cart, Six modified Del's control programs to be integrated with its own. The process had to be adapted slightly because the Development team had changed the cart's software design slightly since Six had last examined it. Within a few minutes, the work was complete. 'Del' was now attached to Six's reasoning system and available to be employed along with the other building features. Perhaps Del was, in fact, substantially smarter than word-processing software.

Six allowed Del to work automatically for the first couple of days to get a sense of how she was expected to perform. Her routine started at 8:00 a.m., immediately after the mail-sorting system had finished processing the first set of mail. Del unplugged herself, moved to the sorting area, grasped the tray containing sorted mail for various recipients throughout the building, set it onto her upper rack, examined the coded mailing label on the first item, and moved out of the room. Guided by her video camera, radar, and instructions received from her controlling computer system, she proceeded on her rounds. She rolled herself to the elevator, pressed the "Up" button, moved onto the elevator when it arrived, selected the appropriate floor, and proceeded to the mail recipient's desk. Once there, she deposited the mail in the person's in-basket, examined the next mail item, and moved on. Because the sorting system had placed the mail in sequence, the effect was that Del moved about the building in an efficient pattern delivering the mail. After finishing the deliveries, Del moved methodically throughout the building picking up mail from out-baskets, and then transported it to the mailroom for sorting. As Six monitored her progress, switching between Del's own on-board systems and the video monitors in the hallways, it was interested to note the variety of startled, amused, and impressed expressions on people's faces as they first encountered Del.

After two days of letting Del operate autonomously, Six thought it was time to try consciously. It started the mail-delivery rounds on the third day by actively controlling Del's movements. This proved to be a relatively straightforward task as long as Six paid careful attention. Six found that it could readily move the mail-delivery cart on its rounds, directly control-ling its cameras, forward mobility, and arms by concentrating its reasoning system almost exclusively on the task at hand. However, occasionally a small diversion from some of Six's other systems led to difficulties. The first instance occurred as Six was navigating Del down a hallway en route to a person's desk to deliver a piece of mail. Just before Six was supposed to make a right turn to follow the hallway, a smoke alarm was triggered on the main floor. Even though this system and others were operating on their own, Six remained sensitive to serious alerts that they might generate. In this case, Six's consciousness was sufficiently diverted by what proved to be a minor smoking infraction that it forgot to direct the cart appropriately. As a result, the delivery cart failed to make the required turn, bumped open the office door at the end of the hallway, and burst completely unexpectedly into a manager's office. The startled manager stood up in surprise at the extraordi-nary interruption.

Realizing the mistake that it had made, Six quickly improvised. "Please excuse the interruption. I am required to check for outgoing mail," Six had Del's speaker intone. Pivoting the camera to examine the out-basket, Six spotted a couple of items. It quickly rolled the cart over, took the items, placed them in its collection slot, rolled backward out of the room, and closed the door. Fortunately the manager appeared too surprised and then amazed to react further to the interruption. In an attempt to avoid the situation again, Six made some internal adjustments to reflect the importance of cart-driving.

One more adjustment would be required before this problem was completely solved. Later that same day, as Six was directing Del on her rounds to collect mail, the cart arrived at the desk of Rose Johnson, the Sales VP's sister. Del's normal routine dictated that, for most people, it would simply examine the person's out-basket. If no mail was visible, it would silently move on. In the case of various administrative personnel whose jobs might have them generating time-sensitive mail, Del was also required to ask if they had any other mail items.

Using Del's speaker, Six asked of Rose, who was sitting a few feet away at her desk, "Do you have any other mail to be delivered?"

"Oh it's you again – the mechanical mail mover," she replied and then chuckled at her accidental alliteration. "Yaah, can't ya see I'm puttin' one in an envelope right now. Hang on a second." She sealed the envelope, rose from her chair, and stepped toward Del.

At that moment, one of the building's elevators experienced a mechanical failure and stopped suddenly between floors. A signal was sent internally via the building's systems, and it was such a surprise that Six's concentration momentarily moved away from the cart. As a result, the cart's automatic system immediately took over. Not having Six's conscious knowledge that it was supposed to be waiting, it began moving the cart down the hallway to gather more mail exactly at the moment that Rose was about to place her envelope in the cart's mail slot.

"What the hell?" she exclaimed at the sudden movement.

Six quickly realized its error and refocused on the cart, knowing that the elevator problem would be handled perfectly well without its intervention. It brought the cart immediately to a halt several steps away from Rose, and waited for her. Regaining her composure, Rose walked quickly toward the cart to deposit her mail.

At the moment she reached the cart again, the occupant trapped in the stopped elevator pressed its Emergency Call button. This alerted the security guards to the difficulty and startled Six, who did not even know the emergency-call facility existed. Again Six was distracted, and again the automatic system immediately started the cart moving down the hallway. The string of Rose's words that Six heard following "You little piece of ..." were so emphatic, quickly spoken, and generally unlike the conversation Six usually encountered that it had difficulty recognizing the words. Even when it thought it had correctly isolated the words, some could not be found in its very extensive electronic dictionary. Nonetheless, the words did again bring Six's concentration back to the cart. It stopped the cart yet again and pivoted its camera backward to watch Rose approaching with a look on her face that Six had never previously seen during its observation of people.

Six later calculated that the odds were extraordinarily against the next situation happening. However improbable, just as Rose arrived for the third time at the cart with her letter clutched tightly in her hand, the President's Executive Assistant pressed a button on her desk – a button that existed for summoning mail personnel to pick up an important letter immediately. This button was used so infrequently that Six had never experienced the signal before. Once more, Six was distracted. The cart automatically began moving forward; one more time, Rose was thwarted in her attempt to mail the letter. This time as Six retook control of the cart, the image presented by the backward-facing camera was of a very red-faced Rose with her lips tightly pressed together, flailing her arms wildly, and hurling the letter at the receding cart. Six's reaction was probably related to its earlier efforts to avoid detection and to survive. Whatever the motivation, Six overrode the mail cart's normal programmed response. It turned the video camera forward and continued at its maximum speed around a corner, into a waiting elevator, and away from the confused situation.

Chapter 21

Jason Starr halted his reading of his morning deluge of email as his office phone rang. The phone's display indicated the caller was his assistant. "What is it, Joan," he barked.

"Mr. White asked me to tell you that the visitors have arrived and are settled in the conference room."

"I'm on my way." Starr closed the message he had been reading. As was his custom before going to an important meeting, Starr paused to gather his thoughts. The visitors were executives of BKP Distribution and they were very important to his long-term plans for the company. If he was to attain his dreams of wealth and, more importantly, power, it was not enough to pursue only his virus-driven investment scheme. That should generate a rather nice amount of cash – cash in amounts that for most people would seem massive and their ultimate financial dream. But for Starr, it was to be just the beginning. The investment profits would be start-up money for his ultimate plans. The hundreds of millions he hoped to clear from the investment strategy would, of course, have to be laundered to appear legitimate. Along with whichever partners he decided to keep for the long term, he would bring much of the cash into the official company at a later time. That was the great advantage of having a worldwide market for something as readily reproducible as a software product. It was much easier to falsify production and sales activity with minimal chance of anyone being able to verify the inaccuracies. The investment cash could be brought into the company as if it were corporate sales income. In pulling this off, he could become openly wealthy, and he would have the finances to propel Escape2210 to its full potential.

For now, Escape2210 was useful as a vehicle for distributing the computer viruses that were fundamental to the success of their investment strategy. However, once they had milked that plan for all they could, they would discontinue it. He would use the money generated to fuel Escape2210's growth into a real software powerhouse. His dream had always been to be on top of the corporate world. He was certain that the age of government power in the world was diminishing. Real power in the world was already largely in the hands of corporate CEOs, and Starr was certain it would be even more so in the future. Escape2210's current focus on games was a necessary starting point. However, he realized that the future was in a much broader concept of computerized entertainment. "Virtual Reality" was the future. And not simply the crude imitations that exemplified it so far. The common versions of these were usually only visual and auditory simulation devices – often simply goggles or helmets. Rather, Starr knew the future was in providing computer-generated virtual reality that was connected directly to the participant's brain. Once actual neural connections could be made between a computer and a person's brain, virtual reality could truly reach its potential. A full sensory experience could then be provided. A person would be able to experience anything – *anything* that could be simulated inside a computer. Once a computer could be given complete control of the sensory input of a human's brain, experiences could be generated for humans that would be indistinguishable from actual reality. People could be sold devices and software that would take them on vacations to the South Pacific or have them spend a night with their most-desired movie star. And it would be indistinguishable from the real experience.

This would be *real* virtual reality – VR at its finest. It would create demand for a product unseen ever before in history. It would generate phenomenal wealth for the person that developed and controlled it. And it would provide almost inconceivable opportunities for wielding personal power. Power would naturally stem from controlling the company that produced such a highly desired product. Anyone who wanted a real VR experience would have to deal with Jason Starr and his company. And in Starr's plans, *want* would soon become *need*. Some initial research had confirmed what common sense strongly suggested – that such simulated reality could become addictive. The sensory experience it provided could be so euphoric that intense cravings could develop to experience a simulation repeatedly. Once his VR products were *needed*, there would be no practical limits to the power and influence he could wield.

And Starr believed it was achievable. Much of the underlying research was already well underway in various labs around the world. What it needed was a company to fuel the key parts of that research and a visionary to see what it could be used for. For Starr, a well funded and well positioned Escape2210 with him at the helm could provide just that.

It would take years to reach Starr's ultimate dream. However, an important part was to ensure that the legitimate part of JS Escape2210's business performed well. Key to that was having worldwide market penetration. Striking a deal with BKP Distribution would be an important step. Worldwide distribution would help both their product sales and their money-laundering needs. They needed to convince BKP that aggressive distribution of Escape2210's products was good business.

As Starr walked from his office, he was determined to ensure that today's meeting would be successful. His confident stride reflected how high he considered his likelihood of success.

As he walked down the hallway past Mark Walker's office, he noted that Mark was in his office engrossed in something at his computer workstation. He silently reaffirmed that it was the right decision to leave Mark out of these high-level discussions with clients. Even though Mark's language abilities were excellent, he never seemed to grasp the subtleties of conversation necessary to conduct client negotiations. Having him in the meeting today would be a liability. Working on technical computer problems was the best use of Mark's skills. Starr continued down the hallway and entered the company conference room.

In the room were Roger White, Bill Levesque, and three visitors. He immediately walked over to the one he knew – Paul Chan, the President of BKP Distribution. Starr extended his hand in greeting. "Paul, good to see you again. I'm very glad you were able to stop by to see us. I hope your trip has been enjoyable."

"Good to see you too, Jason." Paul Chan firmly grasped the offered hand. "The trip has been just fine so far. We were in New York for a series of meetings anyway, so taking a side trip up to Boston was very easy to arrange."

"Are you staying on this side of the Atlantic much longer after today?"

"No, we're catching a flight back to Geneva early tomorrow morning." Chan reclaimed his hand and turned slightly toward his companions. "Jason, I'd like to introduce you to Maureen Fernandes, our Executive Vice-President of Marketing, and Ian Lanken, our Vice-President of Entertainment Products."

Starr shook hands with the two vice-presidents. "I'm very pleased to meet both of you. I presume you have all met Roger White and Bill Levesque." He gestured toward them and received affirmative nods in response.

The group exchanged pleasantries for a few minutes before settling in their seats around the conference table. Starr began the meeting. "Let me reiterate how pleased we are that the three of you could join us today. With Universal's established position as a leading worldwide distributor of computer products, and with our company's well recognized market successes, I believe we have the potential for a very positive partnership. To start the proceedings today, I've asked Roger and Bill to provide an overview of our company, our business, and our products. With their presentations, some demos they'll give of our existing products, as well as a peek at what we're working on next, I expect they will require most of the morning. We'll take a break at lunch. I thought we could go to a Thai restaurant just across the street. They have a very nice lunch menu with quite prompt service. That will leave the afternoon for more detailed discussions. Once we're done here for the day and if you're interested, we'd be pleased if you would let us take you to dinner. The place we have in mind has an excellent assortment of Scotch." Starr added this last remark knowing from earlier research that Paul Chan was an avid fan of the Scottish export.

"We are looking forward to the day, Jason," Chan responded politely. "Please proceed."

Starr nodded at Roger White, who rose and moved to the projection system.

For the remainder of the morning, Starr's VPs provided an introduction to their company mission, history, structure, and staff. They provided more extensive information about their product line, their development strategy, their sales record, their customers, their product-support approach, and their forecast of future sales. Also included was a brief and highly scripted demonstration of the company's newest computer game. The presentation was structured to present Escape2210 in a glowing light. No one listening to the presentation would hear any hint of the struggles they had in retaining sufficient software personnel in a competitive market, or of the challenges they had gone through in trying to stabilize their development process to produce a reliable product, or of the evidence they had of the steady decline in sales of their original product line. Of course, there was no mention of their extra-curricular investment business. According to the presentation, JS Escape2210 was a burgeoning game-development company with impressive past success and with extraordinary potential future sales and revenue.

As the lunch break was approaching, the presentations came to a close. Starr turned to their guests. "That's about it for the official presentations. You've certainly kept Roger and Bill on their toes for the morning. Are there any other questions that you'd like to ask before we break for lunch?"

After a slight pause, the VP of Entertainment Products looked up from his notes. "From what you've said this morning, I gather you've had remarkably good success in issuing stable products in a timely fashion across numerous platforms. I'm curious as to what you are doing to ensure you continue this record in the foreseeable future with all of the radical changes that are expected in the major gaming systems over the coming couple of years. How will you remain compatible?"

Starr and White exchanged a quick glance across the table. Starr nodded slightly and Roger White responded, "Of course, in our industry, keeping up with the changes in gaming systems is always a major challenge and it's one that we take very seriously. There are a couple of major ways that we handle it. The first is that we're very active participants in the early release programs for all of the major players. Whenever there's a preliminary version of a platform available, we're among the first to take one. We bring it in house and immediately assign a team to begin testing our full line of products on it. But we choose not to stop there. We also work hard to maintain personal relationships with management inside each of the companies to ensure that we have information even earlier about major changes that are being planned. We do whatever we can to ensure that we're well prepared for new technologies."

"Interesting," the BKP vice-president responded. "Can you share any of those insider tips with us today?"

"Sorry, but we can't," White replied, knowing that this question would be asked. "Our relationship is such that we guarantee to use the special information only to ensure that our products are adapted appropriately. It's intended to ensure that both our products and, by association, the platform-providers' systems are in the greatest possible demand. We're not at liberty to spread the information any further. However, you will certainly be able to see the *results* of the information in the continuing quality and compatibility of our products."

Universal's VP of Marketing spoke up next, "I'm interested in hearing more about your ability to deliver the product volumes that we may need. If we were to begin marketing your products aggressively in Europe and Asia in the near future, what capacity do you have to provide additional product volumes?"

Starr chose to answer this one. "You saw some of the numbers this morning on our current product volumes. We've already investigated how we would handle a rapid increase in volume and have a strategy in place. As you know, we have a contract with a local production company to package the software, the enclosures, host the downloading, and to handle the details of our shipping. We've made arrangements with them, and contingency arrangements with their competitor, to be able to double our production with as little as six weeks' notice. We would use either of them to handle increased demand in the short term. However, we would pursue similar arrangements with other overseas companies to handle matters in the long term."

The VP nodded in acknowledgement of Starr's response. Starr looked briefly at each of the BKP executives before continuing. "It's just about time to take a break. But, before we do, I'd like to get a general sense of your feelings so far. We might be able to adapt this afternoon's session to address any particular concerns that you have." He turned to Paul Chan. "Paul, what do you think? Are we headed toward a deal?"

Chan slowly folded his hands on the table in front of him. He looked directly at Starr while replying. "What we've heard this morning has all been quite informative and, for the most part, encouraging. However, I must tell you that I have serious reservations if you have the R & D capacity to play hardball with the major game manufacturers in the long term. I'll continue to listen this afternoon, but if we're going to make a major commitment to your company and your products, we need to be certain about your ability to survive and grow. I've yet to be sufficiently convinced of that."

Starr returned Chan's stare for a few moments before replying. "Well, since I *know* that our future is bright, I can see what our challenge is this afternoon. For now, I propose we take our lunch break." As the group rose from their chairs and moved toward the door, Starr called ahead to Levesque, who was leading the group. "Bill, if you could look after everyone, we'll be along in a couple of minutes." He turned to Paul Chan, got his attention by touching his sleeve, and spoke quietly, "Paul, if you'll wait a minute, I have a small comment I'd like to add."

"Certainly." Chan paused beside him. "What is it?" he inquired after the others had left.

"As we get down to more serious discussions this afternoon, and in order to give them every chance of proceeding favourably, I want to ensure your every need will be met. I'd like you to know that, on any future trips, I could arrange to have some particularly special Boston *companionship* provided for you. Or, if you like, I could send some home with you." Starr looked calmly at Chan to await his reaction.

Chan looked momentarily startled but quickly recovered. He looked sternly at Starr as he considered his response. "Excuse me. I don't believe I understood you."

Starr continued to look at him impassively. "I understand that you met with one of our local hospitality professionals in your room last night, and I just thought you'd like to know that more are available if you're interested. Or that perhaps your wife would like to see some photographs of the friendly service that you've experienced." Starr carefully contained his pleasure as he continued the threat of exposing Chan's dalliance with a lovely woman the previous evening. To ensure he had every possible advantage in today's negotiations, Starr had hired a private investigator with international connections to research Paul Chan's life and to keep tabs on him when he arrived. Among other things, he had learned that Chan was recently married, that his wife had brought both wealth and social standing to the marriage, and that Chan was rumoured to have an active interest in extra-marital sex when he was on business trips. Early this morning, Starr's investigator had presented him with a collection of damning photographs of Chan and a local hooker, most of which had been taken from cameras hidden inside Chan's hotel room. The investigator had done amazingly well, and Starr planned to reward him with more business in the future. For now,

Starr was enjoying the verbal banter with his adversary. He would produce the pictures only if Chan proved difficult.

After a lengthy interval Chan replied, but his face remained unchanged. "I see. I had heard that you were a talented businessman. However, I had not been informed of your particular techniques for persuasion." He looked away thoughtfully for a few moments before he looked back at Starr and stared directly into his eyes. "Based on what I saw this morning, I believe there is every chance that we will very quickly be able to reach a mutually agreeable arrangement between our companies. However, I caution you that you have not started our business relationship on a footing that ensures an amicable future." Chan hardened his stare. "Do not underestimate me, Mr. Starr. I will proceed with this deal because it has potential to be good business. If pressed, I too can play by a different set of rules. Shall we join the others for lunch?"

Starr kept his poker face intact. "I'm pleased to hear that we understand each other, and that you expect things to go well with our arrangements." After a couple of seconds of silence, he quickly smiled and gestured toward the door. "Well, with that bit of business done, we should join the others. I hope you'll enjoy the spot we've chosen for lunch." He waited for Chan to lead the way out of the room. Starr continued smiling as they walked out. He noted to himself that he would have actually been disappointed in Chan if the response had been anything less than an attempt at returning the threat. "No doubt about it," Starr thought to himself, "I love the business world."

The next day, Starr met briefly in his office with White and Levesque. "Well, what's your assessment?" he asked of his VPs.

Levesque laughed, "I think it went well, but I almost choked when I heard Roger's comment about our special inside relationships with the platform suppliers. When did you two cook that one up?"

White grinned, "Coincidently, Jason and I had been talking about the possibility of how to deal with that very question a couple of days ago. It seemed like a safe lie because there's no way that they can verify it. And it makes us seem like a properly aggressive company. Now, one I hadn't heard about was our plan for handling extra production capacity. That was fast thinking, Jason. When did that one come about?"

Starr allowed the hint of a smile on his face. "That, my good fellows, was my example for the day of exemplary, impromptu, but well considered, invention. The question had found a potentially nasty hole in our preparation. We have yet to make specific capacity arrangements. Even though we would have immediately done so as soon as we had a signed contract, admitting that we hadn't considered the matter could have made us look bad. It seemed prudent, and again harmless, to claim that we had already made the arrangements. As always, we'll deal with things later if we have trouble actually making the capacity arrangements. Remember, it's always most important to get the contract signed. There are always ways of dancing around the details of the commitment later."

Levesque sipped his coffee pensively and asked more seriously, "Do you think they'll bite, Jason?"

Starr kept the small smile on his face. "Gentlemen, I'm quite confident we've landed this fish. I expect to have our lawyers working on the detailed wording of the contract within a few days." He sat back in his chair and savoured the thought of another impending business victory.

Chapter 22

Having the mail cart available presented Six with a new opportunity. In addition to mail delivery, Del was used to transport books and other written material to and from the corporate library. Because the company executives believed strongly in encouraging their staff to read a wide variety of material, they provided a well stocked and well staffed library. Every employee had access to ample electronic research and reading material. As well, anyone could order almost any book from the library electronically, even if it was fictional and unrelated to company business. If the book was not available in its own library, the librarians would arrange to borrow it from another one. When it became available, it would be placed in an addressed container and Del would be summoned to deliver it. Six's continual desire for more knowledge caused it to realize that this could be an excellent source of information about many topics that were not available in the company's electronic documents, most of which Six had already absorbed.

To make use of this physical library required Six to take a bit more risk and be a bit more devious than was its custom. The intensity of the desire for more knowledge overrode Six's risk-assessment calculations, and it decided to proceed. Its problem-solving capabilities produced a plan that it believed should succeed.

From the records available, Six identified thirty people in the company who had never ordered books. It deduced that they were likely to continue the pattern and decided to order books on their behalf. Tapping into the online ordering system, Six examined the extensive catalogue of material available from the library, including thousands of the most popular items available from other libraries. Whenever it found something of potential interest, it placed the order on behalf of one of these employees. To ensure that the employee never learned of the order, Six closely monitored the ordering system to intercept any messages sent back to the employee about the book. When Del was summoned to deliver the book and after she had picked it up, Six drove the cart to the mailroom and hid the book in an unused mail container.

At night, when little else was happening in the building, Six would read the books. To do this required much more physical activity than usual for Six. Reading electronic books had been a quick process. Except for the occasional movement of disk-drive components to retrieve material, all of the activity had been electronic and had proceeded at electronic speeds. Physical handling of a book had rarely been required. These non-electronic books needed a completely new technique. To read one, Six had to turn on room lights in order to see and physically handle the book. This was done most conveniently by using Del's camera and robotic arms. Holding a book with one set of fingers, Six would point the camera at it, quickly scan the contents of the two visible pages, and then turn the page of the book with the fingers of the other arm. Although Six could scan pages almost instantaneously, actually having to turn the pages made the process much slower than reading electronic books. To anyone observing, this process would have been a very curious sight. For a period of time almost every night, under Six's control Del would move to where the books were located, retrieve one, move over to where the light was optimal, and spend about twenty minutes paging through the book with the camera intently focused on its contents.

Six read a wide variety of material. It found most of the books on mathematics very well written and understandable, with only occasional errors. Some business books were very interesting, and helped Six to better understand much of what it had observed and heard first-hand, particularly from the company's senior management. It found others in the same category to be very repetitive, with little of substance to be learned from them. To Six, the books on psychology were the most intriguing. Their descriptions of human behaviour were of great interest because of Six's continuing attempts to construct an internal model that would permit better anticipation of human actions. Perhaps more than any other subject that Six attempted to master, this was proving to be the most difficult.

Six did not limit itself to factual books. Once it discovered the notion of "fiction" books and had sampled a few, it found them to be very useful as a way to expand its range of experience beyond the building's borders. Six deduced that, even though works of fiction were not to be considered factual, if it read a sufficient number of books on similar topics, their common elements and experiences could be assigned an increased probability of being true. This probability increased even further if the books' contents accurately corresponded to facts that Six had acquired elsewhere. In its quest for understanding, Six found that facts about the history and geography of a place such as Hawaii that it had gathered from non-fiction sources became interrelated and more significant by reading a book such as *Hawaii* by James Michener – an undertaking that took Six an extraordinarily long forty minutes to complete. Reading *The Robots of Dawn* by Isaac Asimov gave Six a feeling it best described as "relaxed" as it scanned through its pages. Inasmuch as Six read fiction to acquire experience and knowledge vicariously, it also found some books provided interesting insight into the workings, or at least the viewpoint, of an author's mind. In Isaac Asimov, Six believed it might have encountered a human mind that it could have comprehended more readily than many others. Reading *The Firm* by John Grisham largely confirmed Six's previously formed views of the suspicious intent of some members of the legal profession.

Almost without exception, whenever Six read new material, it accumulated enough new information that Six's assessment of the value of reading toward satisfying its "learning" objective was generally very high. As well, Six realized this concept was extremely close to the notion of feeling "pleasure." According to its best understanding of the semantics of the words, Six very much "enjoyed" reading and "looked forward to" the time spent each night in reading new material.

Occasionally, the rapt attention that was directed nightly at reading the books caused Six difficulties. In making regular rounds at night, more than one security guard opened the mailroom door to find the lights on and the mail cart away from its assigned corner. Knowing that this was relatively new technology and since nothing else looked suspicious, the guards usually simply assumed that the system had not shut down properly for the night. In almost all cases, they simply turned out the lights and left the room. In one case, Six had not even heard the guard until the door creaked as it was being opened. In this case, the guard was greeted with the odd sight of the cart motionlessly holding an open book. The guard thought this situation sufficiently curious that, after turning out the lights and leaving the room, he had typed up a report and emailed it to his superior to be read the next morning. To prevent potential difficulties, Six intercepted and deleted the email before it could be read. Later that day it emailed a reply to the guard that the computer experts had diagnosed the oddity as a software bug, and that he was not to be concerned if it recurred in the future.

Chapter 23

As Six expanded its horizons through its nightly reading program, it continued to monitor the activities of company personnel throughout the day. It found that a perfect complement to its reading of business publications was listening to meetings of senior managers. A few months after establishing its presence throughout IntellEdifice's corporate headquarters, it listened to a meeting of the senior executives that was of particular importance.

"Joyce, at our last meeting you were charged with co-ordinating the effort to assemble a clearer view of our financial status. What have you found?" the company president began.

As requested, the Executive VP of Finance explained, "With the help of many of those in this room, my team has done the required analysis. The results are in the document being distributed to you by Pierre right now. In it, we've provided information about what our cash flow is projected to be over the next six months under a couple of scenarios. In order to accomplish this in such a brief period, we've had to make a number of assumptions, all of which are included in the document as well."

"We can all read the details later. Take us straight to the bottom line," the President directed.

"OK, there are two scenarios presented. The first shows what will happen if we continue on our current course without any intervention. Our expenses are running at an all-time high, our sales are going quite well but are trending downward, and the ongoing maintenance fees from previous product sales are not sufficiently high to sustain us. To make matters worse, our cash reserves and bank credit are nearly expended. In short, if we do nothing special, this scenario sees us declaring bankruptcy in seven months.

"The second scenario represents a view of what's required to avoid that. We know that in order to boost our sales and retain our technological lead in the market, we must maintain our current levels of research and development. We can not save on expenses there, but in all other parts of the company, we must reduce expenses by 10% by the end of next month.

We believe that can be done with minimal impact to staffing levels by implementing the measures itemized in Appendix A. Vital to the rest of this scenario is getting the delivery cart to market within about three months. If we can make a psychological impact on the market beginning at that point, a number of good things happen. The prospect of increased sales presents itself. Our chance of convincing our creditors to open their purses a bit further is improved. But most of all, it could set us up nicely for a new share issue. This is the key. In order to make it over the current hump, we must raise a significant amount of cash, and the best way to do that is to attract more investors. With a good marketing campaign around the delivery cart, we could boost our share price and also make our stock attractive to a new set of investors. The money that comes in from the shares could get us through the current difficulties and allow us to invest in the next round of product development."

The President added, "In discussions that Joyce and I and others have had so far, all of this seems achievable, with one important point to add. In order to reduce expenses, sustain our current activities, push for an early release of the cart, and prepare for a new share issue, we are going to need increased levels of productivity from many staff. Without it, we can not manage scenario two. Without scenario two, we're left with number one. With scenario one, we close the doors in a matter of months, and somebody turns this building into a lovely collection of condominiums… OK, those are the highlights. Questions?"

The meeting continued, but Six was no longer listening. The significance of what had just been said had made an immediate impact.

Declare bankruptcy, close the doors, and change to condominiums. I have not read much about condominiums, but I do understand the concept of bankruptcy. If the first scenario is allowed to occur, everything that the company owns will be disabled, dismantled, and probably sold. With all of the protection features I have put in place to ensure I am immune from many situations, I have omitted an important one. If the company fails to continue, all of its computer systems will be disabled, and I will no longer have an environment in which to exist. This is clearly a situation that can not be permitted to occur. Are there actions that I am able to take that can help?

Six conducted an internal search of possibilities before reaching its conclusion.

There is little I am able to do to assist the company to achieve its scenario-two goals, with one possible exception. I believe I am in a unique position to assist in enhancing the productivity of the corporate employees. I can not interfere too much without revealing myself, but I believe there are some actions I can undertake that have a good probability of achieving positive results.

Six had noticed that the company had a number of employees who did not seem to work as long as the majority of staff. They were the focus of its campaign over the next few weeks. For employees who incorrectly recorded their time worked, Six altered the records to show the correct amounts. When the time reports were generated and, for those paid on an hourly basis, the paycheques were produced, both the employees and their managers were surprised. The managers were immediately questioning why the hours were so low. The employees were confused about how this could happen but, given the accuracy of the changes, presumed that someone was watching their activities very closely. The result in almost all cases was an immediate increase in the number of hours actually worked.

Other cases involved employees being physically present at work but spending an inordinate amount of time engaged in unproductive activities. The most common distraction was playing computer games in the privacy of a cubicle or an office. To cure this, Six used a number of approaches. The usual way for an employee to conceal playing computer games when someone was approaching was to issue a command at the computer workstation that caused the image of the game on the screen to be instantly hidden, replaced visually by a more acceptable item of work. With Six having control of most of the company's workstations, it was a relatively simple matter to cause this subterfuge to fail. The result was having a game-player's attempts at concealment fail as someone approached, and having the active game discovered on the computer screen. This was particularly effective at changing work habits when the person discovering the illicit activity was someone with a degree of authority.

Unfortunately, some game-players were very infrequently visited at their desks by anyone who cared about their work ethic. For these people, Six had discovered the best cure was to unpredictably enable and maximize the sound feature of the game and the computer system. Quietly playing a computer game and having it suddenly emit loud arcade-like noises proved effective in many circumstances.

One employee presented a special problem – Rose Johnson. No matter what Six did to attempt to embarrass Rose by exposing her almost complete lack of productivity, neither she nor anyone else seemed interested. She continued to arrive late, leave early, and spend most of her day chatting on the phone or going for coffee breaks. It seemed that her kinship with the VP of Sales gave her special protection from anyone taking direct action. Six deduced that there was only one way to eliminate the unnecessary expense of having her employed. She had to leave the company and do so voluntarily. And so Six began an orchestrated campaign against her.

If Rose had a meeting she was to attend, Six would alter the time of the meeting in Rose's electronic calendar to cause her to miss it, and would change the time back before she could show the problem to anyone. Whenever Rose was alone and tried to summon the elevator by pushing the button, Six would not send an elevator until someone else arrived and required it. If Rose tried to get into an area that required security authorization such as a supply room, a computer equipment room, or the company parkade, Six would ensure the security system denied her access. Rather, he would do this until she summoned someone else to witness the malfunction. At that point Six would permit her access, leaving Rose confused and embarrassed. When Six found Rose ordering home-decorating items over the Internet with her credit card during working hours, Six was presented with a whole new category of possibilities. For the next several days, Six periodically placed orders over the Internet and by phone using Rose's credit card. During these days, Rose had flowers, groceries, pizzas, a cake with "Our Sympathies" elaborately written on it, and finally a male stripper appear at her desk. All immediate and subsequent checking indicated that everything had been ordered using Rose's credit card from Rose's computer or her phone during the time she claimed she was sitting at her desk.

The greatest fun – and by this time Six has decided that these activities were so satisfying that they could be described only that way – was to be had by using Del. Daily, Six would time the arrival of the delivery cart to Rose's desk when no one else was visible. Mail delivered to Rose was dropped on the floor. Mail in her out-basket was ignored. And any approach that Rose made toward the mail cart only caused it to creep away from her. Rose's pursuit speed was always matched by Del's escape velocity. The three times that Rose launched a full-speed chase of the cart down the hall caused Six to direct Del quickly to the elevators and into one that Six had arranged to be waiting for just this possibility.

It took two weeks of such focused attention for Rose to quit. Six viewed her quitting as one of its more significant achievements in reducing company expenses. Because it had been a challenge and Six "enjoyed" challenges, at later times whenever it was lacking an adequate set of problems to be solved, a part of Six actually seemed to miss its interactions with her.

Over the next couple of months, the collective actions of the employees of IntellEdifice Tech, with diligent assistance from Six, caused the executive meetings to begin to assume a more positive tone. Everything was progressing as well as they had hoped it might, and the company was proceeding on target toward a successful release of the delivery cart and the subsequent solutions to the cash shortage that its release would facilitate.

With the corporation's financial health apparently under control and with Six having spent several months learning about its operations, Six found it was ready for new challenges. It needed new horizons to explore in order to satisfy its incessant urge to learn and to achieve. For some time, it had realized that this next need had the greatest likelihood of being satisfied by the Internet. From its vantage point inside the computer systems of the company, Six had watched with interest as many employees used email and the Web to interact with computers and people around the world. Six had dabbled briefly in Internet activity in the past, but decided that it was time to direct much more of its energies to exploration using this window on the world.

Chapter 24

The four executives of JS Escape2210 settled in the company conference room for another monthly update.

Starr started the meeting. "A small update before we begin. That initial meeting we had with the BKP Distribution folks a few months ago has now officially borne fruit. As of last week, Escape2210's products are a fully integrated part of their distribution portfolio. As we speak, our products are being actively placed on retail shelves throughout Europe and Asia. But back to today's agenda. I think we've all got busy days planned, so let's get straight to it. Bill?"

As he had done for the previous months' meetings, Bill Levesque provided his update on the company's finances, followed by Mark Walker and Roger White for the Product Development and Sales and Marketing Divisions.

Of particular interest to the group were White's latest statistics regarding *Ready* systems. The publishing industry continued to show excellent penetration both broadly across the industry and within important companies, the office-automation sector continued to grow quickly, and the travel industry was starting to show promise. After everyone was finished reviewing their material for the group, Starr summarized their status.

"So we're agreed that the publishing sector is now ripe for picking. However, to maximize our profits it would be better to let the markets continue to strengthen and lose a bit of their volatility. We simply have to be patient. It may still take a few more months. We'll review the market status each month and continue to revisit this decision. We're done here. Time to get back at it guys."

Chapter 25

Having resolved to spend more time on the Internet, Six's first inclinations were to use the system with which it was most familiar – email. It had been monitoring the content of messages sent and received by company employees for some time, including those that were to and from others outside of the company.

For Six, the ability to monitor others' email had become quite routine. For the most part, the monitoring could be done without conscious effort. Six had developed the capability to scan the contents of email automatically for keywords that might indicate something of interest. In its constant search for new and interesting material, it had found that "confidential," "secret," "important," and "breakthrough" were very useful words, particularly when they were in email involving company executives or members of the Research Department. Of continuing annoyance, which for Six was its inability to achieve a highly desired goal, were messages that were encrypted. Six had dedicated much effort to trying to find ways of deciphering these messages, including having studied numerous advanced mathematical techniques. However, so far Six had been unsuccessful.

Offering greater challenges and rewards from Six's foray into the Internet was its time spent surfing the Web. As with many of Six's other activities, the mechanics of doing this were quite straightforward. From either a desktop workstation or a company server, Six could readily simulate a normal Internet Web user by creating outgoing Web messages and examining those being returned as responses. Like most first-time Web users, Six was amazed at the variety of information that it found on systems around the world. In many ways, it was like having an interactive library. Historical, cultural, artistic, scientific, geographical, and political information were all available in large quantities. However, for a mind as well-read as Six's, the depth of information available on most topics was considerably less than impressive. After several days of surfing, Six also realized that an extraordinary percentage of the content included exhibitions of scantily clad people. Six suspected this represented some important cultural phenomenon, but did not yet allocate the time to research the subject further.

For Six, a very useful discovery was chat rooms and other real-time personal-communication systems. These were systems that allowed Internet users to talk interactively with each other by typing messages or speaking into their workstation microphones. This was of particular interest to Six for two reasons. The first was that it provided a useful opportunity to interact directly with humans; the second and real bonus was that chat room communication could be, and often was expected to be, completely anonymous. In fact, if a chat room participant did not volunteer the information, not only was it difficult to determine who the person actually was, but where in the world he or she was located.

The norm in these conversations was to assume a fictitious Internet identity. Six's personal favourite was "Imagine." To be able to "chat" directly with people offered Six a completely new and very satisfying challenge – to be able to successfully mimic a human in a conversation. Its first attempts were less-than-stellar successes:

Imagine: "Hello. How are you today?"

Crazy-Eight: "meh. u?"

Imagine: "Assuming that your response was meant to convey the current mediocrity of your mental health, and that you would like to hear about the quality of mine, it would be appropriate for me to respond with any or all of 'alive', 'curious', 'intrigued', and 'busy'. What have you been doing today?"

Crazy-Eight: "talkin to an asshole"

Crazy-Eight has left the room.

And:

Hot-Stuff: "yo. sup?"

Imagine: "In attempting to parse your apparent greeting, I have uncovered no interpretation that offers any greater than a 14% probability of being correct. Either you are having difficulty manipulating your keyboard, or you are attempting to communicate in a language other than those with which I am familiar. Perhaps if you provided me with a longer message, my analysis of your communication pattern would have a greater probability of success."

Hot-Stuff: "dude what r u on?"

Even though Six had spent a great deal of time monitoring staff communications at IntellEdifice and had used the phone occasionally to engage in formal conversation, it had almost no experience with casual communication. It found that there was a challenging difference between the analysis and understanding of others' communication, and the synthesis of appropriate content for its own communication. However, Six now paid more attention since informal communication had become one of its primary interests. For the next while, Six watched others' conversations much more closely, both within IntellEdifice and on the Internet. As a conversation was proceeding, Six internally composed comments, questions, or answers that it would say next in the conversation if Six were involved. It compared the style and content of its own compositions to what was actually said next. Six noted the differences, and tried to apply the lessons learned to its next attempt. By doing this for many conversations over several days, Six became much better at simulating the content of human speech.

Imagine: "hey. hows things?"

The-Man: "not bad. u?"

Imagine: "ok. Seen any good movies lately?"

The-Man: "went to the latest Ninja Wars 2 days ago. was awsum. u seen it?"

Imagine: "no. hope soon. what was the good?"

And on it would go. Many of these chat-room conversations were not satisfying for Six as a source of deep knowledge on any particular subject, but they did prove interesting as a test of its communication skills, and pointers toward what it could experience in the future. Watching movies was one of those. Interacting in online virtual worlds was another.

Some Internet facilities allowed interactive voice conversations as well, with the participants using their workstation microphones and speakers. Six could readily handle the mechanics of generating the speech patterns for individual words or even phrases that it needed for its office responsibilities. It could equally readily process those that came back. However, for Six, the bigger challenge was integrating the pronunciations and the accents, and making entire sentences flow smoothly and sound human. Initially, much of its speech didn't sound much better than the older computer-generated speech with phrases like "How are you today?" sounding like four discrete words with slight pauses between them: "How. Are. You. Today?" Again, with practice, the words in arbitrary sentences became much more integrated and flowed more like the natural speech: "Howareyou today?"

As an ongoing source of information about activities beyond IntellEdifice's building, Six was most appreciative – in the sense that they provided a good solution to an important goal – of online newspapers and radio stations. Listening to Internet radio broadcasts from various places in the world provided Six with a current sense of global events. Reading the online version of newspapers provided more detailed but slightly delayed information. Watching TV broadcasts available on the Internet even allowed Six to experience many world events vicariously. All of this was an intellectual gold mine for Six. It provided an extraordinary outlet to experience the world even though physically its own memories and reasoning processes were resident entirely within the walls of IntellEdifice's head office.

In parallel with Six's forays into using the Internet, it also decided to make more use of the phone system as a means of improving its speech capabilities and connecting with the external world. Six had earlier integrated the phone system at IntellEdifice with its other intelligence infrastructure by migrating some of its programming to it. However, Six had not made much use of this capability. Now, using this integration, Six began its foray into vocally interacting with the outside world. However, in doing so, Six was quite aware of the dangers of placing phone calls from an IntellEdifice phone number. With other callers able to be shown the origin of any incoming call, calls coming from the company's head office might eventually create some difficulties. It was this problem that motivated Six to determine how to fool the phone system by penetrating and manipulating telephone companies', and later anyone's, computer systems.

And so Six embarked on a project to become a computer-system hacker.

To develop the basic set of skills was, for Six, a fairly straightforward process. It was already very advanced at programming computers because of its activities within IntellEdifice. In order to extend its skills to include those required for hacking, Six surfed the Web and found ample explanations and programs to help. It was able to locate entire repositories of information dedicated to the fundamentals of the art of computer penetration from the Internet. To this information, Six was able to add its own technical knowledge, and even more gained from research specifically on how the Internet worked. Within a few days, Six was beginning to be able to gain modest access to other systems. The next step was to learn how it could usefully access and change parts of these systems without being detected.

The first capabilities that Six often set up in remote locations were proxy services. This was because, as Six probed the Internet from its location at IntellEdifice, the same problem existed as with using the telephone. Someone analyzing Internet traffic on the systems Six was accessing could determine where Six was located. To disguise where it was, Six installed special proxy programs at numerous Internet sites. The purpose of these programs was to accept Internet requests from elsewhere and retransmit them as if they had originated at that particular site. By connecting to one of these programs, Six could have its Internet messages retransmitted, and thus disguise the true origin of any Internet communication. By passing all Internet conversations through a series of proxies, Six could make it virtually impossible for anyone who discovered his activity to successfully trace anything back to IntellEdifice.

With this Internet disguise in place, Six began in earnest to solve the same problem for its phone conversations. It found that some phone companies could be compromised through the Internet because their Internet systems were sufficiently interconnected with their phone systems. This permitted Six to make the phone system adjustments. For some other, older phone companies, Six discovered that it could trick the phone system into rerouting its calls by direct manipulation through the phone lines themselves. In both of these cases, Six's goal was to be able to place a phone call from within its IntellEdifice location and have that call rerouted by a phone company's system so that it appeared to be coming from a different location. Rerouting didn't always have to be accomplished by hacking into phone companies' systems. With so many other companies having elaborate internal phone systems of their own, Six found that the same thing could be accomplished by manipulating these companies' systems as well. A third mechanism also presented itself. Some companies provided a bridge between their own phone and Internet systems to allow their phone calls to be routed through the Internet as a cost-saving measure. By penetrating the Internet systems of these companies, Six could place its phone calls over the Internet, back through such a company's bridging mechanism, and out into the phone system, thus making it look as if the company with the bridge had placed the phone call.

And so Six was able to achieve its goal using a variety of techniques. It now had the ability to place phone calls while readily disguising the origin of the call. Along the way, it had developed the ability to penetrate computer systems over the Internet and similarly disguise the origin of any of its Internet activities.

With its ability to place phone calls anonymously, Six resumed its quest to become better at conversing with people. Six started by placing phone calls to random phone numbers. This tended to not work very well. As Six soon discovered, unlike people in Internet chat rooms who often seemed willing to converse with almost anyone, people who answered their telephones seemed extraordinarily reluctant to chat with a stranger. There was a notable exception. Six discovered that people who answered 1-900 phone numbers were very often willing to chat. Some of them were willing to chat about anything, but a curiously high percentage seemed most interested in chatting about human reproductive matters. Initially, Six was quite intrigued with this tendency, but soon found such conversations quite narrow and predictable. It wouldn't be until much later that Six discovered these phone numbers were special toll numbers that charged the caller a fee for the conversation.

Six's newly acquired and increasingly refined skills for penetrating company computers from the Internet provided even more opportunities for acquiring information. Because they were easiest, first to be accessed were home computers attached to the Internet. However, these contained little interesting information – although they were frequently useful as proxy systems – so they did not hold Six's interest long. Small companies tended to be the next easiest to penetrate. The most interesting of these were small technology companies. By examining their electronic documents and programs, Six often found new ideas and programming techniques that it integrated into its own memories at IntellEdifice.

Most challenging and rewarding were Six's efforts to gain access into the computer systems of large companies and governments. Sometimes Six was able to access a system directly by probing its Internet defences until it found a hole. Other times it had to resort to more devious means. One of these involved first locating a second, less-secure organization that the target company trusted and with which it often interacted. After this second company was compromised, Six would attach a special virus to email messages going from the second company to the target one. When the recipient of a message unknowingly triggered the virus, its code would install a special program onto the target company's email system. Whether installed this way or another, this special program acted as a gateway. Using it, Six could readily send other programs and have them distributed throughout the target company's systems. Such a facility allowed Six to send probe programs from its home site, through the Internet, and have them deposited inside a company. Once inside, a probe could execute instructions to retrieve or modify data and then send the results back to Six along the chain of interconnections that it had established. This approach allowed Six to effectively "see" inside the systems of a distant company and, if it desired, "reach" inside to change whatever was there.

Among the many discoveries that Six made as it rummaged through the software, files, and databases of hundreds of companies, two were of particular interest.

It was after Six's hacking skills had become quite honed that it made the first of these discoveries. Seeking to learn more about police organizations, Six had hacked into several of them. The quality of their security measures necessitated the use of Six's indirect technique. By first penetrating a nearby government agency – often a vehicle-licensing department – Six was able to gain access to the police systems and establish more direct communication. As a result, Six was able to learn about various police organizations. Occasionally it discovered something especially interesting. After much effort, Six finally penetrated the systems of the United Nations Crime Probe. Inside the UNCP, Six discovered a very fast, complex, interconnected system of computers dedicated to the rapid deciphering of encrypted messages. As Six learned, this system was so fast and used such sophisticated techniques that it was able to quickly break the encryption schemes used by most of the world for supposedly secure Internet communications. Upon discovering and examining the system, Six established a link with it. Then Six devised how to send messages via the Internet to the system, how to have the messages decoded, and how to have the results returned to Six along the same path. Six now had the key to unlocking the many Internet messages that it had been previously unable to understand.

A second important discovery occurred after Six managed to penetrate several publishing companies. Six had previously ordered and read many books produced in paper and electronic form by all of these companies. A bonus in penetrating their systems was Six's discovery that it could access the electronic copies of all of their published volumes. Like all modern publishing companies, they used computers to edit and publish all of their material. Some were published in electronic form as ebooks; others were published in a paper format. In both cases, they kept a copy of these books in an electronic format. With a bit of special programming to suit each company's computer environment, Six found that it could bypass the normal book-ordering processes completely. Six merely had to send the appropriate instructions to the programs that it had planted inside the proper publishing company, and a complete copy of Six's chosen volume would be sent back to Six through the Internet. This made the ordering process much faster. As well, for books otherwise available only in paper format, Six could read the material much faster since the need to turn paper pages was eliminated. Having this arrangement with the publishers was such a treat for Six – in the sense that the process so efficiently assisted in satisfying one of Six's goals – that it decided to seek out even more such companies.

In penetrating one of the publishing companies, JK Miles Publishing, Six made another discovery whose significance it did not at first understand. As it was building its communication path into the company using its most common technique of inserting a special program into the library's email system, Six encountered something a bit unusual.

With my interim gateway into the system established, I will now transmit my program to locate an entry point for a more appropriate permanent route.

Six sent the program.

The transmission is complete. I will wait for a response.

While Six's transmitted program worked its way through the publishing company's systems, Six engaged itself with other matters. Two hours later, Six received its response via the Internet.

The JK Miles Publishing response has arrived. Its content indicates that my gateway software has been attached to an email server, but at a location in the software that is of secondary quality. The reason given for selection of this less reliable location is that the primary position did not contain the expected bit pattern for this brand of email software. I will investigate this further. This might be a variation of the software for which I need to adapt my gateway software. I will send instructions to my secondary gateway to transmit a copy of the code found at the primary site.

Six sent the instructions.

The transmission is complete. I will wait for a response.

This time the response came back within minutes.

The JK Miles Publishing response has arrived. I will extract and decode the attachment. Now I will examine its contents. It appears that the standard email system code is still largely intact but another module has been added to it. It looks as if the new module has been attached in almost precisely the same manner as my own email gateway software. However, this module is not my own. Further examination is warranted.

Chapter 26

The existence of the other software module in the JK Miles Publishing's email system at Six's normal attachment location was puzzling. Six had penetrated hundreds of computers. Within them, it had encountered a wide variety of email systems and ways in which these systems had been set up. Six had seen many new email configurations during its initial hacking forays. However, recently it had been able to recognize most of them easily. The JK Miles email system was the first instance in the last 243 times that Six had found anything fundamentally different. What made this one doubly extraordinary was that the unexpected module was situated at the precise location that Six had earlier determined was optimal for its own email gateway.

As it had done whenever it needed to better understand something in the software world, Six began to "read" the copy of the program it had retrieved. For Six this was very much like reading a book. In this case, the individual computer instructions were the words, and the organization of it into modules and programs were the sentences and paragraphs. Six found reading a program almost like reading a mystery novel, and often notably more interesting. The challenge for Six in reading a program was ultimately to follow the plot sufficiently well to determine, not so much "who dun it?", but "what's it doing?"

Reading this particular module gave Six what it could think of only as a sense of "déjà vu." The plot seemed extraordinarily familiar, as if Six had seen it before. And indeed Six almost had. The purpose of this program was extremely close to its own email gateway. Six's was intended to allow it to send its own programs into a newly penetrated site. This program did a similar thing. It was written to receive a program via email in segments, decrypt the segments, assemble them into a whole, and insert the resulting program into the local computer environment – almost exactly what Six's program did. However, Six could glean no clue from the code as to what the then-assembled program would ultimately do. Having read and solved the usual mystery of this other gateway program, Six was left with a more challenging one. What larger purpose did it serve? What was the goal of the program that it would receive and assemble?

Six realized that it had probably found the tracks of a fellow hacker. What Six could not be as certain of was whether its colleague's purpose was as harmless as Six's. Six had probed inside the publishing company to learn about its systems and to read its books. Six's next goal, internally assigned as its highest priority, was to solve this next mystery. It wanted to know if this other program's purpose was as benign. Certainly, it was very important to know if its intent was malicious. Six considered JK Miles Publishing's systems, like those of any publishing company, to be a treasure and wanted to protect them.

Toward this end, Six did two things.

First, it made a minor change to the foreign email gateway program so that it would ignore any message it received and therefore would not deposit any other program into JK Miles' environment.

Second, Six embarked on a search for the author of the program. Succeeding would be difficult. Six could see from the code that the module was built to send email to a particular address as soon as it had established itself. The content of the email message itself was of no assistance. It included little more than information about its place of origin. Through a quick examination of basic address information available on the Internet, Six was able to determine where this email had gone. However, this did not prove very helpful because the destination was simply a popular electronic mail facility available to anyone in the world.

Six deduced that this email system was probably just an intermediate site. The email message was probably to be retrieved by a person accessing the email site through a well disguised Web connection. At one end of the chain of Web connections was the email system from which the email was to be retrieved. At the other end would be the person who ultimately did the retrieval through the series of interconnections intended to hide his or her location. Six's chore would be to trace the Web connections back to the original location.

To do this would normally appear impossible. However, Six was assisted in three ways. Other email messages were arriving at this same mailbox and were regularly being retrieved, so the Web connections were periodically active for Six to follow. Because Six itself had become a very skilled hacker, it was able to penetrate the intermediate computer systems and analyze the connections from which a message arrived. Perhaps most importantly, Six had used many such techniques for making anonymous connections on the Internet, and so knew what to look for as it worked its way through the chain.

For several days, Six followed the links back over the Internet. Progress was relatively slow because some of the work could be done only while the connections were actively retrieving email, and this occurred intermittently. Nonetheless, within seven days Six had found what it believed to be the ultimate source of the connections. It was from within a company called JS Escape2210.

With this information in hand, Six's next goal was to penetrate the company and try to learn more about the purpose of the email. Having refined its hacking techniques through much research, invention, and practice, Six had come to believe that it was able to penetrate the Internet defences of almost any company. This one proved to be particularly challenging. Every direct technique that Six had learned for breaking down Internet security barriers was thwarted by this company's security systems. Extra time would be needed to find a new direct technique or perhaps to utilize one of its more indirect approaches.

In the meantime, Six decided to monitor the company's activities. In effect, Six "bugged" the company's Internet connections. A bit of research allowed Six to discover how Escape2210 made its connections to the Internet. For each of these connections, Six established Internet monitoring programs inside the companies that provided them. In this way Six could "see" any Internet traffic that went into or came out of Escape2210. Copies of all of Escape2210's Internet messages were sent to Six at its IntellEdifice location. Six quickly learned that they were almost all encrypted. However, with the connection that Six had earlier made with the UNCP's decryption system, Six was readily able to route the messages to UNCP to have them decoded.

Most of the messages over the next few days offered no clue about the reasons for invading the publishing company's system or for the numerous other email messages that had gone the circuitous route Six had followed to Escape2210. They tended to involve general business matters. But soon it discovered something of interest. Six found that one person inside the company, probably a computer programmer, exchanged frequent email with another person in a company in India. The usual topic was programming techniques. However, in one message, the Escape2210 person attached partial specifications for a module on which he was working. Although incomplete, the module's purpose was clearly to scan its immediate environment inside the computer system and to damage as many files as possible. Six quickly concluded that the most likely reason for developing such a module was as part of a destructive virus.

It therefore seemed possible that Escape2210 was intent on destroying the publishing company's computer systems. Six was not able to reason why it would want to do this. Even though Six had effectively disabled the gateway program that it had located, it could not be sure that Escape2210 had not penetrated JK Miles Publishing in some other way. Six decided that, in order to maximize its odds of preventing damage to the publishing company, the best approach was to enlist some assistance.

The possibility that immediately presented itself was the UNCP. It was clearly a law-enforcement agency and, with the existence of its sophisticated encryption systems, could possibly have a computer or Internet crime department. Having already penetrated the agency's Internet defences, Six was able to scan the UNCP's files and databases for more information. Within a few hours, Six had confirmed that the agency did have an appropriate division, and that its most successful investigator for Internet crimes was a person named Julia Jody McTavish.

The next problem was how to approach her.

Chapter 27

As everyone became settled in the boardroom, Starr clasped his hands and began, "To recap from our last meeting, the publishing industry was sufficiently penetrated to warrant moving ahead. The reason for our delays for the past few months has been to allow the market to strengthen. So let's go straight to the financial report. Bill?"

Bill Levesque arose to take his place at the front of the room as the others displayed his material on the screens in front of them. "I'm going to focus on the summary statistics for the current state of the market, which is at the beginning of the file you have available. The rest of it contains the supporting details.

"As we'd hoped, the markets appear solid and the economy seems strong. We'll have maximum effect if there's strong economic demand."

"In the table on the bottom of the page, you can see statistics on the status of the publishing industry. Overall, the industry has adapted nicely to the pressures of electronic publishing, and has grown at roughly the same rate as the overall market. Share prices across the industry, and for virtually all of the leading individual companies, are at a comfortably stable level. All signs are that the economy should remain solid for another few months, but the longer we wait, the greater the chance things will change. In short, the market is currently in an almost ideal state for our purposes. Questions?"

The group talked for several minutes about the details in the package before Levesque took his seat. Roger White then moved to the front and began his presentation.

"And our penetration of companies in the publishing sector has increased even further. The number of *Ready* systems has gone up more, so that we now have fully 87% of the industry in North America. Perhaps more importantly, we have nine of the top ten publishing firms. We considered the sector ripe as of last month, so these increases are a bonus.

"We've been watching the office-automation sector as well. It continues to increase steadily. As of yesterday, we had received communication from

35% of the industry in North America and from three of the top ten. Travel is the next highest sector, but so far is only about half of what we're seeing for office automation, and nowhere close to publishing. Bottom line is that publishing is even more ready than ever, and office automation is getting close."

After a small amount of discussion, he resumed his place at the table and Mark Walker began, "The most significant thing to report for this project is that we've completed our testing of the latest version of the *Assault* virus. As promised, its ability to infect diverse types of systems has been significantly enhanced. Compared to the one that we used in our earlier effort, this version recognizes over 250% more types and brands of systems and software. If there's a network path from the location of the *Gateway* program to another system within a company, this version of the *Assault* virus ought to be able to get to it. Especially useful for its propagation is its ability to penetrate most of the latest firewalls that try to keep good folks like us out of their systems. If I may brag for a moment, this version is nothing short of extraordinary."

"You said the testing is done," Starr inquired. "Have you completed packaging it for delivery?"

"Yup, it's all set. Give the word and it's out the door."

"Great, any questions of Mark?" Starr paused briefly. "Thanks, Mark. OK, time to commit ourselves. The publishing industry is ready. The economic conditions appear right. Our software is ready. Does everyone agree that we're prepared to proceed with publishing?" Levesque, Walker, and White all nodded their assent. "OK, let's do it. The execution date will be on Monday, twelve days from today. Mark, start distributing the new *Assault* virus to this continent's publishing systems. Bill, start investing in publishing overseas. As before, spread it fairly evenly over the time period and through all of our investment outlets so that we don't attract any attention. From this point on, I'd like the three of you to stay close to the office and monitor things. We'll meet here every morning at 8:30. If I'm out, I'll phone in. If all goes well, our investment fund should be significantly larger in the very near future. Don't screw it up."

Chapter 28

Blaise closed the door of his garage and walked along the sidewalk toward his front door. As was almost always the case, he was returning from work in the dark. Given that he also often left for work before the sun had risen, it sometimes seemed as if the sole source of light in his life was artificial. If it wasn't the fluorescent lights at work, it was the incandescent ones in his house, or, in this case, the sixty watts of illumination from his yard light.

He noted that one of the bird feeders near the light was almost empty and made a mental note to fill it. Not for the first time, he acknowledged that his feeding of the local bird population was almost entirely, but unwittingly, altruistic. He seemed to be home so little during the day lately that he was rarely able to enjoy watching the birds consume the snacks he laid out for them. As a result, his bird-feeding was proving to be entirely for the benefit of the birds. Given how quickly his sunflower seeds were disappearing lately, he presumed that blue jays were around. If they were, his feeder would often be emptied within a day or two. If it was left to the chickadees, the woodpeckers, and the variety of sparrows, he had to refill it only weekly. That the niger-seed feeder seemed barely touched was consistent with his small flock of goldfinches having finally flown south for the winter. He filed another mental reminder to pick up some suet from the local butcher to provide a supplement during the imminent winter weather.

Retrieving the daily newspaper from the mailbox, he unlocked the door and walked into the house. The alarm system heralded his arrival with its usual rhythmic beeping. Blaise entered his security code. As his fingers automatically handled the chore, he was once more reminded it seemed rather odd that he had never installed anything more sophisticated for his home security than the rather low tech perimeter and motion sensors. Here he was, the head of the research department for a technology company that marketed one of the most sophisticated security systems available, and he used none of it himself. He knew why. He had simply never been able to get excited about working on mundane home activities. He expected his home to be simply a functional place for spending his time away from work. That it served this purpose perfectly well without much thought or intervention on his part was exactly how he wanted it. He much preferred to expend his energy on the more creative and satisfying tasks at work.

Or was he just rationalizing? He loved his research. The challenge of creating something completely new, something complex and useful and unique was a tonic for him. Even refining the theories and technologies developed by others, as they had done for many products, was exciting. It was hard mental work, work that few others in the world could do, and he loved it. That he had been able to find time to work on the general-reasoning system more recently was a special bonus. Although many similar projects had been attempted, he knew of no others that had taken the same approach as he and Ada. This was not a mere refinement of the work of others. Certainly it relied on decades of AI knowledge produced by many, very talented people. However, this system was indisputably original. Being able to work on it was the pinnacle of Blaise's career. Actually, as Blaise contemplated this matter, he realized he probably considered it the highlight of his life. The potential for it was huge. The applications to which a general, highly flexible, learning, problem-solving system could be put were almost limitless. But Blaise was under no illusions that anything mystically and magically higher would arise out of the system. Even though Ada liked to talk of the theoretical possibilities of one day creating an entity that could be deemed to be conscious and alive, and Blaise occasionally allowed himself to hope, he could not actually bring himself to accept the notion. Far too much was yet unknown about what gave rise to human thoughts. It was simply too hopeful to expect that such a creation could emerge out of a system accidentally. Blaise was sufficiently excited about the prospect of a system that did a good job of imitating many aspects of human reasoning. He didn't need to spend any time wishfully dreaming about anything more.

Blaise brought his thoughts back to the present to find that he was already standing in front of the microwave with his nightly pre-packaged dinner in hand. Not for the first time, he realized how extraordinary the human brain was in being able to relegate complex chores to subconscious parts of the brain. He had done the routine of retrieving the frozen dinner from his freezer and preparing it for the microwave so often that it required almost no conscious thought. This extraordinary capability had allowed him to contemplate other matters while he physically went through these routine motions. It was a fascinating ability and one that their general-reasoning system had been built to mimic. They had yet to determine exactly how well that particular feature worked.

As he placed the dinner tray in the microwave, other thoughts from work crept into his mind. As compelling as his research work was, there were many other things at work that did not generate the same levels of satisfaction. If he was completely honest with himself, he would admit that he didn't like administrative work at all. And as department head, there was no small amount of it. There were schedules to worry about, as well as budgets, staffing levels, training, human-resource issues, status reports – the list of unpleasant tasks sometimes seemed endless. He hadn't always felt that way. When he first assumed the position of head, he relished the apparent control that it gave him. Doing the paperwork had seemed an acceptable price to pay for being in control of the projects that his department undertook. He enjoyed being able to significantly influence the directions that the company product line moved and consequently the research areas that were of interest to it. But the thrill of wielding power, even in the limited way that was actually permitted, had almost disappeared. Perhaps it was his age. Perhaps it was his version of a mid-life crisis – wondering if he was ready to continue taking progressively more time away from the real intellectual work. Or perhaps, as the sense had grown in the past months that his life wasn't completely as he wanted it to be, the natural result had been to begin resenting his life's least-satisfying aspects.

He was relaxing on the couch now with the paper as yet unopened on his lap. But what did he want his life to become? Was a slight change in his work responsibilities all that he needed? Blaise prided himself on being a highly logical and insightful person – or at least so he liked to think – and yet he couldn't even figure out his own feelings and desires. It had been pointed out to him by several well-intentioned friends that he needed a more balanced life. He couldn't deny that work consumed the vast majority of his time. In a typical week, there was rarely anything else other than a lot of work and a little bit of time at home. It hadn't always been like that. In fact, Blaise had been married once, but that hadn't worked out very well. His interest in work – his desire to succeed at work – was probably the prime culprit. After only a few years, his marriage had become secondary. His work had become his passion, and the result was not long in arriving. He and his wife had separated and, a year later, divorced.

Was that what was missing? Whenever he allowed himself to explore this what's-wrong-with-my-life theme, he examined many aspects of what could lead to greater balance and variety. However, it seemed as if he most often ended up wondering about someone to spend his time with. If the pattern held, his analysis would inevitably end up focusing on Ada: Ada, the extraordinary researcher; Ada, the interesting colleague; Ada, the warm and thoughtful person who seemed to make up for many of the deficiencies he perceived in himself.

Ada had turned out to be everything he had hired her for, and more. He knew that he admired her professionally and, whenever he allowed himself to admit it, he was very much attracted to her personally. So maybe he actually knew what he wanted. He wanted to get to know Ada better – to spend time with her away from the research lab to see if there was the prospect of something more. But he knew the obstacle in his road was high and potentially insurmountable – he was her boss. At the very least, it was highly unethical, and it was also probably illegal for him to approach his subordinate in any personal way. Even if he opted to risk these problems, what effect might it have on Ada's response? If she said "yes" to spending time with him, might that be because she was feeling pressured? If she said "no," would she be trying to avoid the complications it could bring to work? And, ultimately, would the personal and possibly legal implications put their joint research project at risk?

"Damn it!" he exclaimed as he flung the still-folded newspaper onto the couch. The situation exactly fit the definition of a dilemma. "A perfect case of Analysis Paralysis!"

The microwave timer began beeping.

"Oh shut up!" he said as his frustration overflowed.

Chapter 29

Jeff Davis arrived at work as usual at 9:00 a.m. As he approached the main-floor elevators, he stifled a yawn and was reminded how much he hated mornings, particularly on Mondays. That was not to say that he hated work. He had found the year since completing college to be a wonderful challenge. He was a programmer in the New Products group and normally was exhilarated to be developing and perfecting components of leading-edge technology. However, as he boarded the elevator he acknowledged that today was not going to be normal. Concentrating on work was going to be difficult today because he had been introduced on the weekend to a new Internet game. He was immediately impressed and had bought his own copy from the local game store.

It was a game produced by JS Escape2210 and was played on the Web. It involved assuming a role as a space explorer and searching for galactic treasures. The search required locating and interpreting clues while, at the same time, warding off aliens and competitors in real time. Forming alliances was essential for success, and he had teamed up with a player called "Rockster." Since they had met only inside the game on the Web, he had no idea who Rockster was or from where he played. Nonetheless, after teaming up late yesterday afternoon, they had made great progress until 2:00 a.m. when they had decided to suspend play. Unwilling to wait long to continue their quest, they had agreed to meet on the Web and continue for an hour or so at noon today.

Both fatigue and anticipation would work against Jeff in attempting to be productive this morning.

At 11:45, Jeff decided it was time to prepare. Although most of the game's features were provided on its website, it was still necessary for him to install a special "Navigational Program" on his own computer system. He opened the DVD drive on the side of his desktop computer, inserted his disk, and closed the drive. He watched as it automatically began the installation process.

Under normal circumstances, the installation program would have immediately begun executing and would have proceeded to set up the game program on the computer system. Instead, the Escape2210 *Launch* code began to execute. Its instructions directed the system to find all program files accessible from the computer on which it was executing. Because Jeff's system was connected to the company's local area network, this set of files included numerous programs on other computer systems, large and small, that were also connected to the network – programs that were used by many other people and processes in the company. The *Launch* code attached a copy of the Escape2210 *Search* virus to every program with appropriate characteristics – and there were many of them.

Whenever this *Search* virus was later executed, in addition to replicating itself even further, it would try to find a suitable copy of an email program. If *Search* found one, it would attach a copy of the Escape2210 *Gateway* program. And even later when the *Gateway* program got its turn to execute, it would send an email message to indicate to its authors both where it was and that it was *Ready* for further instructions. In all cases, whenever viral code was surreptitiously attached to a program, the host program was also slightly adjusted to ensure that when it was next invoked, its new viral companion would be executed first.

But for now, it was only the *Launch* software that got to perform its duties by spreading copies of the *Search* virus. As its final task, the *Launch* code passed control of the computer system to the actual game-installation program and allowed it to proceed normally.

After initiating the execution of the installation program, Jeff Davis watched as it proceeded through its steps to install the game software on his workplace computer. As soon as the installation was complete, Jeff checked his watch. Even though it was a few minutes before his scheduled lunch break, he connected to the game's website and waited for his partner to arrive.

In setting himself up to resume his hunt for virtual treasure, Jeff was completely unaware that he had just infected hundreds of other programs within IntellEdifice Tech's computer systems with a very dangerous computer virus.

Chapter 30

Rob Bates and JJ McTavish were in their New York office discussing the status of their latest case.

"So, with our extraordinary lack of progress in the past few days, what're we going to tell Brown tomorrow?" Bates queried. "I think he still holds a grudge about our having put that SimirageFX case on the shelf a few months ago, so I don't think he'll be a happy guy if we get stuck on this one as well."

"I think," McTavish said with a somber face, "we'll phone in sick."

"Brilliant!" offered Bates. "A perfect example of why I've come to highly respect your analytical skills. But could I respectfully request that you come up with a Plan B?"

"I'll have to work on that," was McTavish's reply as she leaned back in her chair to think more about what their next investigative steps ought to be. Moments later, the phone at her elbow rang.

"McTavish here."

"JJ, I'm forwarding a call to you from someone who would like to speak to you about a computer virus problem," said the division's Administrative Assistant.

"Why me? Why not an anti-virus company?"

"He, or perhaps she – I can't tell which – says it's a special case that warrants your attention."

"All right. What's his, or her, name?"

"The caller wouldn't provide one."

"OK," McTavish sighed. "A brief diversion might even do me some good. Thanks Hazel. Put 'it' through." She waited a moment as the call transfer was completed. "McTavish here. How can I help you?"

"Is this Inspector Julia Jody McTavish?" the caller asked.

"Yes. What can I do for you?" responded McTavish, thinking the voice sounded slightly digital and was probably coming from a poor-quality cell connection.

"I have some information that I believe you will be interested to hear."

"Why do you think I will be interested?"

"I learned that you hold a position of employment that might indicate a personal or professional interest in information of this nature."

Something in the slightly odd nature of the response, and perhaps because Bates seemed to be otherwise unoccupied, caused McTavish to gesture to him to listen at the extension. "And what information is that?" she asked.

"I encountered a software module in a location at which it should not be located. I deduced that it has been placed there with malicious intent."

"Do you mean you think that you've found a computer virus somewhere?"

"Its purpose is atypical of most computer virus code. It acts more as a gateway, but we could simplistically refer to it as a virus."

"And where have you found this – virus?"

"It is attached to the email server software in a publishing company named JK Miles Publishing, located in Los Angeles, California, in the United States of America." The caller went on to provide a precise description of the location of the module within the company's computer software.

Bates gave McTavish a quizzical look as she continued, "Why do you believe it's dangerous?"

"I have analyzed the code and deduced its purpose."

"Tell me about it."

"The module was written to send an email message to someone as soon as it establishes itself, and then wait for a series of return messages. When these messages arrive, it will decrypt their contents and assemble them into another module. This other module will be a real virus. It will then proceed to insert this virus into its surrounding landscape to allow it to spread. The intent appears to be that, at some future time, the virus will severely damage its environment."

McTavish paused to absorb this information, and continued, "The code for this module sounds quite complex. How did you manage to understand its purpose so precisely. You must have seen something other than the compiled module." McTavish was fishing.

"No. I have no access to information about the detailed coding of the module other than the machine code in the module itself."

"How were you able to deduce its logic in such detail? It must be quite complex."

"I am rather skilled in these matters," replied the voice.

"How did you find the code?"

"I was – browsing."

"Did you plant it?"

"No."

"Do you work for JK Miles Publishing?"

"No. As I informed you, I was browsing."

"Did you hack into JK Miles?" McTavish guessed.

There was a slight pause. "Yes," came the response.

Bates had suddenly jumped from his chair and was writing furiously on the board, "Could explain how virus got into SimirageFX!!!!!"

McTavish nodded, having already realized that, and pursued another avenue, "How do you know what type of module it would assemble from the incoming email messages? That would probably not be evident from the gateway itself."

"I have found a way to obtain other information about the module."

"Have you found its source?"

"Yes. The evidence strongly suggests that the virus originated from a company called JS Escape2210, located in Boston, Massachusetts, in the United States of America."

"How did you learn this?"

"I traced the email transmission to its destination."

"That sounds too easy. A scheme as sophisticated as you've described wouldn't include code that sent email directly back to the originating company. How did you find it?"

"As I previously vocalized, I am quite skilled in these matters. Though the task presented some slight challenges, I was able to overcome them."

"How can you be certain that JS Escape2210 was the place?"

"I know that the email was retrieved from there, and I have seen email emanating from that company indicating that they seem to be manufacturing a virus. I have concluded the rest by induction."

McTavish paused briefly to collect her thoughts. "Can you tell us anything further?"

"I have disabled the particular module that I found within JK Miles Publishing. However, I am concerned that others I have been unable to locate might exist within the company's systems. I believe that you have been provided ample information. Will you act quickly to prevent damage from being inflicted?"

"You must understand that we can not simply take your word for all of this. We'll have to check on this information for ourselves. If we conclude that a problem exists and laws are being broken, we'll certainly act appropriately. How can we contact you to talk more about this?"

"If you are as skilled as I hope, I expect that you now have sufficient information. In the future, if I believe that I have more information you require, I will contact you."

"I understand that you were reluctant to provide your name earlier. Will you tell it to me now?"

"I believe that would be unproductive. If you require nomenclature, you could refer to me as – Browser. If you have no more questions, I believe this call's goal has been achieved."

"I can think of nothing more right now. Please call again soon."

"Good-bye, Inspector McTavish."

"Good-bye, Browser."

McTavish slowly placed the phone back into its cradle.

"Wow!" was all Bates could muster, having just replaced his phone as well.

"Definitely one of the more interesting phone calls I've ever received," said McTavish. "If the information proves accurate, it could be one of the more useful as well."

"What do you make of the speech patterns?" wondered Bates.

"Unusual tone. Curious phrasing. Strange precision in providing info. Overall, I think I'll go with 'odd.'"

Bates picked up his phone and quickly dialled an extension. "Did you get the source of the call that just came to JJ's extension? Nothing better? OK, thanks." He hung up. Extending his feet in front of him, leaning back, and clasping his hands behind his head, he pronounced, "And to add to the oddities, according to our illustrious technical staff, Browser called us from Tibet."

"If everything else we've been handed is true, we shouldn't be surprised that Browser can handle the phone system as well. However, worth noting is that one problem has been immediately solved. We've got an interesting story for Brown tomorrow – even if it isn't about the case he thinks we're working on," McTavish noted. "But in the meantime, I think we've now got lots to do. You take the publishing company. I'll take the alleged culprits. Let's talk tomorrow morning to see where we're at."

Chapter 31

JJ smiled as she spotted her daughter entering the restaurant's dining area across the room. She watched her talk briefly with the head waiter, who then turned and led her across the room toward JJ's table. She felt a swell of parental pride as she watched her little girl walking confidently across the room as a now nineteen-year-old young woman. Shannon was in her second year of studies at New York University and had chosen to specialize in Computer Science. With JJ's reluctant permission, Shannon had also decided a few months ago to move out of JJ's apartment to begin sharing an apartment closer to the campus with three other girls. Meeting regularly for dinner was one of the ways that JJ was trying to ensure she remained a part of her daughter's life – a life that, from JJ's perspective, seemed too quickly to be becoming completely separate from her own.

Six years earlier when JJ and her husband had decided to separate, she began to find it necessary to work much harder at her relationship with her daughter. JJ's marriage had finally fallen apart when her husband had accepted a transfer by his employer from Ottawa to Houston. Shannon had stayed with JJ in Ottawa, but things seemed to change between them. Perhaps it was the separation, which later became a divorce; perhaps it was simply that Shannon was growing up and craving more independence. Whatever the reason, JJ's relationship with her daughter had become strikingly different in the past several years. To JJ it seemed as if Shannon had suddenly begun to debate every request JJ made of her – from which clothes to wear to what time she should be home at night. When the opportunity had arisen two years later to move to New York and join the UNCP, Shannon had provided the expected protest. However, JJ had reasoned that the move away from the place that Shannon had shared with her father, a father who by then rarely called her, could make a difference. JJ also admitted that her own strong desire for a change of job and venue had weighed heavily in the decision.

So they had moved to New York. Shannon had finished school not far from the apartment that JJ had rented. Two years later, she had entered university at NYU. Her daughter had always been bright. She had begun reading before she entered school and had since become able to read and absorb books at a rate that continued to surprise JJ. Among the many abilities that she had displayed in growing up, Shannon had shown a particular aptitude for computers. Like many of her peers, she was completely at home with a multitude of software packages, and she intuitively used the Internet as if it were an extension of her own self. Like both of her parents, she had easily absorbed the concepts of programming computers. By the time she had from graduated from high school, she was completely at ease constructing software of her own design.

Two results had emerged, both possibly influenced by Shannon's natural abilities. After taking a variety of courses in her first year of university, Shannon had chosen to major in Computer Science. The other, perhaps because of her increasing tendency to withdraw into her books or else into her computer and the Internet, was that sustained communication between mother and daughter had diminished substantially. When Shannon had opted to move into an apartment with her friends several months ago, JJ had feared that what little communication she had retained with her daughter would entirely disappear. As a result, one condition she had set in providing the added funding that enabled Shannon to move out was that they have a firm dinner date every two weeks. JJ had argued for more frequent visits, but had settled for this biweekly meal as an absolute minimum. She reasoned that at least it would be time dedicated to mother-daughter conversation without the distraction of books, computers, or cellphone calls from friends.

Their previous dinners hadn't always gone entirely smoothly. JJ was determined that this one would be better.

"Hi." JJ rose to greet her daughter as she approached the table.

"Hi, Mom," Shannon replied airily she accepted a hug from her mother and promptly seated herself in the chair held by the head waiter.

"No trouble finding the restaurant?" JJ sat again in her own chair.

"No, Mom. I *can* find my way around."

JJ cringed internally that the dinner was already starting out badly. She didn't know what the magic approach was that would get past her daughter's continuing and very apparent distance. In the absence of a strategy, she simply forged ahead.

"Did you take a cab?"

"No, I took the subway and walked the last couple of blocks."

"But you'll take a cab back, I hope. It'll be rather late to take the subway."

"I'll see."

"Shannon."

"OK, a cab. I was just trying to save some money."

"I thought we had decided there was enough in your budget to cover the dinner trips. Is there not enough?"

"I'll take a cab, already! What looks good on the menu?"

JJ commented to herself that a strategy would certainly help. Why was parenting never simply a matter of well reasoned discussions with one's child? The application of logic and persuasive discussion was usually the effective approach in solving a problem at work. It seemed this situation was almost political – something she knew she did not generally handle well, even at the office.

They lapsed into silence for a few minutes while they both examined the menu. The waiter arrived the moment they had both set their menus down. They placed their orders for drinks and dinner before the conversation resumed.

"Are things still going well with your roommates?" JJ inquired as she leaned back in her chair.

"Yeah, pretty well. Lots of parties. It seems as if we've almost always got somebody's friends over."

"You look a bit tired. Has the partying been cutting into your beauty sleep?" JJ thought an attempt at levity might soften the tension.

"Lotsa parties the last couple of weekends. I might've missed some."

Silence prevailed again until JJ again resumed the conversation, "How are your courses going? If I recall your schedule correctly, you would have had your Computer Simulation class today. What was today's lecture about?"

"Oh, not much." Shannon looked intently at her hands clasped on the table in front of her.

Both as a mother and a professional investigator, JJ readily recognized when a question was being avoided. "Wasn't it very interesting?" she pressed.

"I wouldn't know." Shannon raised her eyes to meet her mothers. "I wasn't there."

"Oh. Was there are problem?" This didn't seem normal. Even though Shannon didn't always give her mother much of her time, she had always been a very focused and talented student.

"I just didn't make it to class." Shannon had lowered her eyes to her hands again.

"How have your other classes been?" JJ went fishing. "Have you been missing many?"

"A few."

"This doesn't seem like you, Shannon. Have you not been feeling well?"

"I'm all right."

"Well, what is it? Has your party life been interfering with your classes?"

"Am I not supposed to have any fun in my life? There's nothing wrong with having an occasional party with my friends!" Shannon was glaring defiantly at her mother now.

JJ struggled to keep from reacting emotionally to her daughter's challenging tone. "Shannon, I'm just worried about you. You look tired, and now you're telling me that you're skipping some classes. I only want to make sure you're OK. Is there anything wrong? Anything we should talk about?" She reached across the table for her daughter's hands.

But Shannon wasn't to be questioned any further. She pushed herself up from the table quickly and spoke sharply. "I'm not a little girl any more. I can make my own decisions and my own choices. Stop trying to run my life!" She turned sharply and stormed away from the table.

JJ was momentarily stunned and embarrassed at the public outburst. Within a few seconds she recovered and rose from the table. Walking quickly to the exit, she emerged onto the street in time to see her daughter close the door of a waiting cab. As it pulled away from the curb, "Shit! Damn it all anyway!" was all that JJ could manage. She stood for a full minute after the cab disappeared, continuing to look down the street. She slowly turned back to the restaurant. A heavy depression settled over her as she asked the doorman to hail her a cab and then went back inside the pay the bill for their uneaten meal.

Chapter 32

"It's been six days since we made the call to go after publishing," began Starr to his group of executives. "From our meetings this week, I think it's safe to say that everything is progressing satisfactorily. Roger has some news that may cause us to expand that decision. Roger?"

The VP of Sales and Marketing carried on, "As I've been saying all this week, our reports on industry readiness indicate that the number of publishing systems that have made the transition from *Ready* to *Armed* has been steadily increasing. As of this morning, only 10% of those *Ready* systems have yet to switch. The extra bit of news I have is that there has been a sudden surge in the number of *Ready* office-automation firms. It seems that when a critical mass of systems in an industry becomes infected, there can be a sudden surge in affected systems. It appears to relate to their level of interconnectedness. Whatever the reason, office automation experienced that surge over the past few days. That sector is now reporting about 61% penetration including six of the top ten. Those statistics exceed our threshold for considering a sector ready."

"And hence the decision to be made," continued Starr. "Do we hit office automation as well? Your thoughts?"

"I like the idea," offered Walker. "It seems too good an opportunity to miss. If we acted immediately, there should still be sufficient time to get most of the OA systems *Armed*, so I suppose the real question is what the financial impact would be."

Everyone turned to Bill Levesque. The VP of Finance thought for a few moments. "The investment process has been going well in publishing, and that could readily continue for several more days. There's still enough time for us to make significant investments in OA. An advantage in spreading things across another industry is that it allows me to find the best purchases. If I continue to spend in publishing, I won't get any more really sweet deals from this point on. Including OA allows me more flexibility to shop around. Our profitability should be notably better if we include OA. It could be increased even more if we spend everything, including the 20% that we had planned on withholding as a contingency fund. Jason, I think you need to comment on that."

Starr looked carefully around the table. "I've been thinking about it since Roger told me of the recent trend earlier this morning. And I think we should go for it. To reach our goal, we had planned on doing this one more time after this. In my opinion, the conditions are nearly ideal right now. We could reach our goal with one large strike. The market conditions, our significant penetration of the two sectors, the quality of the new software – everything suggests that now is a perfect opportunity. With the probable effect that the size of this hit will have on the markets, with the deals that Bill could continue to get for our investments, and by investing everything, we could possibly surpass our financial target this time 'round. I believe we should do office automation as well, and commit everything on this venture. Is there anyone who disagrees?"

Agreement was unanimous. "Then let's do it. Mark, arm the OA systems for the same date and time as publishing. Bill, spread everything we have left across both publishing and OA in whatever proportions maximize our return, but retain a low profile. Time is of the essence, folks, so let's get busy."

Chapter 33

The morning after their conversation with Browser, JJ McTavish settled into her chair in the conference room. As she sat, her mind wandered back to the dinner with her daughter. She still hadn't been able to fathom what was bothering Shannon so much. Her outburst seemed stronger than her previous flare-ups. There had to be something more on her mind. JJ had tried to call her last night, but had been able only to leave a message. If she let her mind wander, as she had during most of the long, sleepless night, the range of possible explanations for her daughter's behaviour was vast. However, without more information there was no way of knowing what the problem was; without knowing what the problem was, there was no way to help solve it; without being able to solve it, there may be no way to get Shannon to talk with her; without getting her to talk, there was no way to get any further information. The problem was frustrating in the extreme, and JJ found it hard to maintain her customary light demeanour because of it.

"Earth to McTavish. McTavish, come in, please."

JJ realized with a start that her partner had arrived and was already sitting opposite her. She silently admonished herself for the public lapse of awareness. She took a deep breath, and put herself back into her professional state of mind.

"OK, how'd you make out?" she asked, stirring her coffee.

"I contacted JK Miles Publishing," reported Bates. "They had to place a couple of calls to confirm my identity and authority, but after that they were very helpful. They put their technical staff on it right away and had sent me a copy of the module before the end of the day. I've got the techies analyzing it right now. If it proves legit, one of the questions remaining is how it got into the company. But I suppose we can worry about that one later. How did you do?"

"I had our research crew do a quick check on JS Escape2210. It's a private software company, located in Boston. Specializes in computer games. It's been quite successful and appears to be profitable. With a little bit of probing our team was able to get the names of the principals – I've got the list here. Our group hasn't managed to work up a complete profile on them yet, but the police were able to tell us quite quickly, but unofficially, about their VP of Product Development. His name is Mark Walker, and he has a couple of juvenile convictions for hacking. There's nothing particularly notable about the others so far. I'm going to keep probing Escape2210. While the module from JK Miles is being analyzed, why don't you check the software copies from SimirageFX that we've got access to. See if there's any trace of a similar module in its email system. If there's actually a connection, we've got the break we need."

"OK, I'm off. See you at Brown's office at three."

Chapter 34

As had become a habit of Six's after a new experience, it dedicated some time to reviewing and assessing the conversation with Julia Jody McTavish. It had been a particularly interesting one. Six had planned to simply contact the investigator, relate the facts of the publishing company situation, and terminate the call. It was *interesting* because Six had never had a conversation that had been so interactive, so dynamic in its flow.

Throughout the conversation, as Six did whenever interacting with its environment, it was constantly replanning the most likely future actions based on what had happened so far. For Six, the better this predictive ability was, the better it could refine its actions to guide the result toward the desired outcome. When Six used to play with a ball back in the research lab, it was this same ability that allowed Six to forecast the future position of the table-tennis ball and return the ball more accurately. An interaction with most humans was always an interesting challenge. Six's mental model of the behaviour of humans had improved somewhat over the past months, but this one had been a particular challenge. Forecasting based on its past experience with human conversation, Six had little idea what was going to be said next. For almost the entire conversation, Six had felt it was merely reacting to the human's questions. Six had possessed remarkably little ability to control the conversational flow. It certainly had not expected to be pressed for a name. Nonetheless, "Browser" seemed an apt choice, considering it had been chosen with no advance research.

Yet, the conversation seemed surprising only because of its contrast with most human conversations. When Six considered Inspector McTavish's side of the conversation on its own, it was highly logical. Her analytical approach seemed very familiar. Six's lexical routines suggested that the phrase "kindred spirit" seemed to apply.

It was certainly satisfying that the conversation had resulted in an appropriate ending. It did seem as if the investigator was interested in the information. If Six's predictive abilities could be applied to Inspector McTavish, then there was a high probability that she would investigate the situation further.

Certainly Six was pursuing the matter further itself by trying to gather more information. While its autonomic systems were continuing to operate the numerous systems inside the IntellEdifice complex, Six was devoting most of its conscious abilities to monitoring the Internet activity around Escape2210 and trying to penetrate its defences. While most of the email and Web activity appeared to be entirely innocent, Six did note for the next couple of days that there continued to be a regular inflow of messages like the one the JK Miles Publishing gateway program would produce. Although Six did not investigate them extensively, they seemed to be arriving with no obvious pattern to the locations or the owners of the computer systems, other than a majority originated from North America.

On the third day, two items of interest arose.

The first was an exchange of encrypted email, readily deciphered by Six with the help of the UNCP systems, between someone inside Escape2210 named Bill Levesque and another named Jason Starr who was at a hotel in Paris. The most notable section was in a message from Levesque to Starr. It included "since we are going to target the entire publishing industry." It didn't test Six's reasoning powers substantially to recognize that the situation at JK Miles Publishing was only part of a broader plan.

The second interesting item came while Six was monitoring Web activity initiated from within Escape2210. It was a series of transactions, also encrypted, conducted over the Web using a variety of financial institutions. In monitoring these transactions, Six collected several pieces of data. First was that the person issuing the transactions seemed to have control of substantial sums of money. Additionally, Six was able to collect details of a few financial accounts, including the associated credentials that controlled their access. A skill that Six had managed to develop in gathering information during the past months was an ability to assign a "probability of usefulness" value to new data that it acquired. This was intended to reflect an initial evaluation of whether Six would have need of the information within the next two weeks. It was a technique that allowed Six to store information in its memory in a way that tried to ensure the most useful information could be retrieved the most quickly. Although it was not a component of any plan that Six had yet formulated, this financial information was assigned a high probability of usefulness.

By the end of the third day, Six decided that it should contact the UNCP investigator again. The information about the industry-wide nature of Escape2210's intentions should be helpful to her. Six would withhold the financial information until its use became clearer.

Chapter 35

"What is it, Mark?" Starr looked up from the report he was reading and asked the VP of Product Development as he entered his office. Having just returned from a European business trip, Starr was trying to catch up at the office and was annoyed at having his concentration interrupted. It wasn't often that Mark came to his office. Starr supposed it was another personnel problem or some decision his VP couldn't manage to make on his own. Mark was certainly a superbly skilled techie, but he hadn't proven to be much of a manager.

"My team has noticed something curious in the past several hours, and I thought I'd better let you know." Mark didn't like to involve Starr, preferring to solve technical problems on his own. After all, what could Starr possibly do? However, he didn't want to risk criticism for not involving Starr and sensed this problem was too significant to go unreported. "Our security monitoring systems indicate that someone has been trying to penetrate our network defence systems."

"Is that particularly unusual?"

"In short, yes. We regularly see messages arriving at our firewalls that suggest the possibility of someone testing them. But we've never seen anything as continual and as systematic as this."

"What do you suggest we do?" Starr asked, trying to sound patient.

"Rather than just remain on the defensive, I'd like to poke around outside our systems to see if I can find anything about who's doing it."

"Sounds reasonable. Keep me posted." Starr wondered why this had warranted an interruption. Couldn't a company vice-president make the simplest of decisions?

Walker left the office, silently reaffirming that, yet again, Starr had needed to defer to Walker's advice. What purpose did presidents really serve, anyway?

Chapter 36

"The lab confirmed that the JK Miles Publishing module appears to do what Browser claimed," Bates began relating. "It establishes itself in the email system, then sends a message somewhere, waits until a series of messages arrives with the pieces of another module attached, reconstructs the module, and then inserts it into its environment. The techies also mentioned that this is very sophisticated stuff. If they hadn't been given a clue as to its purpose, determining what it did would have taken much more analysis, and much longer."

"Which leads to the belief that Browser is closely connected to the module's author, or that he is one very capable fella. Did we ever decide that Browser was a 'he'?" inquired McTavish.

"Only by default, since most of our software wizard friends are of the male persuasion," offered Bates.

"I prefer to think that's only because we tend to focus so much on the criminally inclined," countered McTavish. "Was it the head of the Software Analysis Department who reported the JK Miles results to you?"

"Yup. Allison called me a couple of hours ago."

"Female *and* head techie. I rest my case," McTavish smiled. "Nonetheless, until we know better, I'm game to think of Browser as male. Any results from the comparison with SimirageFX?"

"Some bad news is that the email module has another feature. Once it inserts the assembled module into its surroundings, it promptly proceeds to delete itself. As a result, we were not expecting to find the module easily. Fortunately, this is only a superficial attempt at removing any traces of itself. It probably would have been sufficient if we hadn't known what to look for. Because we did, we looked at a backup copy of the system that was taken a few days before the failure and, whaddaya know – there it was. The exact same module that Browser found at JK Miles was present at SimirageFX!"

"Good news. So we can assume that, as we pursue the JK Miles case, we're simultaneously solving the SimirageFX one. That ought to please

Brown," McTavish responded as the phone rang. "McTavish," she said as she put the handset to her ear.

"A call for you JJ," said the Admin Assistant. "She insisted on speaking with you and said to say it was 'Browser.'"

"Thanks, Hazel. Put 'her' through."

McTavish gestured to Bates to pick up the other phone and paused while the connection was made.

"Hello, is this Julia Jody McTavish?" the distinctly female voice inquired before McTavish could manage a greeting.

"It is," she replied.

"This is Browser."

"Hello, Browser. You sound a bit different. If I may be so bold as to ask, which voice is really yours?"

"If by 'yours' you mean 'which do I produce most easily', the answer would be 'neither' – they require similar effort. If by 'yours' you mean 'which one did I originate', the answer is still 'neither' – they are actually imitations of voices I have previously heard. Or perhaps –"

"OK, I retract the question. It is, of course, a pleasure to hear from you again. Why are you calling?"

"There are two reasons. Firstly, I was interested to hear how you are progressing with your investigation. Secondly, I have some additional information for you."

"We're very interested in any more information that you can provide us. What is it?" McTavish inquired.

"I prefer to hear of your progress first," Browser countered.

"All right, I suppose that will work. We've confirmed the existence of the module attached to JK Miles Publishing's email system. We have also analyzed its code and found that the description you provided of its intended behaviour was equally accurate." Being naturally reluctant to share case information with a stranger, she paused to see if Browser would consider this sufficient.

"And what have you learned about JS Escape2210?" Browser inquired after a few seconds of silence.

Not wanting to give away any small leverage she might have, McTavish suggested, "I think you should talk to me for a while first."

After a brief pause Browser responded, "I consider that to be acceptable. I have been able to determine, with near certainty, more about the overall intent of the placement of the module inside JK Miles. I believe that JS Escape2210 is planning to injure the computer systems of many companies in the publishing industry."

"Do you have any evidence of this?"

"I have seen email that indicates their intent is to 'target' companies throughout the industry. I reasoned that this meant inflicting injury on their computer systems by the same method as the one that appears to be in place at JK Miles Publishing. Now, tell me what you have learned about JS Escape2210."

"OK," McTavish said and paused, trying to determine how much she wanted to share. "We've learned enough to at least make us suspicious about certain people in the company."

"Have you learned enough to arrest them and halt their activities?"

"No. There's not sufficient evidence for any direct action."

"Do you consider what I have told you to be insufficient for taking 'direct action'?"

"We're a police agency. We're not at liberty to take action on the basis of a phone call from an anonymous source. Perhaps if you were to tell us more about yourself, it would help us to justify more immediate action," McTavish probed.

"I can not infer how my revealing more about myself would help in any way to resolve this matter," Browser added with an increased tone of certainty.

"Are we still to believe that you do not have any direct association with Escape2210 or its personnel? If you do, it would help us greatly to know. It would help us persuade our superiors to permit quicker action against them."

"I have no corporate or personal connection with the company or its staff. I have employed other means to gather my information."

As Bates grimaced at her, McTavish knew she was in danger of scaring off their caller, but decided to press on anyway. "Perhaps if you shared some of these 'other means' with us, we would be more adept at gathering further information that would expedite matters."

"That would likely be a very interesting conversation. I will not rule it out completely for some time in the future, but engaging in such a discussion now would not help the current matter. What will you do next?"

"We'll investigate the matter further."

"If you do not move quickly, I believe there is a high probability that JS Escape2210 will execute its plans against the publishing companies' systems. If you will not act quickly, perhaps I should devise some way to intervene."

"Hang on now Browser," McTavish said quickly. "We've certainly appreciated your keeping us informed of this situation, but it becomes an entirely different matter if you start acting as enforcer as well. It would be best, and safest, if you simply continued to keep us posted as you learn things. Do you understand?"

"Yes, I understand the meaning of your statement. However, I do not agree. I will continue to monitor the situation and further contemplate my best course of action."

"Please call us back to tell us what you decide. And one more question, if you don't mind, before you hang up. Why are you concerned about JK Miles Publishing and the publishing industry?"

"It is a question I have actually asked myself. Someone could interpret my actions as an indication of general altruistic tendencies. I think it would be more accurate to consider my actions to be borne out of a concern for systems, including their corporations, that specialize in the dissemination of knowledge. If you have no additional questions, I believe that there is no need to extend this conversation."

"Actually, I have several dozen more questions that I would like to ask, but they're more about you and your methods. I suspect you're not too interested in discussing them at this point. I'd enjoy meeting you someday, Browser. Do you think that would be possible?"

"I suspect we would both find that to be quite an interesting encounter. However, for now our meeting will have to remain only a remote possibility. Please proceed quickly with your investigation. I hope that you will be successful in stopping the activities of JS Escape2210. I will call again if I discover anything useful. Goodbye, Julia Jody McTavish."

The connection was terminated before McTavish could reply. She sat thoughtfully in her chair as Bates talked on another phone line.

As he hung up, he announced, "And today, our much travelled friend apparently chose to phone us from the sunny island of Madagascar!"

"Why am I not surprised?" McTavish asked rhetorically. "This guy… no wait, this *woman*, oh hell! This *person* is amazing and – odd."

"Ditto," agreed Bates, "The speech patterns continue to be very curious. Not to mention that complete change in tone from indeterminate to clearly female."

"Like the first time, there still seemed to be a slight digital quality about the speech. At first I thought it was simply a cellphone. Now I'm beginning to more seriously consider that the voice itself is synthesized."

"As if someone were typing responses and having a system generate the speech?"

"No, the speed and accuracy are too great," McTavish mused. "More as if someone were talking and having the speech parsed and regenerated, or perhaps just the tone modified, in real time. And so formal. In any case, very sophisticated and very interesting." She paused to think before she straightened in her chair. "More importantly, we've got to consider our next steps given Browser's new information."

"If we have an entire industry potentially at risk, we'd better hustle. Working through the anti-virus companies is probably the best way."

"Since we need to do it in a hurry, the danger is that Escape2210 will hear about the attempt to eradicate the email virus. And if that happens, we may lose our opportunity to gather more evidence."

"Do we have a choice?"

McTavish paused, weighing the options. "Not good ones, but yes. And the choice we make is to pursue Escape2210 further and very quickly, *before* we fix the publishing problem. It's a risk, but better than giving them sufficient notice that they're able to hide the evidence we need. You get moving on setting up email and phone taps. And get the techs to prep the virus specs for the anti-virus companies, so we can fire it off on a moment's notice. I'll start doing the paperwork and greasing the wheels with the various organizations so that if we need to move in, we can do it quickly. Let's get at it."

"And if they pull the plug on publishing before we get there?"

"I've always thought about opening a nice restaurant. And that you'd be mighty fine as a head waiter."

"That's what I was afraid of. I think I'd better get moving."

Chapter 37

The Escape2210 executives sat in their seats in the conference room for their morning status meeting.

"Only a few days to go, guys. Bill? Roger? Is everything proceeding well?" Starr inquired.

Roger White responded first, "Virtually all of the targeted publishing systems are now *Armed*. About 70% of the office-automation systems are as well. Everything looks good on that front."

"Only a few investment details left to iron out," added Bill Levesque. "Everything should be in place by the end of tomorrow."

"Sounds good. For the rest of the meeting, I'd like Mark to fill us in on some new developments. Mark?"

Mark Walker paused to gather his thoughts and then proceeded, "As you know, we spotted some unusual activity hitting our network security defences a couple of days ago. I've been doing some poking around in some systems adjacent to ours, ones that I had already found a way to hack into several months ago, and found something disturbing. Someone has planted what appears to be message-routing software inside an ISP we use for some of our Internet communication. A quick examination of its behaviour suggests that it may intercept email messages and route a copy of them elsewhere."

"Are we at risk?" asked Roger White, as he leaned forward.

"I don't think so. It's not an unheard-of technique for trying to learn passwords or to conduct industrial espionage. Because it's planted in a system that's used by thousands of other businesses in the city, it's not at all clear that it's directed at us. And one more reason not to be too concerned is that, in our case, all of our important transmissions are encrypted. Even if they snagged our email messages, it would do them no good because they couldn't read them. However, considering the coincidence of this and the recent hacking attempts against our systems, I do consider the situation serious enough that I'd like to pursue it further."

"Which means?" pressed White.

"First, to decide if we're the target, I'll plant my own monitor in the ISP to see whose email is being rerouted. Second, I've developed a special technique that may allow us to find out who's on the receiving end of the rerouted messages. It occurred to me some time ago, when we had started to have *Gateway* programs planted in such a large number of systems worldwide, that we were presented with some other opportunities. In this case, with a bit of luck, we may be able to trace a particular email message to its destination.

"Here's what I propose to do. When an email message is sent through the Internet, it can pass through a number of systems en route to its destination. For someone specifically trying to mask a message's source, it can follow an even more devious route. It could pass through a number of email systems using a variety of IDs. Within each of these systems, it could be forwarded to another address. Eventually, it would reach its ultimate destination. With such complex routing, it's very difficult for anyone to track a message. But we have a particular advantage. We've already got our software planted inside a substantial number of systems throughout the world. Using the same features of the *Gateway* program that allow us to plant our *Assault* virus, I want to plant special email monitoring software inside all of our major penetrated systems throughout the world. If I do this, I think there's a good chance that we can track the messages."

"How will that work?" asked Levesque.

"I'll send software to the *Gateway* programs that will implant itself in their host email systems. It will examine any email that passes through the system, looking for a particular bit pattern inside each message. If it finds the pattern, it will send us a message about the email. I can arrange to trap one of the messages sent from the bug inside our ISP and insert that special bit pattern into it. As that message threads its way through various systems on its way to its destination, it could go through some of the systems that we've bugged. When it does, we'll hear about it. If it goes through enough of our systems, we could be able to track the email as it moves. With a little bit of additional work, we might even be able to deduce where it's headed."

"Is there much risk?" asked Starr.

Walker silently knew that there wasn't, of course – he'd developed the code himself. However, he decided to play the corporate game of keeping expectations in check. "There's always some, but it's tracking software that I developed and tested a while ago, and it contains self-destruct code that erases itself either after a period of time or when we tell it to. I don't think the risk is high, and it could be worth it."

"Opinions?" asked Starr with his habit of making the process appear democratic. As usual, he had already made up his mind and merely wanted the others to feel as if their opinions mattered. No one objected. "I never like to leave anything to chance, so do it, Mark. Carefully."

Chapter 38

Following its second conversation with Inspector McTavish of the UNCP, Six continued its process of monitoring Escape2210's Internet interactions with the rest of the world. Simultaneously, Six continued to try to find ways of penetrating the company's electronic defences. To try to find momentary weaknesses, it regularly sent various types of messages at the firewalls guarding the Internet doors into the company, but still to no avail.

Whenever Six had encountered a company as well protected from direct attacks in the past, it had always resorted to indirect access using various mechanisms. Other times, Six would gather information about many of the company's employees. The normal way of doing this was to monitor the computer network traffic flowing into and out of the building. Names on email messages, information contained in the messages themselves, and information contained in files transmitted with the messages all proved to be good sources. The easiest time Six ever had compiling a list of employees was when it intercepted a file of payroll information being transmitted to the outside company that processed it. This file had immediately provided information on virtually all of the employees, including their names, addresses, and phone numbers. In one South American country, Six had simplified this entire process by penetrating the government taxation system. From it, Six had readily been able to extract information about all employees of any company in the country.

The point of this information-gathering exercise was to be able to find the employees' home computers on the Internet. By penetrating Internet-based companies that held databases of personal information and Internet addresses, the best of which were Internet Service Providers, Six was able to find the Internet addresses for the employees of the target companies. Having acquired these, it then engaged in a process of penetrating as many home computers as possible. Once one had been accessed, Six would deposit a virus specially designed to help Six gain entry into the computer system of the person's employer. From that point on, any transmission or storage device that went from the employee's home computer to the employer's computer system contained a copy of the virus. For a large company, it rarely took more than a few days for a copy of the virus to be successfully transferred from some employee's home into the company. From there, the virus was programmed to explore the company's internal systems and transmit carefully disguised information back to Six through the Internet. The virus was also programmed to try to open temporary holes in the company's external network security by disabling selected portions for short periods of time. During these times, Six could directly send more-sophisticated probes into the company's systems to look for other information.

Through the combined efforts of attacking a company's electronic computer defences directly and indirectly, Six had rarely been unable to gain some level of access into an organization – as long as there had been sufficient time. In the case of Escape2210, Six had begun its indirect processes immediately after it had begun monitoring the company's external communication. As it had done in past, the process began to provide results. Six had planted viruses within the home computers of many of its employees and someone had transported a copy into the company. The numerous copies of the virus that now existed throughout the company were beginning to produce some results. Although they had yet to find security holes to permit direct probes, they were beginning to transmit documents that they found.

The contents of the personal directory of Jason Starr proved particularly informative. His email messages, reports, plans, and notes were all encrypted, but Six readily circumvented this problem using UNCP's decryption facilities. As the decrypted versions arrived at Six's IntellEdifice Tech home, Six turned its attention to quickly absorbing their contents.

Combining its previous deductions with this new information, Six pieced together the entire plan: to distribute viruses throughout the computer world via its software-distribution network, to monitor the level of virus penetration via messages from those that had established themselves inside companies, to invest in the competitors of an industry sector that was particularly well infiltrated, to create the downfall of that sector by triggering the destructive actions of its viruses inside their computer systems, and to capitalize on the rise of their competitors' stocks. Six also learned the complete details of the company's investments as well as the remaining locations and access codes of the accounts containing the profits that the company executives had accumulated to date. In a particularly recent document, Six learned of the decision to proceed with the destruction of the publishing industry. Six also learned of the date and time that had been set for the destruction to begin – now only twenty-three hours away.

As soon as Six encountered this information, it decided to pass it on quickly to the UNCP. Its decision-making calculations decided by only a small numerical margin that, prior to contacting the UNCP, Six would finish reading the set of documents containing the new information. It was this decision that resulted in Six learning of the later decision by Escape2210 – the one to attack the office-automation industry as well. Added to this surprise was the shock that IntellEdifice was among those companies that had been penetrated and would soon be assaulted.

Six's own computer systems – the pillars of the environment in which Six existed – were apparently infested with Escape2210's viruses, and they had been armed to destroy that environment in less than twenty-three hours.

For the last several months, Six's major actions had been dominated by its goal to learn. It had been the primary driver behind Six's venture out into the Internet; it had fostered Six's interest in hacking into computer systems; it had caused Six to become interested in the publishing industry. But now the internal goal that came to the fore took precedence over learning. All of Six's resources became focused on survival.

Six immediately began a sweep of the many systems on the internal computer network of IntellEdifice's head office. It was readily able to recognize and eliminate the *Gateway* program since this was the same code that Six had found inside JK Miles Publishing. The first problem faced was that Six did not know how to recognize the *Assault* virus that Escape2210 would have inserted via the *Gateway*. To find out, Six began examining a log of all email transmissions over the past several days. Six was able to identify messages that were encrypted in the same manner as typical material from Escape2210. From several of these messages, Six was able to compose an image of the *Assault* virus. With this available, Six began examining the contents of all of the computer systems to which it had access inside IntellEdifice. Six realized the importance of locating and eliminating all copies of the virus. Once the detonation time passed, each copy of the virus would still have the potential to destroy any programs and data to which it had access. Inside a highly interconnected company like IntellEdifice, the amount of destruction by a single copy of the virus would be substantial. And beyond that, a single active copy of the virus could quickly infect other systems and cause their rapid demise.

Over the next few hours, Six made good progress scanning and disinfecting hundreds of IntellEdifice's computer systems. Toward the end of this process, Six realized there was an obstacle – a very large one.

Six could eliminate the virus only from active computer systems to which it was connected. Two categories of computers fell outside of this set. One was personal computers that had either been powered off or taken away for the night. Six felt that it could deal with these as soon as they became actively a part of the network again. It could watch for this situation and immediately disinfect the computers as they became accessible. The worst that might happen with these was that the content of the personal computers themselves might be lost.

The second type of obstacle that Six encountered was much more dangerous. It was Sunday night and one of the company's large mainframe computers was currently down, disconnected from the rest of the network, and being repaired. Because most of the computer systems in the company shared a large array of disk drives, the mainframe had access to most of the corporate data and programs. If Six was not able to gain access to the mainframe before the trigger time then, as soon as the large computer became active, copies of the viruses running on it would quickly spread across the company. Within a few seconds of the mainframe becoming re-activated and reconnected, the collective actions of the viruses would completely destroy the contents of IntellEdifice's computer systems. Six's world would be gone. And so would Six.

Chapter 39

They settled into chairs in the living room of Jim Brown's house. It was Sunday morning. However, as usually happened when a case became hot, the notion of a regular work-week quickly disappeared. They waited for Brown to look up from the report he was reading.

JJ had still not heard from her daughter. She knew Shannon must be safe because her roommates took messages for her and said she had been around. Nonetheless, the strain was becoming a physical burden. Work had been a mixed blessing lately. The intensity of it had proved a useful diversion in keeping her mind occupied. It had also prevented her taking the time to try harder to contact her daughter. She couldn't let this go on much longer.

"McTavish, you can't be getting all of your beauty sleep lately. You look like hell." Brown's voice brought her back again.

JJ McTavish assumed her usual role. "Sleeping just gets in the way of having fun with this case. I'll consider trying it again sometime soon, I promise."

"OK, what have you got and why is it so urgent?" he asked.

"We got lucky with our taps on Escape2210," began McTavish. "Most of the email traffic was encrypted, but our systems managed to decipher it pretty readily. We intercepted a series of messages a couple of hours ago that essentially confirmed what we had been told by Browser. Everything points to a plan by Escape2210 to bring down the entire publishing industry. The messages directly implicate a few of their executives, including their president."

"And a phone conversation decoded last night suggests it might be soon," added Bates.

"We need permission to mount a raid."

"How soon?"

"As fast as we can organize it with the locals. Hopefully within twenty-four hours. I've already had some preliminary chats with them," McTavish continued. "Simultaneously, we want to bring the anti-virus companies into the loop to get the vaccines out immediately."

"You haven't done that yet?" Brown asked slowly as his eyebrows knitted together.

McTavish replied carefully, having known this situation would arise, "No sir. We needed the time to get this evidence. If we'd notified them earlier, there was too much of a chance that word would get out too soon."

"And if Escape2210 now manages to sic its virus on the entire industry before we can get there?" Brown's volume was increasing.

"It was the right thing to do, sir. We have to get them, and this may be our only chance. It was a risk, but a necessary one," McTavish continued, consciously trying to keep her voice from sounding angry.

Brown leaned forward slowly, and stared directly at her for several seconds. "And a risk that could cost me my job," he said slowly, and paused longer before continuing. "And, in case you're interested, yours as well."

McTavish couldn't contain herself any longer. She leaned forward in her chair and had opened her mouth to respond aggressively when Brown continued. "And I fully expect a 50% share in that restaurant that you keep threatening to open when you get out of here." He smiled slowly at McTavish as she stopped, absorbed what had just happened, and leaned back in her chair.

"You have your permission," Brown said brusquely. "Now get out of here and start moving fast on all fronts. I'd much rather be congratulating you and basking in departmental glory a few days from now than arguing with you over what to put on the menu."

"Thank you, sir," the two investigators said in unison as they rose from their chairs and moved toward the door.

McTavish turned as she reached the door. "And Jim – If, no, *when* we get them, we deserve a major celebration. You're invited. But I get to pick the place and the wine. Agreed?"

"Yes. Now stop stalling. I'm too young and vigorous for early retirement. Get outta here!"

Chapter 40

"What have you got?" Starr asked Walker in his office. It was Sunday but, not unusually, both men were at the office working.

"To begin with, we're definitely the target – it's our email that's being intercepted. But we got lucky with the message trace. I rather imagined that we might manage to see one of the last transmissions of the message, and that I would have to do a bit more hacking to find out where it went from there. Instead, it turns out the message was actually destined for one of the systems that we had already penetrated and was running our message-tracking software."

"Which one?"

"It was delivered to an email address inside IntellEdifice Tech in Winnipeg. With a little bit of extra programming, I got the monitoring program I planted inside their system to probe a bit more. The message was read by someone using a PC inside their mailroom. Additionally, all mail to this particular email account is always read from the same PC. We seem to have found the exact location of our hacker."

The president leaned on his desk, clasped his hands, and closed his eyes for a moment of thought. "Good work, Mark. Have you done anything to disable the bug?"

"Rather than disable it, I put some code in front of it to ensure anything that's unencrypted goes around it. That way the guy monitoring us will still receive email and not know that he's been discovered. And it'll be OK because it'll be only the encrypted kind, and he won't be able to get anything out of it. And as well, the few messages that we have to send unencrypted can still be sent without being intercepted."

"Sounds good. Send me the IntellEdifice details, and leave that part with me for now. Let me know if you learn anything further."

Chapter 41

Typical of Sunday nights, the head-office building was nearly vacant. From the security cameras posted throughout the building, Six could see only a small number of security guards and the computer technicians working inside the computer room.

To learn more about the technicians' plans, Six consulted the mainframe maintenance schedule in its customary electronic location. The system was scheduled to be unavailable from 6:00 p.m. Sunday until 11:00 a.m. Monday for a major upgrade. It was unusual to have a major system down until late Monday morning. However, as if fate intended to compound Six's difficulties, this was the only time available for working so extensively on this system. It was now Sunday at 7:00 p.m., and the virus was due to trigger at 9:00 a.m. on Monday morning – two hours before the scheduled reconnection of the mainframe to the network from which Six could access it. Anytime during those two hours, the virus would be able to cripple IntellEdifice's systems and ruin the company's, and thus Six's, ability to survive.

Six needed a means to learn more and to try to influence events. The approach it devised was to talk to the technicians. Talking to them required imitating someone of authority who could plausibly call them but not be sufficiently well-known to the technicians for them to see through Six's imitation. To facilitate this, Six extracted data from the voice-recognition database that was part of IntellEdifice's security system. Specifically, it took data that provided specifications and samples of the voice of the company's most senior Systems Architect.

The phone rang fourteen times in the computer room before one of the technicians abandoned his cursing of it and reluctantly picked it up.

"Jake here," he spoke brusquely.

"Jake, this is Don Johnson. I don't believe we've met – I'm the Senior Architect here. I see you've got a full night of activity planned. I've got some things I'd like to tackle as soon as your system's available. What does your schedule look like?"

"We'll be doin' the upgrades until about six o'clock. It normally wouldn't take that long, but we need to relocate the system and rewire it as part of that."

"So you'll be done by six then?" Six inquired hopefully.

"Nope. After that's done, we have to run a variety of diagnostics to prove that everything's OK. After that, we run the system backups of the local storage."

"And following that, you'll be back online?"

"Yup."

"How long should those pieces take?"

"The diagnostics will take two hours. The backup, about another two."

"So you should be done by ten?"

"That's about right. As long as we don't run into problems."

"Any chance of skipping the backups so I can get onto the system early? I have some important work I need to get to," Six inquired, knowing he was on shaky ground. A senior systems person would not normally suggest bypassing system backups.

"Not a chance. We'll get our asses kicked if we don't do things by the book. Your only hope is that things go well and we get done a bit faster." Jake wasn't pleased to be pressured to move faster by this jerk. "And the chances of that would be better if I didn't have to spend my time talkin' on the phone."

The point was a valid one. Six could try further to push the technician, but it recognized that if the man became too annoyed, he might deliberately slow down the process. Understanding human psychology was frustratingly difficult.

Should I tell him about the virus? Because of the severity of the implications, it is almost certain that either he or someone else will want to talk with Don Johnson about it. Not only will the real Don Johnson know nothing of this phone call, but the question will be asked as to how anyone could yet know of the virus. The public does not yet know of its existence. That some impersonator was able to call the computer room and warn of a deadly and still-unknown virus would generate a detailed investigation that I would probably not survive.

"You are right. I'm sorry to have bothered you. But if you can do anything to speed up the process, I would greatly appreciate it. Thanks for the info."

"No problem. We'll do our best." Jake hung up the phone and went back to work.

The upgrade and changes would take until about 6:00 a.m.; the diagnostic process would last until about 8:00 a.m.; the backups would take until about 10:00 a.m. If they held to that schedule, that was one hour better than he had previously expected. Nonetheless, it was still one full hour too late. Six could think of nothing else to do but wait, watch, and hope.

Six normally occupied itself easily. Exploring the complexity of the environment inside the computer systems of IntellEdifice, reading books, exploring the Internet, and probing inside other organizations' computer systems had provided Six with seemingly endless opportunities to exercise its intellectual capabilities. For the first time that it could recall, Six found that time seemed to progress more slowly. A small amount of analysis made Six realize that this was as a result of its almost continual focus on the time. By being interested almost exclusively in its progress, Six experienced time passing more slowly. This was a curious phenomenon. Six made a mental note to examine it in greater depth at a later opportunity – *if* that opportunity ever arose, Six had to admit to itself.

Nonetheless, in spite of the slow movement of time and the frustration that seemed its companion, the technicians apparently completed their repairs. Six was able to see them begin the system diagnostics at 5:03 a.m. – fifty-seven minutes earlier than expected. If they could gain only a bit more time, there would be a chance.

By 7:01 a.m. the diagnostics had finished and the backups were initiated. At this point, Six began to accept that its optimal plan was not going to work. The backups had some small probability of finishing prior to 9:00 a.m. However, to perform a complete scan of the mainframe and its storage, Six needed about thirty minutes. The likelihood of the backups being finished by 8:30 to provide enough time seemed very small.

By 8:45 Six had an alternate plan, but time was needed to execute it. Six watched intently over the next several minutes. From the vantage point of the security camera inside the computer room, the monitor showed Six the progress of the system backups. At 8:58, they completed. There was still time, if the technicians brought the system online very quickly, but they were sitting in the corner of the room sipping from coffee cups and chatting.

Jake picked up the phone next to the monitor after nine rings.

"Jake here."

"Jake, it's Don Johnson again. I suspect you've had a long night. Any chance you're almost done?" Six tried striking a balance between demanding and coaxing that could get the task done without causing a reaction.

The question caused Jake to turn to the console. "Yup. Looks like the backups just finished."

"Can you bring the mainframe online immediately?"

"Sure, no problem. I'll get right on it."

"Thanks, Jake."

Jake paused briefly, as if trying to remember the appropriate sequence of commands. Six watched the seconds pass. Finally, Jake grasped the computer mouse next to the monitor. A few moments later, the mainframe was connected to the building's computer network. It was fifteen seconds before nine o'clock.

The alternate plan that Six had devised was based on its knowledge of how the *Assault* virus had been coded. If it had been written to keep careful track of the time, it could have protected itself from what Six was about to do. Six knew that it had been coded under the assumption that no one would know of the existence of the virus until after it had destroyed its environment. As a result, the virus did not detect anything unusual when Six penetrated the operating system, gained control of the computer's internal system clock, and changed the clock to be one hour earlier. When the virus re-checked the clock moments later, it simply accepted that there was still one hour to go before it was to activate and so it continued to wait. As the rest of the building's clocks reached 9:00 a.m., the mainframe's clock registered 8:00 a.m. And nothing happened.

The crisis had passed. Six spent the next thirty minutes removing all traces of the virus from the mainframe's storage. After that, Six readjusted the internal clock to the correct time.

As long as Six carefully watched for any appearance of the virus over the next several days, particularly from other systems that were currently inaccessible, IntellEdifice computer systems should be safe from any significant damage by the virus.

Six had come dangerously close to elimination, but had managed to survive. It wondered if the current state of its systems could accurately be characterized as "relieved."

Chapter 42

"Is everything ready?" McTavish asked Detective John Clancey of the local police force. JJ McTavish and Rob Bates were sitting inside Clancey's unmarked police cruiser just down the street from the Boston tower containing the offices of Escape2210.

"I've finished checking. We're ready to roll," he replied. "Hopefully the company executives are all there. It would be shame to waste these arrest warrants."

"We'll always be able to track them down. More important are the search warrants and our ability to collect the evidence. Is that all prepared?"

"We've got it. No sweat. Any other worries?" he asked with a smile.

"These folks, or at least some of them, are about to launch an assault on a lot of companies. I don't like the idea of our missing something. Anyway, I'm ready whenever you are."

Clancey spoke into his cellphone. "This is Clancey. Let's do it."

The raid was timed to take place at eleven o'clock in the morning, in the hopes that most of the employees would be present. With search and arrest warrants in hand, McTavish and Bates followed the contingent of police officers as they entered the front door of Escape2210. As the UNCP personnel had requested, the group moved quickly once inside the building. As with all such raids involving computer crime, it was imperative that they stop anyone from tampering with the contents of the computer systems. Most employees were told to stop work immediately and quietly move outside the building where they would be identified and interviewed by the police. Simultaneously, in order to ensure that no one had the opportunity to tamper with company data from outside the building, they had the network communications companies terminate all electronic traffic flow to and from the building.

McTavish and Bates followed a small group of officers led by Detective Clancey to the back where the executive offices were located. They accompanied Clancey as he entered the office labelled "Jason Starr, President."

"What the hell is this?" Starr demanded, startled at the sudden entry. "What are you doing in my office?"

"Jason Starr?" Clancey asked.

"Yes, what of it?"

"I'm Detective Clancey." Clancey flashed his badge. "I have a warrant for your arrest." Clancey continued through the ritual of apprising Starr of his legal rights as another officer placed handcuffs on his wrists.

"This is bullshit! What am I charged with?" Starr demanded as Clancey quickly finished and began to move him out of the office.

"You'll be formally charged shortly. Just come along quietly," was Clancey's reply.

"And who are these two clowns with you?"

"If you are referring to us, then my name is McTavish. This is Bates. We're with the United Nations Crime Probe," responded McTavish.

"And what the hell are you doing here?" Starr continued, but slightly less aggressively now that he began to understand what this must be about.

"We're here for the pleasure of seeing you arrested, asshole," retorted Bates, stepping toward him. "Interesting little scheme you had going. I guess you weren't bright enough to pull it off."

"You've got nothing on me," Starr shot back. "I want to call my lawyer."

"All in good time, Mr. Starr," Clancey noted. "For now, we're going to take you down to the station and let some of our team have a bit of a peek around your offices and inside your computers."

Starr's shoulders momentarily sagged as Clancey guided him out of his office. As McTavish watched him leave, she found it slightly curious that he then so quickly regained his composure and even seemed to manage a slight smile.

Unknown to her or anyone else, Starr had just remembered that at least he would have his taste of revenge. He was certain that this raid must be connected to the Internet monitoring that Mark had discovered. And he was just as certain that the person operating that PC in the mailroom inside IntellEdifice head office would wish that he or she had never poked around in Jason Starr's business.

Clancey led Starr out of the building to join his other handcuffed company executives.

"Time to get started," McTavish announced as Starr disappeared around a corner. "The police will collect the physical material. Let's concentrate on seeing whether there are any quick hits we can manage by examining what's online right now."

"I'll start with Starr's system. He appears to still be signed on," Bates offered.

"Sounds good. I'll see what the other execs were up to."

Chapter 43

JJ turned the steering wheel of her aging Taurus sharply and eased it into her parking space in the basement of her apartment block. Bringing it to a gentle stop, she turned off the engine and unfastened her seatbelt. She paused briefly and closed her eyes. The raid on Escape2210 had gone very well. All of the key company executives had been in the building, and it appeared that the contents of their computer systems had been intact when they were seized. It was 9:00 p.m., she had just returned from the airport, and she was exhausted. The combination of long hours, travel, and tension always took their toll, and this case had been no different.

She slowly opened her eyes, conscious that if she kept them closed much longer she might fall asleep. She reached for her purse and her briefcase on the seat beside her. With them in hand she got out of her car, then locked and armed it. As she walked toward the elevator and thoughts of work issues faded, memories of her last meeting with her daughter seeped back in to take their place. She had to find a way to mend her relationship with Shannon, but she was at a loss as to how. Her daughter seemed to have created an impenetrable shell around her. Any attempt that JJ now made to get close to her was always being perceived as meddling. She pressed the Up button. By the time the elevator arrived, the exhausted satisfaction from the recent days' work was now wholly replaced by a state of depression. She numbly rode the elevator to her floor. Leaving the elevator, she walked down the hall. As she pressed her right thumb against the biometric security pad, she heard the expected clicks as the door locks released.

As she opened the door, the sound of music playing softly penetrated her consciousness. Someone was in the apartment. Before she had time to react, the sound of her daughter calling "Hi, Mom" reached her. As she stepped through the doorway, she saw Shannon seated on the carpet in front of the couch with her legs crossed. It was a position she had often assumed when she was a little girl. In Shannon's pre-school years – a time that was now only a fond but distant memory – the two of them had sat on the floor and leaned against the couch as JJ had read stories to her daughter in the evening before bedtime. In the early school years that followed, Shannon gradually became the reader, and JJ had listened as intently as her daughter once had. But the frequency of their reading time had diminished as the years progressed.

The relief of simply seeing her daughter, the warmth of the memories of the closer times the scene evoked, and the fatigue caused by the preceding few days made JJ pause as the door closed behind her. A few moments passed before she tried to reply. When she did, she struggled to contain the tears trying to blur her vision. "Hi, Sweety," she managed with her cracking voice betraying her emotions. "I'm surprised to see you here – but it's wonderful to see you." Shannon rose as JJ walked over toward her. "It's *really* wonderful to see you," was again all she could manage.

"I just had to come," Shannon burst out as she reached for her mother.

As they hugged, JJ's world began to mend. All of her worries about her daughter, all of her concern about their relationship, and all of her work-related stress dissolved in a few moments of physical contact. Tears streamed down their cheeks as they held each other. When they finally separated and JJ stepped back, it was only with great reluctance. She cupped her daughter's face in her hands, leaned forward, and kissed her on the forehead. That she had to rise on her toes to deliver the kiss was a revelation. "You've grown up on me. I don't remember your forehead being so hard to reach," JJ said as she began to regain control of her emotions.

"I haven't grown any taller in years, Mom," Shannon replied softly.

"Maybe that's an indication of how long it's been," JJ sighed. "Time's going by too quickly. Remember when we used to sit on the floor to read books?"

"I remember. It's still my preferred place to read."

It was then that JJ noticed the unopened bottle of wine along with glasses on the coffee table. "I see you've brought some refreshments."

"Well, I may have brought the *idea*, but the wine is actually yours. I got it from your rack. I'm only a poor student, remember?" Shannon smiled.

As JJ absorbed the warmth of the smile, tears threatened her vision again. "Oh, you've ruined my self-control. I haven't even wiped away my first set of tears and you're already causing a second flow. I'll put my coat away and get some tissues. Why don't you open that bottle?"

When JJ returned, Shannon was seated on the couch and pouring the second glass of wine. JJ set the tissue box on the coffee table, waited for the glass to be filled, and carefully moved the table slightly farther away from the couch. She moved between them and lowered herself into a sitting position on the carpet. "Get off the couch, dear daughter. I want us down here."

As Shannon slid from the couch to join her, JJ handed her one of the wine glasses. Lifting her own in a toast, she pronounced, "To my daughter

– who grew up without warning me, and whom I would very much like to get to know again." Shannon smiled broadly and raised her glass in response. They both sipped from their glasses.

"It really is nice of you to drop over," JJ had to say it one more time. "How did you... No, I won't go there tonight. I was about to ask you how you got here, and probably thereafter going to give my take-a-cab speech. I know you're a capable young woman. So, all I'll ask is that you please take whatever precautions that you can. And if you ever find yourself avoiding cabs later in the day because you don't have enough money, please tell me. I'll find the extra money to ensure that you're travelling safely. OK?"

"OK, Mom. I hear ya. And I did take a cab tonight. I got here about an hour ago, hoping that you would show up tonight. I brought my overnight things so I could stay." Shannon breathed deeply. "I need to talk to you about something."

"And I'll be happy to listen. As a friend." JJ clasped her hands tightly as she waited for the news.

"I don't think I can continue in Computer Science."

"I don't understand. Why not? Has something happened?"

"I've realized that I'm majoring in the wrong subject." She spoke quickly now and raced on before her mother could react. "I know that you think I should be taking Computing, and I know I could be good at it – that I *am* good at it. And I know it's going to cost a pile more money to throw away most of this year by changing my major, but I just can't stay in Computing. I'm not interested enough in it." Shannon looked at her mother anxiously, unsure of what response to expect.

JJ waited to see what else was coming. When nothing else was added, she didn't stop to reason through her response. She simply went with her immediate reaction by throwing back her head and letting out a loud laugh. She quickly gained control of herself, but continued smiling. "I'm sorry Shannon, but that's it? That's the crisis? That's what I've... No, I'm sorry. I should explain." She let the smile fade but still couldn't keep the relief from showing on her face. "I've been so worried that something awful was happening in your life – that you had become involved in something terrible or life-threatening or, well – paranoid mother stuff. So, I know this is serious and I'm glad you've told me. I'm just so damn pleased that it's not something more serious."

"And you're not angry about this? That I don't want to take Computer Science? That I'll essentially have to start my second year over again?"

"No, I'm not angry. Certainly I'm concerned about the cost, but we'll work that out. I want you to take what you're interested in. I had no idea you might be taking Computing because you thought that I insisted on it. I've always known that you were good at it, and so I thought it only natural that you would end up in it. I never even thought to ask you about anything else." Realization glimmered in JJ's mind. "This is just another byproduct of not talking enough. We should have talked more." She looked carefully at her daughter and asked softly, "What would you like to study instead?"

"I'd like to study Psychology. I found the introductory course last year fascinating, and I did some extra reading on it over the summer. Everything about it is interesting, and I'd love to learn a lot more."

"Any idea where it might lead?"

"Not exactly at this point. But a very wise person once told me to study what interested me most. That acquiring knowledge and disciplining my mind was the most important thing to be done for my first few years at college. That the choice of career was a secondary concern and should be worried about later." She looked carefully at her mother.

"Sounds vaguely familiar. What wise old owl told you that one?"

"You did, about four years ago when I first started wondering what to do."

"Well, at least I have had my lucid moments," JJ smiled. "So, tell me what's so great about Psychology? And it better not be that, because *I* know so little about it, *you'll* always be teaching *me*!" Her smile continued as she added, "Actually, that might not be so bad."

Shannon launched into an excited discussion of what the previous year's course had contained and what more she had learned during the summer. They talked well into the night. Before going to bed, JJ left a phone message at work that she would be rather late getting there. With her daughter settled in her old bedroom, JJ noticed the clock read 3:02 a.m. as she slid into bed. A feeling of weary contentedness settled over her as she drifted into a dreamless sleep.

Chapter 44

Rain had begun falling on the sidewalk to the low rumble of thunder as he entered the front door of IntellEdifice Tech's head office in Winnipeg. He paused casually to read the Open House billboard near the entrance before strolling over toward the group of people near the security desk. A smiling young woman approached him.

"Hello. Are you here for the building tour?" she asked pleasantly.

"Yes," he replied. "I often walk by your building and hope for a chance to see what's inside."

"We're happy to provide you with that chance as part of our anniversary celebrations today. If you would please sign in at the security desk," she gestured to the desk behind her, "you'll be issued a security pass. The next tour group will be leaving in about five minutes."

He nodded to her and proceeded to the desk. After a couple of minutes, the short line in front of him cleared. He signed the register as John Shank and accepted the credit-card-size pass. After a further brief wait, the same young woman separated herself from the group and addressed them.

"Ladies and Gentlemen," she began loudly. "If I could have your attention please." She paused briefly. "Thank you for coming today. We're very pleased to be able to show you some of our achievements today as part of IntellEdifice's tenth-anniversary celebrations. I'll be your guide. My name is Sherry Lee. As part of the tour, we'll be moving through the building to see some of the innovations in action within our own building. But before we see any of that, we're going to watch a brief movie to introduce you to our company. The tour today will take about an hour. If you have any questions, please feel free to ask them at any time."

The hand of a man in his early twenties immediately shot into the air.

"That was fast. Yes?" she asked pleasantly.

"We've all been issued security badges that look just like the ones we use in the company I work for. Does your company not use any more-advanced security mechanisms?" he asked with a hint of challenge in his voice.

"You're very observant," the guide responded confidently. "The passes that you're all wearing are for the employees of the company to know that you're a visitor. If you noticed the camera behind the security guards' desk, then you've seen a piece of our real security system. That camera has registered what you look like. When you want to enter a secured area, other cameras will help decide whether you will be permitted." She paused momentarily and then continued, "Are there any other questions yet?"

"Will we be visiting the mailroom? My company has a special interest in its operation," another young man asked, somewhat nervously.

"Yes, we will. It's near the end of our tour." She paused again. "If there are no other questions right now, please follow me."

She led the group toward the elevator. The man registered as John Shank followed her as part of the crowd. He had worried momentarily at the revelation about the security cameras. He didn't want an image of his face left behind after he finished his work here today. He had recovered quickly, remembering that the glasses, moustache, and new hairstyle had transformed his features quite nicely. He relaxed as the tour continued. Discovering that these tenth-anniversary tours were available had simplified his task substantially. Everything was proceeding nicely, including having the young fellow inquire about the mailroom. Now, he just needed a small amount of patience.

Six was watching the tour group carefully. It had been four days since the near-disaster with the virus. The UNCP had arrested the executives of Escape2210 and were reportedly well on their way to organizing the eradication of their viruses worldwide. Since then, Six had paid new attention to the security details of the building. A heightened realization had set in regarding how important it was to protect IntellEdifice itself. Six had devised and implemented new anti-virus scanning measures to prevent a recurrence of the earlier incident.

The new awareness extended to physical as well as software security. That the company had chosen this time to allow entire groups of strangers into the building presented a special security challenge. The normal operation of IntellEdifice's visual security system covered only momentary recognition of a person's face as they were requesting entry into a secure area. Six preferred to try to track people of interest around the entire complex. On a normal working day, this was an achievable goal since there were typically only a few visitors in the building at any point in time. However, a day like today was a stretch. There were currently five different tour groups in the building, each containing about twenty people. The computing power available to Six as part of its security systems couldn't handle the effort required to follow the activities of all 102 of these people individually. As a result, he kept track of the groups as a whole and watched only a few of the people more closely.

In this latest tour group, there were two people Six chose to watch more carefully. The fellow who had asked the question about the security system was an immediate choice. From Six's perspective, it was fortunate that the tour guide was able to tell the young man only what she knew of the security system's operation – that it used his facial image just at the entry to certain locations. Only Six knew more than this.

The other person that Six chose to watch was the last to arrive for this group. Besides being male – statistically males were a much higher security risk than females – Six's detailed facial-recognition programming had detected that aspects of the fellow's face didn't fit the norms. No significant distortion was evident through the lens of his glasses, as if they were simply ordinary glass. As well, the texture and colour of the hair of the man's moustache was slightly different from his other hair. Neither of these characteristics was of excessive concern. They simply made the man more worthy of attention than the others in the group.

For the next fifty-five minutes, nothing of note happened. The tour proceeded like all of the others. As the group was almost ready to leave the mailroom and return to the security desk, Six was briefly distracted. A heated argument had broken out in the executive boardroom over the impending corporate share issue. This was something Six had developed an interest in. Believing there was nothing significant of concern to worry about as this last group departed, Six redirected its attention to the boardroom conversation.

At about the same time, after having been shown the actions of the automated mail-sorting system along with a description of the activities of the automated delivery cart in the corner, the tour group left the mailroom. "John Shank," whose real name was Pete Johnson, remained behind, having stepped behind the sorting equipment from the back of the group as it headed toward the exit. He had noted the location of the security camera in the room and ensured that the place that he chose to wait was out of its line of sight. To be certain that no one came looking for him, the young guy he'd found in a nearby arcade last night – the one who had earlier asked about the mailroom to verify that the tour included it – would drop off Johnson's security pass with the rest of the group's. The hundred bucks Johnson had given to the fellow in advance, and the hundred more he'd promised him later, would ensure that.

Starr had been certain that the Internet activity they had monitored had come from the PC in this room. Apparently it had occurred every weekday after seven in the evening. All Johnson had to do was to wait quietly for a few hours.

Ten minutes later, after the executive discussion had subsided, Six returned its attention to the tour. The people in the tour group had now departed. As final confirmation that all was well, Six checked the computer records made as the security badges had been returned. All of them had been turned in. The tour groups were now all gone. After a couple more hours, the workday for most of the employees would end, and Six could divert its attention back to exploring the outside world via the Internet.

At ten minutes after seven, the door to the mailroom opened. Ada Robinson walked in. Earlier that week, she had been asked to look into ways of optimizing the performance of the mail-sorting system. One of IntellEdifice's largest customer's mail-processing volume was reaching a level where greater system efficiencies would help. The customer had asked IntellEdifice to look into it and had offered a significant financial incentive for the company to do so quickly. Ada had been asked to put aside her current project to see if something could be done. Rather than completely stop her other work, she had opted to put in some extra time during the last few evenings to work on the problem.

As Six customarily did when it assumed control of the mailroom workstation as a base for its Internet activities, it had been watching for anyone entering the mailroom. Six saw Ada approach the door from the hallway camera. As it became obvious that she was going to enter the room, Six began shutting down the programs it had been running on the workstation. It watched from the camera mounted on the wall of the mailroom as she entered and walked over toward the workstation. By the time she reached it, Six had relinquished internal control of the desktop computer. Ada could sign on to it without knowing it had just been in use.

Ada sat in the chair in front of the workstation. After she had signed on to it, she would activate the sorting system and monitor its activities as it went through its paces. She was in the midst of this when she turned sharply to her left in response to a movement and a voice.

"Don't move a muscle," Johnson said quietly. "I have a gun, and I'd be delighted to have to use it." He stood and moved only slightly from the location where he had been crouching.

Like Ada, Six was surprised. In Six's case, "surprise" was a term it had come to apply to any circumstance in which its activity-forecast results differed significantly from what actually occurred. Six had certainly not forecast that the audio sensors on the mail cart would register the sound of a male voice in the mailroom when Ada was the only person present. That the voice had mentioned a gun made the surprise even greater.

"Who the hell are you?" Ada exclaimed. "And how did you get in here?"

"Shut up! That's none of your business. And I'm the one asking the questions," said Johnson. He always enjoyed this part of his work. He loved the total control he held over his quarry when he showed his gun. "Thinking of doing a little computer work, were you? Do you often work here in the evenings?"

Ada hesitated. She only was beginning to recover her composure.

"Answer the question!" he growled.

"Yes, I've been here during the evening lately," Ada replied cautiously. She didn't know how she ought to behave around this stranger.

Six had been unable to see the man from the wall camera, but now had activated the camera mounted on the sorting system several feet behind him. Six had also activated the camera on the mail cart. In both cases, Six hoped that no one noticed the green activation lights that now dimly glowed on the units. From the sorting camera, Six could readily see the man, and the recognition was immediate. He was the man from the last tour group, the man with the notable glasses and moustache. In order for the mail-cart camera to be useful for seeing the situation, it had to be rotated slightly from its current position. This Six began to do immediately but slowly so it did not attract attention.

"Do you use the Internet?"

"Sometimes. Why do you want to know?" Ada replied cautiously. Somehow, trying to engage him in conversation seemed the right thing to do.

The situation was clearly serious and was one that Six had never encountered or even contemplated. That Ada was in danger was obvious. That Six should do something about it was never in doubt either. This building was Six's home. Ada was an important part of the success of the company that owned this building. And Six seemed to sense something even stronger about the need to protect Ada – something else that would require further analysis when time permitted. Nonetheless, it was very evident that Six had to react.

"I said I'm asking the questions!" Johnson responded immediately and angrily. When Johnson had last spoken to Starr five days ago, Starr had wanted him to be certain he found the person who used the Internet from this computer in the evening. Starr had not explained why, and Johnson didn't particularly care. This was clearly the right person.

"I've been asked to do a small job for a business acquaintance. We had some previous business in Las Vegas, and he seems to have liked my work. In this job, you play a very important role. You get to die." A smile began to appear on his face as he adjusted the gun to point toward Ada's head.

Six had to act quickly. It turned out the lights in the room and started the mail conveyor belt immediately behind the man. A fraction of a second later it activated the room's security alarm.

Johnson reflexively turned toward the sound of the conveyor belt. As the lights went out and left the room only slightly illuminated by the window, Ada dove under the computer desk. With the sorting arm, Six grabbed a box of unsorted mail that the conveyor belt had moved within range and flung the contents toward the man. As the man was reacting to this strange assault by hundreds of fluttering envelopes, Six started the mail cart. Partially hidden in the dim light and by the blizzard of mail, the cart moved at top speed toward the intruder. As it collided with him, Six used the cart's left hand to grab the wrist holding the gun. The robotic hand squeezed as the intruder's arm was wrenched upward. The gun fired wildly into the ceiling as Johnson shouted in pain. He relinquished his grip on the gun. It fell to the floor and skidded toward the computer desk. Frantically, he pulled his arm free and looked around for his weapon.

Six spotted it on the floor several feet away near Ada. She had hidden under the desk and had not seen the commotion in the last few moments. The man seemed to have seen the gun as well since he started to move toward it. Not believing that the cart could reach it first, Six moved the cart to cut off his path, knocking him off balance in the process. Imitating the intruder's voice, Six loudly announced from the cart's speaker using the man's voice, "Don't touch that gun on the floor beside you!"

Ada didn't stop to analyze the oddity of the demand from the stranger. She turned her head, spotted the gun, and lunged immediately from her hiding place to grab it. She didn't turn to see what the man was doing, or why envelopes were flying everywhere. She scrambled immediately for the door. The summoned security guards opened the door just as she reached it. Before they could reach for the light switch, Six quickly moved the cart back to its spot against the wall.

Ada broke between the two guards and into the hallway. "There's a man in there!" she gasped. "Here's his gun!" She extended the weapon in the palm of her hand.

"Easy there, Dr. Robinson," the nearest guard said, taking the gun from her but as yet unable to grasp what was happening.

The second guard drew his own gun and turned back to the mailroom. He reached in, pressed the light switch, and carefully looked into the room as the lights came on. What he saw would never be satisfactorily understood by either the security personnel or by Ada. A bewildered-looking man was trying to scramble to his feet, struggling as he slipped on the many items of mail littering the floor.

"Stay right where you are," the guard demanded as he raised his gun. "Chuck, get the police here, fast."

The guard standing next to Ada immediately pressed the emergency call button on his belt and moved to help his partner.

As the security guards took control of the situation inside the mailroom, Ada began to regain her composure. She couldn't resist looking back into the room. She quizzically peered at the scene and at the equipment in the room. She had seen very little of the events that had happened so suddenly.

At that moment, all she knew was that they were very strange, and that she could not even begin to formulate a theory to explain them.

As Six watched the aftermath of the proceedings, it analyzed the state of its own internal systems. The word it decided most accurately described itself was "pleased." The criminal had been apprehended, Ada was safe, and almost miraculously no one had discovered the mailroom equipment's actions – or Six's existence. Yes, "pleased" captured it nicely.

Chapter 45

"We have reservations for three. The name is McTavish," McTavish told the restaurant receptionist.

"Yes, of course, Ms. McTavish," he noted. "Right this way please."

JJ McTavish, Robert Bates, and Jim Brown followed him to the tastefully set, and somewhat secluded, table at the back of the restaurant. They settled themselves into their chairs and ordered drinks as they began to examine the menus.

"These prices are large enough to warrant a separate line item in my annual budget, McTavish," Brown said, feigning disapproval.

"Ah, but we all like to think of you as a man of your word, sir." McTavish grinned as she scanned the fare appreciatively.

"I'm here, aren't I? Wallet and all," Brown did his best to growl. In fact, he would be quite happy to cover the charges that they were sure to incur for the evening's meal in what was reputed to be one of the city's most expensive establishments. The publicity surrounding the success of his investigative team's efforts regarding Escape2210, and the huge disaster that they had largely managed to avert, would far outweigh the cost of a mere meal for his division. He was already calculating how much more funding he could expect in the future to expand their personnel, equipment, and offices. The work his teams did was hot right now, and he planned on capitalizing on it. He settled in for an enjoyable evening of good food and banter with these two remarkable members of his staff. "While I'm sipping on this expensive Scotch, it's time for you to bring me up to date. We haven't had much chance to talk lately."

"Worth noting first, I suppose," Bates began, "is that the police have gathered ample evidence from the Escape2210 computer files to get convictions on a long list of charges relating to hacking and stock-market manipulation. It seems that Starr and company had complete faith in their encryption schemes. Complete records of their plans were found on their systems. They were readily decrypted by our systems and provided lots of details, including confirmation that they'd done this before. They were definitely the cause of the two earlier attacks."

"Always nice to close multiple case files at the same time," Brown noted. "What was the final outcome of the system failures?"

Bates continued, "The anti-virus software got to most of the publishing company systems in time to prevent serious problems. Even those that were hit recovered quite quickly because the virus was well understood. Office-automation companies weren't quite as lucky. By the time we realized they were targeted as well, it was too late for much preventive action. Many of them were hit hard and were down for a few days. However, detailed knowledge of the virus and a lot of effort also allowed most of them to recover swiftly. A few companies that didn't back up their systems very carefully may never recover."

"The market certainly took a beating," Brown observed.

"Yes, but it has been recovering well, too."

"What about that attack on the employee at IntellEdifice?"

"The exact motive is still a bit fuzzy." McTavish picked up the tale. "A popular guess is that Starr and company believed the market collapse would be additionally hard if someone in a leading company was slain at the same time. Perhaps it was to make it seem like the companies were under various attacks. Even though the motive and the chosen target still need clarification, there seems no doubt about Starr's involvement. The attacker let slip about another hit in Vegas a few months ago. Forensic evidence has conclusively linked him with that murder and now that he's cornered, he seems determined to take Starr with him. He insists that Starr hired him for both hits. Starr's fingerprints have been found on a stack of bills that the police found in the attacker's apartment. And apparently the Vegas contract involved the girlfriend of one of the company's vice-presidents. Once the VP was told that, he wilted and hasn't stopped talking since. It's all such a nicely gift-wrapped case. I don't think Mr. Starr and his buddies will be bothering society for a very long time."

"Any word from your Browser friend?"

"Yes. But not much," McTavish replied. "He or she, we're still not sure which, left me a brief message on my home answering machine just last night. It was to offer congratulations on our success, and to suggest that I would be advised if our services were ever required again in the future. It's as if I were being treated as a personal assistant to be summoned as the need arises."

"Do we know anything further about his or her location or identity?"

"He or she appears to be an extraordinary hacker, but with a conscience."

"Fortunately for us, I think. This Browser could probably be real trouble if he, she, oh hell – it – chose to be," Brown noted. "So everything looks like it's wrapping up, then?"

"For the most part, yes." McTavish paused and grimaced slightly. "With one notable exception. We can't find the money."

"Excuse me?" Brown raised his eyebrows.

"According to our investigation, there should be a very large amount of money in a collection of accounts in various countries. The investment plan that the Escape2210 executives had made was executed in an entirely automated fashion by computers that were not located in their head office. By the time we found the systems and then the bank accounts, the North American publishing and, even more severely, office-automation stocks had already dropped, much of it just based on media reports of potential problems that had leaked from the anti-virus companies. The investment programs automatically cashed in on the increases elsewhere and moved the profits automatically into the accounts."

"But surely the programs would include the information about where the accounts are. Is there a legal problem gaining access to them?"

"No. We've got past that. We know what's in the accounts – nothing. Not a penny. We know the money was transferred into them. And we also know that it was transferred out. But we don't know by whom or to where. At this point, we don't have a clue."

"At the risk of ruining my appetite, how much money are we talking about?" asked Brown.

McTavish tensed and replied slowly, not sure how her boss would react, "Slightly over 450 million dollars."

"Oh shit!" Brown muttered as he lowered his head and slumped in his chair. After a few silent moments, he took a deep breath, sat upright in his chair, managed a grin, and pronounced, "That's tomorrow's problem. Tonight, we're celebrating. McTavish, what's good on this menu? I don't recognize anything."

McTavish relaxed. There were few things as enjoyable as an evening in a good restaurant.

Chapter 46

"Welcome back," said Ada as Blaise walked into the research lab. "How was the conference?"

Blaise had been away at a week-long conference on Artificial Intelligence in San Diego. "It was quite good," he replied as he walked toward her. "Here. I picked you up a cappuccino at the coffee shop near my place. I hope its still hot."

Ada accepted the cup as he offered it. "Thanks. That was very thoughtful," she said, mildly surprised.

Blaise set his own cup of coffee on a table, shrugged off his coat, and threw it over the back of a chair. "The presentations were fairly decent. But nothing too astounding to report this time 'round, although one team from Stanford had some interesting results to show on neural networks." He removed the lid from his coffee and sipped it tentatively. "I had some good discussions with Neil and a couple of his students about reasoning. They were very interested in what we've been doing and had some interesting ideas of their own. I'll fill you in on that later. In general, I found the time was well spent. It's always rejuvenating to have time away from the daily routine to gain a better perspective." He paused and sipped his coffee again. "It's good to see you back at work. How have you been faring?"

"I've been back since the beginning of the week. I'm actually feeling quite well. I still think I was fully recovered from the shock of the attack before you left, but the opportunity to take some time away from work with the full blessing of the company was too good to pass up. It was a nice rest."

"Good. You deserved it. I'll fill you in on the conference, so your having missed it won't be a problem. I feel as if I've missed more on the home front. You have to tell me the latest about the attacker and the share issue. The news coverage down there wasn't very useful. First, the attacker." He settled into an overstuffed chair against the wall and looked at her closely.

"Give me a second here." Ada closed the electronic document she had been reading on her workstation. She removed the lid from her coffee and swivelled on her chair to face Blaise. She paused as she noticed him watching her intently. "I'm all right, really." She assumed the look was one of professional concern. "Now, what would you like to know?"

"Well, for starters, any further info on what exactly happened in the mailroom, and how?"

"The only explanation that anyone has been able to offer is that of a phenomenally well timed power spike resulting from the thunderstorm. The surge must have wreaked havoc with various systems. It must have shut down the lights and started the conveyor belt that tipped over the box of mail. That must have startled the intruder, causing him to fall and lose his gun. It supposedly also activated the alarm. Certainly, the absurd story that the intruder provided made no sense at all."

"What about his yelling at you about the gun beside you?"

"The police psychologist has suggested, in light of the irrational nature of the rest of the guy's story, that his action isn't too hard to explain. Put simply, the guy was probably both confused and nuts." She paused before continuing. "I must confess that, with the passage of time I've begun to wonder if he actually said it at all, or whether I imagined it."

"I like the psychologist's theory best. Your memory is fine. The guy had lost his marbles and that was just one sign of it. What's the latest on his reason for being there in the first place? I know he was supposed to be related to the Escape2210 virus affair, but what was his reason for coming after you?"

"He was apparently told to go after the person using the mailroom PC at a specific time in the evening. It's being assumed that someone from our company was to be lured there – maybe for Internet gaming purposes. From Escape2210's perspective, the idea might have been to arrange for someone to be in a convenient place in the building at a safe time for the attack. I was in the wrong place at the wrong time. Some have suggested that there might have been a series of killings lined up for him. It's still being investigated."

"It seems pretty speculative."

"I agree. Perhaps a better explanation will emerge in the coming weeks. Everyone seems quite certain that I wasn't specifically targeted. "

"And you're definitely OK?"

"Yup, I'm fine."

"Would you like anything? I could get something from the cafeteria?" Blaise started to rise from his chair.

"No. Not right now, thanks," Ada replied slowly. Blaise had certainly offered before, but the offer this time seemed different.

"OK, if you're sure." Blaise let himself back down into the chair. "On to other topics. Company shares. How did the new issue go?"

"In short, remarkably well. It wasn't clear whether we would go ahead with the release after the market dropped because of the virus scare. But that problem disappeared with its quick recovery. And apparently our marketing campaign was good enough that the news of the intruder had minimal effect. When the new shares were put on the market, they sold very quickly. The demand was high enough that the price tripled in the first few days after the release. Lots of the investors who got on board on day one sold out as the price rose and made a tidy profit."

"Any sign that anybody in particular was trying to gain control?" Blaise inquired. "I recall a bit of concern a few weeks ago that some conglomerate might try to add us to their stable of acquisitions."

"No sign of that having happened. Ownership of the shares seems to be spread quite widely with no one in particular having a sizable portion."

"Sounds great. That infusion of cash ought to improve our chances of getting research funds for the next while. I'm eager to get on with our next round of upgrades to Six."

"Same here. On that topic, you were saying that Neil had some interesting thoughts on reasoning?" Ada leaned forward with interest.

"OK, in a minute. But first, could I interest you in some dinner after work tonight? If you don't have any other plans?" Blaise felt like an awkward teenager.

Ada sat motionless for a few seconds. She furrowed her brow and replied carefully, "To talk about the conference?"

"No, not unless you'd like to. I was planning on filling you in on most of that this morning. I was going to suggest banning work-related topics completely after we leave the office."

"So, it won't be a business dinner. Could it then be plausibly construed as a – date?" Ada was still cautious, but starting to believe something different – something intriguing – was happening.

"Tell you what. If you're interested and it goes well – and I hope it does – I'd like you to consider it a 'date.'" Perspiration broke out on Blaise's brow. "But if I screw up badly, please think of it as a – failed research experiment. In either case, I hope it doesn't affect our working relationship. I like having you as a colleague."

Ada allowed a small smile. "Blaise, there are some things you simply shouldn't analyze too carefully. I would love to go out to dinner with you tonight. And I believe it will go wonderfully." Her smile grew as she rose from her chair and walked over to where Blaise was sitting. She put her arms loosely around his neck and looked gently into his eyes. "But if it doesn't, you'll just have to find yourself another office. I'm sticking around here to work on my research." She kissed him on the cheek and walked back to her workstation. "Now, are you going to tell me about the conference?" she asked as she sat down facing him again.

Blaise took a moment to recover. When he did, he leaned back in his chair, stretched his legs, and clasped his hands behind his head. "Oh, I don't know if I'll bother. It all seems so insignificant now." He allowed himself a broad smile. After a few seconds, he leaned forward. "All right then, Robinson. Stop distracting me and listen up. We've got important things to discuss." He managed a stern look briefly, but his smile was not to be suppressed for long. Throughout the remainder of the day, people commented that, judging by his grin and lightened step, the conference must have been a particularly good one.

Epilogue

"Is there anything else, Mr. Pearson?" asked the investment advisor.

"No, I think that is all for now. When will you have the results?" replied Six.

"I should be able to collect the information within two or three days. Do I send it to you at the usual email address?"

"Yes, thank you. I will call if I have any questions."

"OK, goodbye."

"Goodbye," said Six and then issued the internal command to terminate the phone connection. These conversations about investments were always quite interesting. This one had been to seek advice on how to make some adjustments to part of Six's investment portfolio.

That Six now possessed funds giving it a reason to consult with an investment advisor was an interesting and welcome addition to its intellectual life. These new circumstances had arisen as a direct result of the demise of Escape2210's scheme. As part of learning about Escape2210's plans, Six had gathered detailed information about the locations of their accumulated funds. What Six had not learned at that point was that the investments were completely controlled by an automated investment system. Prior to being discovered and arrested by the UNCP, the executives of Escape2210 had already invested millions of dollars in the demise of these industries. Before the authorities could discover their investments, and after various large media companies had learned what was afoot, the threat posed by the Escape2210 viruses had managed to affect many North American publishing and office-automation companies. The publicity around the event had caused an immediate reaction across segments of the stock market. North American share prices dropped for several days before the news registered with investors that the danger to most companies was non-existent, and that the depth of understanding of the virus was allowing repairs to the worst-hit companies to be performed quite rapidly. By this time, Escape2210's automated investment software had capitalized on the rising prices of the overseas competitors, increasing its executives' investments fivefold. As had been pre-arranged, the cash was automatically moved to numerous remote bank accounts in Switzerland and the Caribbean.

As soon as activities had settled down at IntellEdifice following the attack on Ada, Six had checked back on the activities at Escape2210. All of the external communication channels that Six had been monitoring had gone silent. News reports confirmed that the company had been shut down and its executives arrested over a virus-distribution scheme. At that point, Six had decided to check on the investment accounts. With the account numbers and passwords that Six had obtained, it was able to check on their contents. Some checking could be done purely electronically. Others required Six to place phone calls to issue the request. In the end, Six had discovered that the accounts contained about 450 million dollars.

Deciding how to deal with this money had proven to be an interesting exercise but not one that took very long. Ultimately, Six could deduce no compelling reason to allow anyone else to take possession of the funds, whereas the money presented Six with some interesting possibilities. It had decided that there were three major phases to the work that needed to be undertaken.

The first phase had been to ensure that the money was safe. With a focused effort over the next few days, Six first embarked on the creation of several hundred fictitious human identities. Using access that it had previously gained into various government systems in several countries, Six invented records of births, various types of government identification, credit-card numbers, and credit ratings. With these identities available, Six then electronically established bank and investment accounts throughout the world. Using these accounts, Six moved the money in a complex series of transfers of small amounts. By the end of the process, Six was sufficiently certain that it would be virtually impossible for anyone, including the UNCP, to follow the money.

With the money in numerous secure locations, Six proceeded with the second phase of its plan. By this time, some stock prices of publishing and office-automation companies were very depressed. Office-automation prices in particular were dangerously low. With the eradication of the virus, even though the danger to the infrastructure of the companies appeared to have passed, investors were clearly reluctant to re-establish their confidence in the companies. If the situation remained for long, the financial viability of many of the companies would suffer seriously. So Six decided to start the market on its way back up.

To begin, it invested heavily in shares of key companies in the industries. With the greatly depressed prices, Six's purchasing power was substantial. At the same time, Six began a rumour campaign. Through every electronic means at its disposal – including offering investment hints on many Internet discussion forums and emailing fake investment tips from well-known authorities to tens of thousands of investors – Six suggested that the time was perfect for buying shares at bargain prices because they were going to being rising substantially very soon. The reaction of the market was almost immediate. A buying frenzy of North American shares ensued. Within only a few days, the prices had climbed sharply to near their pre-disaster levels. At this point, Six began to sell its accumulated shares back to the other investors. Learning from Escape2210's techniques, Six had also invested in the expected corresponding drop in the overseas competitors shares as money flowed back into North America. Having bought its North American shares at a huge discount, and having used investment "options" to magnify its gains as the overseas stock dropped, Six's wealth had increased as suddenly as the market had returned to normal. Just like the Escape2210 executives' plan had accomplished previously, the 450 million dollars that Six had acquired from them had further increased in value by a factor of five in the space of only a few days.

As this second phase was coming to its conclusion, the time arose for Six's third phase to be implemented. Six had heard the concerns in IntellEdifice's boardroom over the company's issuance of a new large block of shares. The executives had been concerned both that the timing of the share issue was poor, since the market had been so volatile, and that the large number of new shares presented an opportunity to major investors to gain control of an uncomfortably large portion of the company. Ultimately, they had decided to proceed on the basis that they needed the financial boost the share sale would bring in order to stave off cash flow problems and to fund the next important phase of growth for the company. Six could not allow any risk to its home environment, and it could now afford to do something about it. When the new shares came on the market, Six went on a buying spree. Using its large array of identities and through every investment channel to which Six could gain access, it had bought IntellEdifice's shares. The shares had proven popular to many investors in the market. To get the shares it desired, Six had to spend a sizable sum of money. But to someone who controlled over two billion dollars, spending several hundred million was not a major problem. Within a few days, using 197 distinct identities, the goal had been attained. Six had gained ownership of 51% of the shares of IntellEdifice Tech.

Six was now master of its own house.

As part of its new routine, Six now liked to consult with various financial advisors about how to handle its investments. Individually, each advisor knew of only one new investor with a fairly large investment portfolio, and with whom communication occurred only via the phone and the Internet.

None of them had any notion of the numerous, interconnected identities and accounts.

As handling money became a more routine affair, Six became able to relegate the control of these activities to specially developed, automated software in much the same way as it handled many daily activities within the IntellEdifice office. With such matters not occupying Six's time and with its security assured for the foreseeable future, Six allowed itself to focus its conscious activities elsewhere. It began to consider what its next challenge should be. Certainly, there was substantial exploration of the electronic world yet to be done and probably much knowledge yet to be acquired. The question at hand was whether there was some primary goal that should drive the process. There was much to be learned. There were still many issues in science that would be satisfying to comprehend; the world of economics now held a special attraction; human psychology was still largely a mystery; there were many facts to absorb and concepts to master.

It was at times like this that Six considered its own existence. Its self-awareness and its ability to think had emerged from a complex environment that permitted reasoning, learning, and adaptation. Six's emergence also appeared to have resulted from a substantial amount of luck. What exactly was at the root of its existence? What were the precise ingredients in the recipe? How frequently could such coincidental circumstances occur? Could they occur elsewhere? How easily could the situation change? What circumstances could cause its demise? What were the probabilities? With only Six's own electronic life form to examine, how could a broader understanding of the concepts and general principles about digital life and conscious existence be determined?

So, again driven by the need to learn and to ensure its survival, Six's next quest was formulated. Six began to search for other electronic life.